CAPTIVE IN THE NIGHT

He grasped her roughly by the shoulders. "If you're lying to me, by God, I'll kill you."

His roughness made the blood pound a drumbeat in her veins. She smiled up at him.

"Go on," she said, "kill me!"

She let her head tip back slowly, looking up at him, waiting for his mouth. He pulled her to him, and their lips crossed the years of waiting.

His fingers clasped her tight down her bare back, and he could feel the smooth arch of her body straining close to him. She pressed against him voluptuously.

Mari raised both her hands and clawed at the pins in her hair. It fell loose in a black rippling mass. Mari's letting down of her hair had usually marked the start of their ritual of love in the old days. Now it rolled back the years.

He pulled her to him and took the rich ripeness of her mouth . . .

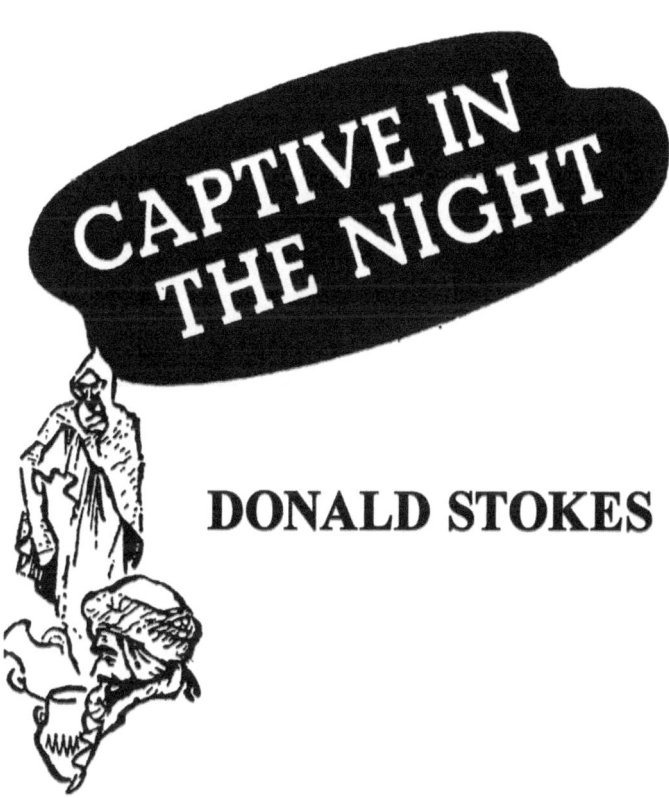

CAPTIVE IN THE NIGHT

DONALD STOKES

WILDSIDE PRESS

Chapter One

Hansen opened the shutters of the French windows, and moonlight streamed through the vents, marking his nakedness with pale stripes. He stepped out on to the terrace, and the touch of his feet on the cold marble made his overheated body shiver pleasurably. Below him lay Algiers. The two great curves of the city, swelling up to its twin-breasted hills, were like a spangled bosom on the night, above which the eyes of the stars stared down feverishly.

After the intimacy of the bedroom, it was as if he were perched on the tip of some cosmic thumbnail. From out of the blue-blackness of space came a coolness that reached through the lacy carvings of the balustrade and played over his sticky skin.

Behind him, in the bedroom, the girl's voice interrupted his thoughts. "Come back to bed," she said.

"In a minute. Want to finish my smoke." Hansen sucked on his cigarette, so that she would see the glow and leave him alone. The coolness was stirring the leaves of the false pepper trees in the gardens below, bringing him the perfume of oleanders, the cloying sweetness of heliotrope.

Lightning ripped silently along the crystalline horizon, where the Mediterranean met the farthest fringe of the stars. Hansen waited for the thunder to follow, tensing himself to release, with it, some of his pent-up urge for action. Instead there came another stab of white, weak against the moon. Just like the ack-ack when we landed here, thought Hansen.

Down below was the harbor, where the troop transports had docked. He could pick out the El-Djefna pier, where he had come down the gangplank. Near it was the stucco hall

5

in which the French Foyer du Soldat had given dances for the GIs—until things got out of hand, the cocottes being in such short supply. That was, let's see, eight years ago. Eight years and nothing much to show for them. But there would be from now on. Tomorrow was his big chance, he would see Kuhn.

What had Kuhn been doing when the Americans were landing here? A safe bet he was making a fast million, opening those turtle eyes just wide enough to see the main chance, feeding his elephant body with pills to keep himself alive.

If Kuhn had been in Algiers he'd have stayed right here in this hotel—nothing but the best for Kuhn. No, Kuhn couldn't have. This hotel had been Allied headquarters during the war. All the big brass, and the staff cars sprouting stars all over.

Hansen remembered driving up to this place, skidding round the bends of the Rue Michelet. He'd gotten a kick out of seeing the minor brass move like hellbats when he had showed them his Counter-Intelligence identification and told them he had a priority dispatch for the big chief.

Hansen leaned forward to study the bright necklace of lights over to the east, which marked the coast road. It seemed only yesterday that he'd driven along there in a convoy, away from the blacked-out city toward the front line, marveling at himself for not having put a bullet into Mari. What a fool he'd been, taken for a sucker when everybody had warned him.

He had thought he would forget her as soon as his unit went into action, but instead there were the long hours of slow burn, of having to sit and think—the images running through his mind of Mari's white body up against Martello's. Even now, he could remember every detail of her face, the exact pitch of her voice. Memory was queer; something that happened eight years ago could be more vivid than yesterday. Even now there was that pain in some part of him. He never thought he would ever return to Algiers. He had sworn he wouldn't.

Hansen looked across at the other hill of the city. Just around that sparkling curve was Mari's house. Was she still there? Had she changed? Not she. He would probably run into her, if he were to work in Algiers for Kuhn. She might even be useful, in whatever scheme Kuhn was cooking up.

Useful? Hansen made a jeering groan at himself. If he let Mari give him the green light again he'd be finished.

"Come on," called the girl from the bed.

"Half a minute."

Seemed queer to hear her prissy Parisian accent in this tropical darkness. Where had this girl been eight years ago? Probably in pigtails, too young even for the GIs, and that meant plenty young. There was something about Algiers that had made all the men as keen as bulls; maybe it was the long voyage, or the battle not far off.

Hansen peered down at the city, searching for the baroque immensity of the Sambetta among the lime-washed minarets and domes, which returned the insistent stare of the stars. Oh, of course, it had been rebuilt. There it was, turned into one of those ugly functional jobs. That place could tell some stories. The biggest *maison de tolérance* in town, seven whole floors, with *divertissements exotiques* on the top floor (only the topkicks could afford that, at fifty bucks a time).

The Passion Pit—that's what the GIs called it. They kept it busy as Macy's day and night. The madames jammed you into an elevator that was stifling hot, like being slid into a crematorium, and took you to every floor, looking for the shortest wait in line. You could get it quicker and cheaper in the Arab quarter, if you weren't the worrying type.

Hansen turned his head and could see the Rue Thuillier, in a semicircle of perspective that made its arcades bend in curves that grew smaller and rounder. And above this frontier of the European section reared the Casbah, like a great carbuncle, festering and malignant, ripe to be lanced.

Lemmie had tried it in there. He had got past the M.P.'s on guard at the Off Limits sign by wearing an Arab burnoose. It had taken a squad of M.P.'s and French poilus a whole day to find his body. By that time it was stripped of everything, even the identification disc.

Hansen stared down at the teeming hillside, which erupted here and there in the pustules of mosque domes. In this wan glow the Casbah looked decayed, yet even now, long after midnight, when the alleys were thick with homeless sleepers and fat rats played tag over rotting garbage, Hansen knew the horror and the pain and the evil were still pulsing.

The old-guard French were right. They knew the Arabs were ripe for trouble. Trouble, and so here was Kuhn, the old vulture, ready to stick his beak into the carrion.

Hansen's restlessness jarred him again, and he counted how long he had waited for Kuhn to arrive in the city. Five whole days. But tomorrow he would see him, unless Kuhn postponed his arrival once more. No, it had to be tomorrow. He gripped the carved balustrade of the terrace in a surge of impatience, exerting the powerful span of his hands against its delicacy.

"Why don't you come?" The girl's voice was sharp.

"I'm restless."

Restless—that was putting it mildly. What was the word when you'd had an ache inside you every minute for eight years, when you felt that if something didn't happen soon you'd split wide open?

Tonight the ache was worse than ever, in spite of knowing that he would soon see Kuhn. Must be this damned city—it seemed to bring back all the torment to his mind.

. He looked again at the other great breast of the city, which was nubbed with bold light. Mari's house was just round the other side of it. Was it because of her that he was het up? Was it the knowledge that a taxi could get him to her in ten minutes, that he could see her, touch her, once more?

"What's the matter with you?" The girl's voice had edged.

The bed creaked, and he knew she was coming over to him. He pretended not to know, he wanted to hold on to this moment and the realization that he felt was about to explode in his mind.

The girl's voice came from close behind him: "You look like a great bull with those shoulders." She slid her arms round him and he could feel the points of her breasts against the small of his back, the tickle of her hair on his shoulder blades. She brought with her the warmth of the bed.

"You must come," she said, and began to tug him.

Her eagerness repelled him. There was something jarring about her lack of reserve, and once more suspicion of her coiled in his mind. She'd been too easy a pushover, right from the moment when she'd sat next to him on the bus from the airport. Maybe that wasn't an accident. She had never mentioned again, after that, the girl friend she said she'd hoped to meet on his plane. And she'd always been so willing.

Maybe she was playing some little game of her own.

Was she mixed up in this mess in Algiers? She'd been full

of guff about the Arabs—she got a great kick out of them, like many Frenchwomen who wanted a new thrill. Maybe she was one of these bleeding hearts, the fake intellectuals who were working for the Arab independence movement. Snooping was the Algerian hobby, everybody had to know what everybody else was doing. Perhaps she was doing her stint by finding out why he had returned to Algiers. She'd been full of questions—and she'd known too much about Kuhn for a casual tourist who'd only been in the city three weeks.

The girl began to pluck gently at his skin with her lips, and he could visualize the wet redness of the mouth—a sentient little being with an appetite of its own.

Hansen flipped away his cigarette, watching it arch to the fountain that hissed in the gardens below, then he turned and looked at the girl. Her body was marked diagonally by the light that fell through the vents. The straight lines were bent by her curves, and reared sharply over her breasts, making them striped domes. He grasped her by the shoulders and turned her round, then gently pushed her in the direction of the bed. She obeyed the unspoken command and trotted ahead of him, and he heard the springs give under her weight.

Yes, she was too eager. She was up to something. What was her game? As he followed her into the dimness he decided to find out. "I'll be with you in a second," he said, and went into the bathroom.

"Hurry!" Her voice had an urgent edge to it.

As soon as Hansen was inside he turned on the faucets to drown his noise, then went to the other door, which led into the dressing room. Maybe he could find a clue from what was in her handbag. Hansen turned the handle of the dressing room cautiously, so that the girl would not hear. He realized that the catch had been turned. Strange. The girl must have done that—she was the last one in here. Why had she fastened the door? There was nobody in the dressing room. Unless . . .

He pulled back the catch, with elaborate softness, and turned the handle. He went in crouching.

The moon set the room in silver and black, but there was something else in there, a blur of white over by the chest of drawers, A moment poised, and then the whiteness rushed at him.

Chapter Two

Hansen had time only to distinguish that there were two figures—in Arab robes—and then they were on him.

He threw himself forward, aiming at their legs. His head and shoulders struck sharply and splinters of pain went through him. Their bodies fell with his, and for a moment there was one violent mass of movement. Through his mind flashed, "Knives, they're sure to have knives."

He had to finish this quickly. He smashed out furiously with his fists.

He saw the glint of the blade too late. A cold agony ripped his shoulder, and then rage took hold of him, possessing every nerve in his body. He scrambled up and went in with both fists driving. He felt his knuckles jar on bone, and he smashed harder, in savage fury. One Arab crumpled and lay still, the other turned and ran toward the bedroom.

All that Hansen could see was a pale movement of robes, but the sight of his prey escaping galvanized him into a tackle that flung him on to the white-covered body.

Hansen pinned his arms round the man, and they fell together. The Arab squirmed frantically, threshing his wiry body, freed his right arm, and stabbed viciously. Hansen felt a searing pain in his hand, but with the other seized the knife arm of his opponent and strained with all his strength to pull back the fingers. He heard the wrist crack and the Arab began a shriek, but Hansen grasped his throat and throttled the sound. He brought up his slashed hand to tighten his throttle; the blood from his cut fingers made his grasp slippery. He felt a terrible compulsion to squeeze the life out of the Arab, but some flicker at the back of his blazing mind warned him. Instead, he staggered to his knees, hauled the Arab round and smashed him full in the face. The man fell to the floor and lay still.

Hansen lurched to his feet and saw the other Arab was also motionless. The room was deathly quiet. A reaction flooded through him, and he tottered to the nearest chair and fell into it. For several minutes he slumped there, sucking great breaths into his lungs. Gradually, his nerves slowed their jumping. His right shoulder felt as though a lighted cigarette were being pressed against it. When he touched the wound his fingers came away reddened. He went into the bathroom and saw in the mirror that his chest was covered with blood. He soaked a towel under the cold faucet and pressed it against his shoulder, to stem the flow of bleeding. He wrapped the end of the towel round his slashed right hand, then twisted his head in the mirror to see what was making the throbbing in his face. There was an ugly red mark in the hollow of his cheek.

Hansen went back into the dressing room. The two intruders were still motionless, their limbs thrown out at grotesque angles, as if their bodies had been carelessly flung aside. Were they dead? Hansen knelt beside each man in turn and examined him carefully.

No, they would be okay, except that the older one's wrist was obviously broken.

Hansen noticed that both men had the sallow complexion of the city Arab. One of them was about thirty—a powerful heavy-headed man—while the other was not more than twenty and unusually tall for an Arab.

Hansen picked up their two knives and sank back into the armchair. He sat there for several minutes, watching the men and gathering his strength.

He saw one of the Arabs stir. He went over and saw he was the one who had been felled first, the tall young man. The Arab's black eyes were open, staring up blankly.

Hansen prodded him with his foot. "Get up," he ordered.

The youth moved his head from side to side weakly, and tried to lift it, but failed. His lips were puffed and a little spurt of blood was pumping rhythmically over them, coursing down his cheek.

Hansen pulled up the young man's *ihram*, a seamless garment, and searched through his pockets. They were empty. His hands were clean and smooth—obviously he did no manual work. His clothes were of good quality. While he was being searched, the Arab's eyes followed every movement.

Hansen noticed that the door of the closet was open. He went over and saw that his suitcase had apparently not been touched, but he could tell that the intruders had been through it, because the zipper of the inner pouch, which he remembered putting in the locked position, was not quite fastened. Nothing had been taken; the fountain pen, the wrist watch that needed a new strap, the cuff links, all were in the same place. So the men were not thieves. Why had they come?

Kuhn? Was the old man trying to check up on him? Perhaps Kuhn wanted to find out if Hansen planned to operate on his own, as he had threatened several times. No, Kuhn wouldn't have employed Arabs. The old man palm greased the police, who could have done a much better job. And the police had stopped using Arab agents, for far too many of them had turned out to be members of the Arab independence movement. He'd make these guys talk.

Hansen went into the bedroom and for the first time remembered the girl. She was crouching up on the bed, with her reddish-brown hair falling forward over her eyes, which were staring at him in terror. Her smeared little mouth was hanging open, tremulous.

"What happened?" she quavered.

"As if you didn't know. I'm giving a party for your friends who dropped in." He opened the bedside closet and got out the bottle of *eau de vie*. He took a deep swig, and the fiery brandy sent roots of stimulation down into him. The girl looked round wildly, and he shook his head. "Don't try to go away," he said. "I haven't finished with you."

Hansen took the brandy bottle into the dressing room. He went first to the older one, Big-Head, whose broken wrist was bent back at an unnatural angle. Hansen forced open the man's lips and poured some of the brandy into his mouth. He felt a sardonic pleasure in forcing him to drink liquor, forbidden to him by his religion. The Arab spluttered and coughed, and his large head rolled from side to side in pain. He spat out the brandy, and its stain on the carpet was tinged red from his bloodied mouth.

Big-Head's white kaffiyeh headdress had jerked off in the struggle, and Hansen ripped away the agal cord that had kept it in place. He passed the cord round the Arab's throat and said, "Who sent you here? Tell me, or you'll die the death of an unbeliever."

Big-Head stared up at Hansen and faintly shook his head. "*Nekaf*," he said, "I am afraid." But there was no fear in the black eyes, only obstinacy.

Hansen realized that he was taking the wrong line. "You are no robber," he said, "you are a man of quality. Why do you creep in like a carrion dog?"

Even as he spoke a realization came to Hansen. The clean-

liness of the intruders' hands and clothes proved they had
not climbed any pipes to get in. They must have gotten in
before he entered with the girl. The Arabs had no springers
or celluloid with which to open the doors themselves. So
somebody must have let them in with a passkey. They had an
accomplice here in the hotel. These Arabs all stuck together.
Their underground grapevine was quicker than the phone.
Underground . . . Hell, that was it.

Hansen took a chance. "I know who they are," he said,
"I know who sent you and how you got in here. You come
from the *s'iba*, the rebels"—he corrected himself quickly—
"that is what the French call you. You are patriots who serve
Messali Hadj."

The dark eyes flickered and Hansen knew he was right.

"You were told to find out what I am doing in your country," Hansen went on. "Your friends who work in this hotel
opened my door for you—they're also working for Messali,
aren't they?"

Big-Head looked him stolidly in the eye. "*Mish haraf*,"
he said, "I don't know." Hansen fought down a murderous
desire to smash the man's obstinate face.

"You'd better rest, so you can remember," said Hansen. He
helped the Arab to get up and sit in the armchair, then picked
up the girl's slip and wiped his bleeding mouth with it. The
man kept his lips together, trying not to show the pain of his
broken wrist.

Hansen felt his reaction intensifying into an acute weariness.

"I'll attend to your friend," he said. He brought a glass of
water to the younger Arab, who was still dazed, and dashed
it in his face. Globules of the liquid glistened in the gullies
between the youth's mashed lips, and on the bruised flesh
round his left eye.

The young Arab's face became twisted by pain, as he tried
to lever his body up on to his elbow. He collapsed, his lips
drawing back from his gums as if he were about to cry out.

"Be quiet," said Hansen, "unless you want the police to
come."

Big-Head hobbled over, holding his shattered arm out from
his body, as if not to jar it. He squatted on his haunches and
muttered haltingly to his companion in Berber. Hansen
guessed that he was using that tongue instead of Arabic, in
order to conceal from Hansen what he was saying. It was

something about the wounded man keeping his mouth shut.

"Enough of that," said Hansen to Big-Head. "You'd better go to the hospital as soon as you can. Don't try any of your Arab home treatment, or you'll never be able to use your hand again."

Both pairs of eyes looked up at him. He could tell that they were surprised he did not call the police.

"Go back to your leader," said Hansen to Big-Head, "after you have had your wrist treated. Tell Messali Hadj that I am his friend, that I wish him no ill. Say that if I can do anything to help his movement I shall be proud. As a proof of that I am letting you both go free. You know that if I were to pick up that phone I could have you both sent to prison. But I don't like the police any more than you do."

Big-Head shrugged. "*Maleesh,*" he said, "so be it,"—the Arab term of supreme fatalism.

"Get up," said Hansen to the youth. He tried to obey, but swayed dizzily. The older Arab used his sound arm to steady his companion.

Hansen remembered the knives. He hesitated, and he noticed that Big-Head was looking at them anxiously. Hansen remembered that the dagger was the Arab symbol of masculinity; if he kept the knives he would be humiliating the men.

He picked up the daggers and handed them back. "I thought you were thieves," he said, "I did not know that you were from Messali Hadj. Your friends who let you into my room will help you to leave the hotel."

Big-Head took the younger Arab's arm round his shoulder and helped him out into the bedroom. The girl was standing up with the sheet draped round her, and the contrast of the whiteness against her tanned skin made her look like a savage. Her face was naked of any pretense—she was terrified. Hansen sensed she was about to shriek, so he said to her, "Not a peep out of you. Stay where you are, you little Delilah."

Hansen motioned the Arabs to wait while he unbolted the door and glanced along the corridor. All was quiet. He nodded his head and the two Arabs moved out. Big-Head hesitated and looked up at Hansen. "*Salaam aleikoum,*" he said, "Peace be with you."

"And to you peace," said Hansen. He shut the door behind them, and grinned. Coming from them, that farewell was mighty big.

He turned and saw that the girl was scurrying into the dressing room, with her reddish hair bouncing on her shoulders, and her rump like an ace of spades turned upside down.

"Where are you going?" he asked.

She turned and said in an uneven voice, "My clothes—"

"Come back. You forgot something."

Her mouth formed a red O of alarm. She reached the dressing-room door, but Hansen beckoned her, bending his fingers in a gesture commanding her to come to him. The girl's arm dropped from the handle and she turned to face him, slowly, as if mesmerized. The door of the dressing room continued to swing open and the spreading bar of light gradually exposed the girl's nude body.

All of Hansen's faculties had sharpened suddenly. The fight had left him keyed up to every stimulus. He could hear her rapid breathing as she stepped, trembling, toward him, and as she came close he could even detect the scent of fear on her. When she came within reach of him she stopped. She was breathless with terror.

"Delilah," said Hansen softly, "you're going to get yours."

He raised his arm. She knew the blow was coming but she was too rooted to duck. He cuffed her hard with the heel of his hand. Her head rocked, and she toppled back onto the bed. She cowered, wiping the blood from her mouth. Her eyes stared wildly at his body, and as she stared she ceased to cower. She lay back, waiting for him.

Hansen went at the girl brutally. As he lunged toward her he felt her arms pull at him, joining his urgency to her own. As his lips crushed upon hers he could taste the blood she had wiped there.

Chapter Three

Hansen pushed open the frosted glass door marked SYNDICAT DES ENTERPRISES ALGERIENNES, and a cold gust of conditioned air enveloped him. Kuhn always took care of his asthma, he thought. Wonder why the old man stuck it out here, in the dust and the stink of Algiers, when he could live like a prince anywhere he chose.

The brunette at the reception desk flashed a mechanical

smile, which gained warmth as her wet eyes took him in.
"I'm Blair Hansen," he said, "I'm expected."

"Oh, yes, you're to go straight in." She rose and led him
down the checkered light and shade of a corridor, past a row
of cubicle offices. A Havas tape machine was busy chatting
to itself in a corner, spilling out its grayish roll of news tape.

The girl made a diffident tap on a door marked ERNST
KUHN, and bent her dark head to listen for a reply. As she
did so, she rolled her fine eyes sideways to look apprecia-
tively at Hansen.

"Here, let me try," said Hansen impatienty. He opened
the door and walked in. The old man was sitting at the far
end of the room, outlined against slithers of sunshine that
managed to elude the lattice blind.

"Ah, Mr. Hansen!" wheezed Kuhn, in a voice that was
blurred by asthma.

Except for the great desk and two chairs, there was no
other furniture; Kuhn feared anything that might harbor
the deadly dust that provoked his disease. Hansen's heels
sounded loudly on the tiled floor as he crossed over to the
desk and looked down at the old man.

The sun was brutally frank with Kuhn. It emphasized his
bald head, which was speckled on top with patches of brown
age-pigmentation, and gave to the fluff of weak hair over
each of his ears the appearance of white mildew. His skin
hung in loose folds from his cheekbones, and his mouth was
buried in puckered slack. The old man was still a ponderous
figure, but the former elephantine bulges seemed to have
shrunk a little, as if somebody had let air out of him. He
had been very ill, and showed it.

"Sit down," said Kuhn. He motioned to the visitor's chair
which was placed well away from Kuhn—another precaution
to avoid the dust he feared. "Hello, you've been in a fight?"
He leaned forward to peer at Hansen, and his hands, as they
took the weight, became ridged with veins.

Hansen explained briefly what had happened. "I thought at
first they were from you, checking up on me," he said, "but
I discovered they were from the Arab rebels."

Kuhn's lips showed for the first time, out of the folded
slack of crepy skin—two thin lines of pale mauve flecked
with mucus. This was Kuhn's smile.

"I never use such crude methods," he said. "The rebels are
very anxious to find out what I plan to do in Algeria. They

went through my things in the hotel. I've had to hire a guard. Why should you think I wanted to check up on you? I know all about you, without resorting to melodrama."

"Well, why did you send for me?"

"You can be useful to me here."

"You're having trouble, I know that."

"You have shown reasonable intelligence, and some animal courage. That, and your command of Arabic, did the trick in several of the negotiations. On the other hand, you have a regrettable tendency to needless violence—it was lucky for you that the Tangier affair turned out so well. You almost killed the man—"

"I'm allergic to knives, especially when they're stuck into me."

"I prefer my subordinates to act through their brains, not their glands."

"My methods pay off. When your manganese project in Tangier bogged down I got it moving. When the officials tried to hold you up with the antimony deal I—"

"Yes, yes. That's what I paid you for, handsomely. But you must not be too impatient. There are difficulties here that have licked some of the best business brains in America. They spent several years as I have, in trying to get to first base, and finally they went back to America in disgust."

"You mean the Arab trouble that's blowing up here—it's stopping plans for development?"

"Partly. I'll explain the setup later. First of all, I want you to understand that I want no recklessness. You must follow my orders strictly, and above all avoid strong-arm stuff."

"You make me sound like a gangster. I've never got into trouble yet nor tangled up with the police."

"I wouldn't have sent for you if I didn't think you could do what I want."

"Good! Now, what do I do?"

Kuhn picked up his blotter pad and laid it on end beside his chair, so that the desk was bare except for the phone. Under the glass top, the entire surface was taken up by a large-scale map of Algeria, which went flush to the edges. The old man's paunch was pressed against the southern extremity of the map, where the outline of the great desert was relieved only by a few dotted lines to mark caravan tracks. Kuhn stretched out his hand to the dark-brown stippling that marked the central massif. The wet heat of his palms left a faint vapor on the glass, which remained for several seconds. It was as if Kuhn were caressing the reluctant curves of the country, leaving his own brand on it.

"Just here," he said, his soft hand resting on the glass. "The El Hazy Bloug valley. It's the biggest development I've ever planned."

"What is it?"

"Iron ore, Mr. Hansen. A very great deal of it." He fished in one of the drawers of his desk, pulled out a folder and opened it. "Here's the latest report from the geological team we sent there," he said. "They've taken drillings for fourteen months over an area of two hundred square miles, and have bored down to four hundred feet. Listen to the assay report." He read out: " 'Average approximates 58 per cent iron, 1.2 per cent manganese, .17 phosphorus, and 6.11 silica.' That, Mr. Hansen, is as good as the Mesabi range of America, which is running out. And the whole world is looking for iron ore."

Hansen peered down at the map. "Your valley is in the heart of the Berber country," he said. "That's rebel territory. The French never dare patrol there except in battalion strength, with armored cars. You'll never get any iron ore out of that valley."

"I can and I will," said Kuhn. "That's why I want your help."

"I know. I go and tell the rebels they can't intimidate you. I've heard that joke before."

Kuhn's rheumy eyes fixed Hansen. "There's a great fortune to be made out of this," he said quietly.

Hansen grinned. "You've talked me into it. The only chance would be for us to contact the central committee of the rebels. Explain it's for the good of the Arabs. Promise to hire only Arab labor, trained by Americans, as you did in your Egyptian plant."

"You think you can persuade them?"

"Frankly, no. But it's worth a try."

"I am willing to back you heavily."

"You mean with—" Hansen twiddled his forefinger and thumb together.

Kuhn nodded.

"Good. You need plenty of folding money with the Arabs."

"You know the old saying—'If you can't beat them, join them.' That's what we must do with the Arabs."

Hansen shook his head. "Too late for political tricks. This country is a powder barrel waiting for somebody to light the fuse."

"That's why most American capital fights shy of Algeria. But I figure that in the long run Algeria is the best bet. After all, it's a department of France, as much French as Long Island is American. The French will never give up an actual part of France itself." The old man said this interrogatively.

"The French have created their own monster," said Hansen. "They've built clinics and hospitals for the Arabs and cut down their death rate, so that Algeria is now swamped with eight Arabs to every Frenchman. The French, of course, are hopelessly split on what to do about it. Those in Paris try to bribe the Arabs with still better social conditions, while the French here are all for a strong hand with no nonsense."

"You think there will be armed revolt again? The fighting two years ago set my plans back for years. Some of my best technicians were killed—"

"Not to mention the small item of hundreds of French and God knows how many thousand Arabs," said Hansen drily.

"Already my field teams have had trouble—only a little sabotage and sniping so far, but I don't like the smell of it. It's growing. You can see the signs everywhere. That huge store of explosives the French discovered the other day. The hundreds of arrests made by the French Security Brigade. The rebel slogans you see painted up on all the walls. The sniping that goes on at French soldiers in the country districts. . . ."

The buzz of the phone cut into the still coolness of the room. Kuhn answered, and instantly his face lightened. "How good of you to call, madame," he said.

The tiny microcosm of a woman's voice vibrated in the earpiece.

"A wonderful idea," said Kuhn. "I'd love to." He listened for a few more moments, then he rolled back his head and wheezed out a laugh. The sharp line where his dentures met his gums could be clearly seen.

"Yes, yes, I will," said Kuhn, " and may I ask you a great favor, madame? I'd like to bring along a young man who has just arrived in the city. Eh?" Kuhn grimaced as if the person he were talking to were present. "Oh, he's an American. His name is Blair Hansen."

The disembodied voice in the instrument suddenly cut

short. Kuhn's eyebrows, which looked like coarse gray weeds sprouting out of the decay of his face, moved toward each other. He lifted his hand as if to jiggle the receiver, but in that instant the sharp little diminuendo of the woman was heard again.

Kuhn raised his voice: "I said his name is Hansen, Blair Hansen . . . yes, American." The old man looked across at Hansen and said into the mouthpiece, "Yes, very tall, with black hair. Can you hear me . . . Hello? . . . Oh, you've met him? That's fine. You would. Fine. At eight this evening then, both of us. Enchanted!"

Kuhn put down the receiver, and the vertical gullies lined his face again, erasing the semblance of a smile.

"You know her?" the old man demanded. "You know Madame Mari Lander?"

Hansen felt his breath catch. "Yes, I know her," he said.

"How well?" Kuhn looked angry. "Listen, she's not another of your women, is she?"

Hansen felt as though he were poised in the center of a storm, in danger of being caught up by it at any moment. He spoke swiftly, before his thoughts could be whirled away. "It ought to be an interesting dinner tonight. I can't exactly call her a social acquaintance. I once had the pleasure of arresting her."

Kuhn's mouth reappeared, an oval of surprise. He recovered himself, and his tone grew more friendly. "Ah, I see, during the war, you mean, when you were with Counter-Intelligence. I suppose Madame Lander was mixed up with the Vichy crowd?"

When Hansen nodded, Kuhn went on, "That was a damned mess. When soldiers try to meddle in politics they usually ruin everything."

"You mean me? It wasn't politics. Just a moral delousing of the civilian population—routine security work." The storm was crowding him closer. He marveled at himself for being able to make conversation.

"What happened to her when she was arrested?"

"She was deep in with the Fascist crowd here, so deep that you'd have to hold your nose, but we got nothing on her. She was clever, and she had sex appeal—what more did she need? I guess the bloom is off the peach by now."

"She is still a very beautiful young woman."

"Young? Her daughter must be nearly twenty by now."

Hansen had to force himself to speak casually. "Anyway, Mari Lander went free. In fact, if the Army had been here a little longer I think she'd have hooked my commanding officer—yes, wedding bells and all trimmings. We used to call her the Merry Widow. A bit corny, but it stuck."

Kuhn cleared his throat, irritably. "All of that happened eight years ago. A lot of people—big people—backed the wrong horse in those days."

"Listen, I'm not criticizing her. She took care of herself, the way she knew best."

Kuhn looked mollified. "She is one of the cleverest women I know. It won't be, er, awkward, when you meet tonight?"

For one moment Hansen had on his tongue the words that would have excused him from going. "No," he told himself, "she'd think I were scared."

"It won't be awkward," he said, "it ought to be interesting."

"Good. I want you two to get together. I'm sure she can be very useful to us."

"Now wait a minute! You're not bringing her into your plans, are you?"

"Of course not. I just want her advice, that's all. She knows everyone worth while in the country. With her influence we'll be able to find out where we stand, support the right people, plan our moves."

Hansen felt his stomach muscles contract with mingled anger and alarm. "You'd better keep your shoulder blades to the wall," he managed to say.

Chapter Four

MARI LANDER'S HOUSE was exactly as Hansen had seen it for eight years in his memory—a veil of pink oleanders softening its whiteness, intricate filigree ironwork masking the outer doorway. The gray-haired maid who answered his ring spoke in the slow drawl of the Midi, and he remembered that all of Mari's staff had been French even when he knew her—and that was before the Arabs had begun to get restive. Mari distrusted the Arabs too deeply to hire them as servants.

He followed the maid through toward a central garden, which formed the core of the square-shaped house. While his eyes were adapting themselves to the dimness he realized that another maid, an older woman, was standing in an archway that led off from the main passage. Her bright old eyes stared at him, with a growing look of horror. To his amazement she made the sign of the cross.

She clicked into place in his memory. She was Yvette, Mari's personal watchdog. Hansen grinned, and Yvette averted her eyes. I must have made quite an impression, he thought.

Through the delicately fluted Moorish columns that surrounded the central garden, he saw the fountain sending a lacy cloud of spray pattering softly into a pool of porphyry, in which glided purple carp. The whisper of that spray had been in his ears for years; he looked up at her room—the window was open.

The grass was so brilliantly green and smooth, the flowers so brilliant, that they looked artificial. Patterned across the garden, in the formality instinctive to the French, were bitter orange trees and bushes of jasmine, mellowing the dry air.

"Ah, M'sieur Hansen!" came a girl's voice, from a room that opened on to the garden. She walked out from the shade to greet him, a slim little figure who seemed the same as when he last saw her eight years ago. Céleste, daughter of Mari Lander.

As he took her hand he said, "M'selle is *ravissante!*"

She smiled nervously. "M'sieur is very easy to please. Please come in. M'sieur Kuhn is already here, and Mari will be down in a moment." Her small teeth showed in a smile, and only then could he detect the faintest resemblance to her mother; Céleste's mouth had the same full sensuous bow.

Except for her mouth and her large gray eyes, Céleste might have been a delicate boy. Her honey-colored hair was cropped short in the gamin style, and though her calf-length evening dress, of some frothy white material, did things for her figure, it seemed to accentuate her coltishness.

"You'll have an *apéritif?*" asked Céleste, as they entered the reception room and she seemed relieved when Hansen said, "Please." He guessed that she wanted to have something to do with her hands.

Kuhn was sunk in an old-fashioned wing chair, looking like a waxen Buddha starting to melt.

Hansen tried to put Céleste at her ease by asking her about her university. She told him she had arrived back by plane the previous day from Paris, where she studied at the Sorbonne.

"What are you studying?" Kuhn asked her heavily. "What do you want to be?"

Céleste shrugged. "I have no talents," she said.

"Then you must go into Government service," smiled Hansen. "You will be able to build a fine career at the Quai d'Orsai."

She laughed in a pleasant low pitch, and seemed to gain confidence. While he talked to her there floated into the back of Hansen's mind an impression of the real Céleste; she was a stranger here, her world was in the dingy crowded cellar clubs of the Left Bank of Paris. He could imagine her happily arguing with fellow students in the little restaurants round St. Germain-des-Près.

She sat with her feet well apart, resting her forearms on her thighs, and Hansen realized that this was probably the first time in months she had worn an evening dress. In the Latin Quarter they went for sweaters and corduroy skirts. He noticed that the girl's gray eyes were faintly tinged with pink, as if she had been crying.

"Hello." It was the voice of Mari.

It came from beyond an arched half wall that divided the room in two. The rustling of a dress could be heard, till it was overborne by Kuhn's wheezing as he pulled himself up from his chair.

"Her old trick," thought Hansen: "she has to make a big entrance."

Mari appeared and poised for a moment in the frame of the arch, collecting the focus of their gaze. "Sorry I'm late," she said, "I'm a terrible hostess." She came forward in a movement that rippled the perfection of her full curved lines.

She wore a black strapless dress, the dull sheen of which made a live counterpoint to each curve below her flared skirt, and emphasized each one above.

Hansen bent over her hand, in the formal French greeting, and when he straightened up he kept his face from betraying any expression.

She gazed at him intently, as if trying to gauge her effect on him. By God, the same old come-on. Her black eyes still gave the appearance of being flexible in depth—flat if she were bored, deeper as her interest grew. As she looked at

Hansen, her back to the old man, the pupils seemed to expose their deepest depths.

"Oh, you bad, bad bitch," he thought, "you're trying the quick treatment."

"You're much thinner," she said, "and you look more sad. And you've hurt your hand!" She laid the tips of her fingers on the bandages of his right hand, and he had the sensation that their skin had actually touched.

"I am flattered that madame remembers me."

She gave that full smile. "One never forgets a friend as close as you."

She used the intimate "toi!" Hansen glanced involuntarily at Kuhn; the old man would not like this familiarity between them. As if in answer to his thoughts Kuhn said, "Mr. Hansen has been warning me, madame, that you are a very dangerous woman."

She laughed, her ripe mouth showing perfect teeeth. "I hope he's right," she said, and made a complete turn, smiling over her bare shoulder at Hansen as she did so.

She revolved with such smooth swiftness that the flare of her dress closed in a swirl and outlined the full symmetry of her figure. She knew how to use her body. "Well?" she said, "Do you think I've changed?"

Hansen was suddenly keyed by her challenge. There was something different about her, now that he could see her more closely. Something had changed, changed for the worse.

"Nothing could ever change my opinion of madame," he said.

"That is very qualified praise. So you have told M'sieur Kuhn that I am dangerous?"

She beckoned with her bare arm to the ottoman, which was strewn with fat, silk-covered cushions. She piled several of them together to make a rest, then patted the place beside her for Hansen to sit. She arranged herself so that she could look at both men.

"Why am I dangerous?" she asked turning to Hansen.

"I am sure that madame is under no illusions as to what I think of her."

Her mobile lips made their pleasure again, and she leaned back on one elbow. Her breathing made two crescents of shadow ebb and flow in rhythm below her breasts, accentuating their firm swell. Hansen was suddenly aware that there was no single part of the woman that was not a curve—the shoulders, the chin, the bold wing of the eyebrows, even the light that glittered richly in the chignons of thick black hair.

Kuhn cleared his throat importantly. "Men are always afraid of women who have beauty and brains," he said.

"Afraid?" she said. "That is not the way I want you two to feel about me."

"I don't," said Hansen. "I feel admiration, for your success is apparently defeating time."

"Ah, your cynical smile again," she replied. "You still haven't explained why I'm dangerous."

"A woman who is capable of holding off the years is capable of anything."

"I hope to prove that you are right."

Céleste brought her mother's drink, and when the two women were caught in the pool of light from the lamp, Hansen was struck by the contrast between them—the girl's fair hair and skin and gray eyes, against the black iridescence of Mari's hair, the primal red of her lips, her dark complexion.

As Mari sipped the drink, the light played over the rounded grace of her arm, forming loops and bows of shadow. The line of her cheek looked as smooth as Céleste's. Yet there was something that was new about her. He would find it soon.

"Oh, look!" cried Céleste. "The birds are here."

The girl rose and moved on tiptoe to the arch that opened out into the garden. Hansen leaned sideways, and could see mosque swallows swooping down onto the fountain, bouncing up again and again as they touched its delicate veil. The wings of the birds caught the dusk light, and flashed like fireworks.

Madame Lander joined her daughter under the arch. Hansen was amused to notice how Kuhn's eyes ran slowly over Madame Lander's body, savoring each curve. The moist turrets that held Kuhn's eyeballs swiveled with his hungry gaze.

The two women became silhouetted against the white of the courtyard walls, accentuating the femaleness of Mari's figure and the slender boyishness of her daughter's.

Hansen crossed the room to them, and looked out over their heads into the cool scented twilight of the garden. Mari's vivid pile of black hair was only a few inches from him, and her scent was disturbing. It was the same one she had always used.

"If only Algiers were all like this," said Céleste.

Hansen glanced down at her, surprised by the fervency of her tone. The girl's profile was remarkably pure in its lines and seemed to make her youthfulness a tangible quality of light. In contrast, Mari's face seemed voluptuous and sultry.

On the still air, from afar off, the wild cry of a muezzin could be heard faintly, with the sundown call to the faithful: *"La Illah il Allah, Mohammed rassoul Lah".*—"There is no God but God, and Mohammed is his Prophet."

"That always makes my spine prickle," said Céleste. "It's like a battle cry."

Mari made a noise of contempt. "The Arabs have forgotten what battle is," she said.

"They still fight you when they get the chance," said Hansen, trying to provoke her.

"Fight? You mean murder. That cowardly slaughter of the French at Kabylie—"

"But, Mari, the French are always repressing them," Céleste burst out, "they massacred the Arabs at Sétif in '44, they shot them down in cold blood at Fez—"

"A few scared conscripts fire in panic! If we wanted to massacre them don't you think we would have done so? Remember we have raised the living standards of these creatures so high in the short time we've been here that there are now eight Arabs for every one when we came. We've given them universities and hospitals—"

"And slums and sweated labor," said the girl.

"Céleste!" The anger was clear in Mari's voice. "You talk of the French as if you are not one of them."

"Sorry, *maman*," said Céleste, barely audible.

Hansen saw a surge of red appear on the girl's neck and cheeks. He wondered, *"Why does she feel so deeply about the Arabs?"*

Mari looked up at Hansen. "You see what a few years in Paris do for a girl?" she said. "It's always those who have the least to do with the natives, who regard themselves as experts on how to deal with them."

The tension between Mari Lander and her daughter tightened its web all during the dinner. Céleste was sitting opposite Hansen, in a cocoon of silence, speaking only when she was directly addressed. The other three had made several attempts to draw her into the conversation; she made replies that were polite but nothing more.

"It cannot be that you are sulking, Céleste?" asked her mother at length. "That would be a strange attitude for a girl of twenty."

"I'm sorry, Mari, I'm very tired from the journey. I had very little sleep last night."

"I'm sure our guests will excuse you after dinner," said her mother coldly. The two women exchanged glances in which Hansen could sense combat.

Mari gave her low-pitched laugh. "Besides," she said, "Céleste must get plenty of sleep—she has an important engagement tomorrow. She's spending the day with an American— the whole day, mind you, though this is the first time she has been home for six months. She must have a great amour!"

"Oh, Mari!" The tide of red again colored the girl's neck and cheeks.

"Oh, yes," said Kuhn, "you were telling me about this man, Spenser Boward, did you say he was called?"

"Spenser *S*. Boward." Mari accentuated the initial. "A very ambitious young man. He was telling me what he would do if he were running Algeria. He seems to think he will be very soon. Well, you know what we call Americans behind your backs"—she gave a long look at Hansen—"*les maîtres futurs du pays*. Maybe M'sieur Boward is right."

"Oh, you were drawing him out," cried Céleste, "trying to make him look silly."

Kuhn took in a wheezing breath. "Our State Department makes me sick," he said. "They send these young college boys over here for a couple of years, and then they're America's experts on the Arab world for the next twenty years."

Mari laughed. "Then I'm very glad you are cultivating him, Céleste," she said. "I think we should, for the sake of France. M'sieur Boward will probably be a power in the State Department before long."

"Don't try to ridicule me," said her daughter, "M'sieur Boward is merely an acquaintance, I happened to sit next to him on the plane coming here. He is extremely *sage*. He knows more about Algeria than I do. He was telling me what a great man Marshal Lyautey was, and why there wouldn't be this trouble today between the French and the Arabs if he were still Governor General here."

"If your American diplomat is so entertaining, why won't you bring him to lunch tomorrow, as I suggested?"

"You would mock him again. I'm sure he noticed your sarcasm this morning."

"Céleste, I do believe you have a maternal instinct! That reminds me—I insist you take the chauffeur when you go into the Casbah. M'sieur Boward's eloquence would not be any use if trouble were to start."

"Oh, we shan't go to the Casbah."

"Not go to the Casbah?" said Kuhn. "But that is the first place every visitor wants to see."

"That's why." The girl's tone was curt. "I hate the fat tourists who go staring round, with guides bawling at them and cameras slung round their necks. They act as if it's a zoo."

"Well?" said Mari. "Zoo is an apt description."

"I'm ashamed to take a foreigner there," Cèleste went on. "I'm ashamed of the filth, the poverty, and the misery. I don't want this American to see children blind from trachoma, or hundreds of homeless sleeping in the gutters—French citizens sleeping in the gutters!"

"These are the radical ideas they teach you in Paris?" asked Mari, her voice dangerously soft. "These Arabs were barbarians before we came, do you think they were better off then or now?"

"Were the French better off under the Nazis? The Arabs are suffering now just as we did then. We even have our French Gestapo, the Security Brigade, to keep down the Arabs."

Mari reached out her hand and patted Céleste's wrist. "That is enough," she said in a tone of satin, "our guests don't want to hear our dreary domestic disputes."

Soft tongues of flames from the candles licked shadows under Mari's high cheekbones.

Compared to Mari, Céleste seemed to be out of place. The purposeful way the girl wielded her knife and fork, keeping her eyes on the plate, the hungry rapidity with which she put food into her mouth, made her look unformed.

Mother and daughter held each other in a silence of opposition for a minute and then Céleste looked up with a smile that was bright but blank. "I'm sorry," she said. "Perhaps we'd better talk about something else, instead of Arabs."

"Let's have coffee in the other room," suggested Mari. She

rose and led the way through the arch into the main *salon.*

The focal point of the room was a *saniya,* a circular tray of beaten brass, wide as a cartwheel, carved with intricate Arab patterns. The four people ranged themselves around it, as the maid served coffee. A small patch of sky was visible from where Hansen sat, and stars were scattered in it like asterisks.

After they had drunk their coffee Céleste said, "Please don't think I'm rude if I ask to be excused now, I am terribly tired." Both men rose to take her hand, and Hansen wondered again about the faint pinkness in her eyes. Why had she been weeping?

Kuhn's moist eyeballs followed the girl till she was gone. "Your daughter is a clue to what we're up against, Madame," he said. "If that's the way they're talking in France, how can we expect this country ever to be developed?"

Mari joined her gaze with Hansen's over the rim of her glass. The intimacy in her eyes brought him a sharp reminder of the last time he had seen her in this room, when she had tried to sell him the idea of the cozy threesome—she, Hansen, and his commanding officer.

"We colons—we French who were born in Algeria—must make our own destiny," said Mari.

"Show me the colon who'll lead you and I'll back him," said Kuhn. "But what have you got—a horde of graft-ridden civil servants. Maybe our only hope is DeGaulle. He didn't stand any nonsense when he was in power here. He exiled Messali, this fellow who's causing all this unrest—packed him off down to the jungle two thousand miles away."

"No," said Mari. "The French always go for an orator with *mystique,* especially if he's a military man, but DeGaulle is too frigid. The French like to suspect that their men of destiny have a harem." She smiled at Hansen. "It's a pity you're not French, Blair," she said, "you might have become a power in Algeria."

Kuhn made a growling cough. Hansen sensed that the old man had noticed the way Mari smiled at him.

"We must rule out the colons and the Arab stooges," said Kuhn, "they've proved themselves to be ineffective. That leaves us with only this fellow Messali and his independence movement. Can we get a tie-up with him?"

For the first time Mari lost her calm. The bows of her lips tightened and her voice was sharp. "Are you crazy?" She rose lithely and faced Kuhn. She was breathing so hard that the shadow which poised over low décolletage contracted and broadened in a rapid motion.

"Help for Messali would mean civil war in Algeria—it would devastate the country," she burst out. "A million colons would fight the Arabs, they would never accept Arab rule. Then what would happen to all your development plans?"

Kuhn flexed his fleshy arms on the arms of the chair, pulling himself up, but Mari had already moved away to the arch that led out to the garden.

Hansen watched quizzically as Kuhn clambered to his feet and went to placate her. The old man was several inches shorter than Mari and his gross bulk looked venal against her lines. "I was only thinking out loud," said Kuhn apologetically.

The old man kept on talking, in a tone that grew more earnest, and Mari softened as swiftly as she had flared up. "I can see that I shall be able to save you from drastic mistakes," she said.

Hansen made no attempt to hide his sardonic grin as she graciously allowed the old man to lead her back to her seat.

Chapter Five

MARI ESCORTED Hansen and Kuhn to the door. She had thrown a lace mantilla over her shoulders and it was delicately suggestive, webbing an arrow-shaped shadow over the cleavage of her bosom.

The light from the hallway spilled out into the indigo night, spreading long glistens on Kuhn's automobile in the driveway. The chauffeur helped the old man to pull his great bulk into the car, and then Kuhn leaned forward, his face waxen in the light. "I'll give you a lift to the hotel, Mr. Hansen," he said.

"That wouldn't be smart," Hansen replied. "If I came in with you the whole place would be buzzing with the news in five seconds."

"Oh, come on, I can drop you off somewhere near." The

hooded eyes revealed that Kuhn didn't like the idea of leaving Hansen alone with Madame Lander.

"Thanks, but I feel like a walk," he said.

He had to get on his own. He wanted to cool his mind and his senses. Somewhere deep down was the wish to remain with Mari, but he fought down the impulse. He waved farewell and strode off toward the outer gate.

Kuhn apparently had more conversation with Mari, for Hansen was halfway down the driveway before the old man's limousine purred past him, its tires making a noise on the gravel like slitting silk.

A flash of something moving caught the corner of Hansen's eye as the car headlights swung round the curved drive—something white. "An Arab," thought Hansen.

He wondered whether he were being watched by the rebels again. These Algerians were all the same—they watched you like a convention of Pinkerton men, and had a grapevine that made the phone look sick.

Hansen stepped onto the crisp well-watered lawn and peered along the pergola that supported the oleanders, but the moon had not risen and he could see nothing. The grass was easier to walk on than the rough driveway, so he moved over it, noiselessly, toward the main gate. Then he heard voices, a man's and a woman's. Hansen peered again, his curiosity aroused. He strained his ears but heard only the noises of the night—a chirping and croaking of furtive things, which seemed muted under the forest of stars.

Mari? No, it couldn't be she. He looked back to the house and saw that the door was still open, pouring out a bar of glowing amber into the night. There was a blur of dark superimposed on the light, and he realized that Mari was still standing there, waiting.

Hansen thought he heard her call out something. He stopped, and the quiet was painful to his ears. She was there, wanting him to go back; he knew that, and the knowledge pulled him. He thought of her with the lace mantilla softly rising and falling, with that moving arrow of shadow cleaving her breasts. At the end of a moment he quickened his stride and passed through the gates, out onto the macadam road.

He forced himself to think about the white-robed intruders in the garden. Sounded like a man and a woman—who could the woman have been? Perhaps it was she who was wearing the white. The memory of a frothy white dress slipped into his thoughts. Céleste—she had worn white at dinner. Maybe she had slipped away to meet this American of hers.

Hansen looked back to see if Mari was still waiting, but the palms and shrubbery had closed out the house from view. He walked rapidly till the road began to dip down toward the sparkling city. Then he heard a car behind him. It rounded a bend and its headlights impaled him, pushing out his shadow to a fantastic length, which rapidly grew denser and shorter as the car drew near. Hansen tensed, listening to the beat of the engine, expecting to hear it slow down at any moment. The car rushed by, leaving an acrid taste of dust and exhaust fumes. Even when it was far ahead, its lights transfixing each of the telephone poles like exclamation marks, Hansen still half thought the car would slow down, but gradually the fingers of the night closed over it.

He admitted to himself that he was disappointed. He had expected it to be Mari. "That bitch, I must stay away from her," he said to himself. He gave in to the insistent thread of thought and let his mind run free, speculating about her. She seemed to be exactly as he had always remembered her, except for that something he couldn't place. Her face sharpened in his mental focus. He could see her olive skin, smooth over the bone formation, setting off the wicked ripeness of the mouth, the black ovals of the eyes. And then his memory gave him the answer that her presence had obscured. He knew how she had changed. It was in those very things—the red mouth, the black eyes. That was it; she hadn't corrupted on the outside, only inside, and the effect of that change had transmuted the quality of her eyes and mouth.

He remembered the ripe red little cavern of her mouth, how the very touch of its voluptuousness had seemed to sap his whole being of everything except his need for her. That something must have been inside her even then. Was it a tangible thing? Would it corrupt his own lips?

He realized that he had been walking mechanically, oblivious to his surroundings. His long stride had taken him down the hill and now he was climbing the slope on the other side, up the Rue Cantaur, which writhed over the hill like a serpent.

It was farther than he thought. He strode as fast as he could, feeling pleasure in extending his muscles, and working out the disturbance that filled him. He kept his eyes on the tall clumps of eucalyptus that could be seen afar off, for the coarse branches were powdered with white dust, glittering like snow. He watched the clumps move against the deeper perspective of the city, which was gradually falling away beneath him as he ascended. It was as if he were using each plant to lever himself up, mentally, to the top of the hill, where his hotel perched; he was escaping from Mari's curved figure.

By the time he reached the marble archway of the hotel, he was tired and calm, and all he wanted was sleep.

The knowing eyes of the desk clerk met him. "A lady has come for you," he said. "She's waiting up in your suite."

Hansen sensed immediately that it was Mari. The car, he thought, she was driving the car that passed me.

The clerk's eyes were inquisitive. "The lady sent her car away," he said.

"Call a cab," Hansen ordered. "She'll be going right back." He walked to the elevator with his indecision gone, anxious for the pleasure of throwing her out.

Mari Lander dropped her cape onto an armchair and looked round the bedroom. On the escritoire over by the window was a small pile of oddments—a handkerchief, some crumpled notes, a battered old hairbrush with one of Hansen's coarse black hairs still in the bristles. She felt them with her fingertips, very gently. Then she went to the French windows and looked east at the hill round which he was walking.

He's coming nearer, she thought, in ten minutes he'll be here, in this room. Mari crossed over to the little closet beside the bed and felt inside. She found the *eau de vie* she expected and lifted it to her lips. She did not drink, but moved her lips against the rim.

She looked round the bedroom, and her memory was a bridge to that other bedroom in which she and Hansen had first met.

She had been sitting up in bed, sipping her morning coffee, and the window panes were throbbing with the roar of American planes. The Allied forces had landed in Algiers a week previously, and the city was still stunned by the sudden appearance of thousands of GIs and British, fat planes thundering low day and night, and—most of all—the security check that was rounding up those who had collaborated with the Nazis.

Mari had looked over the rim of her cup as Yvette, her elderly maid, burst into the bedroom and said breathlessly, "He's here! Captain Hansen is here!"

Hansen's name was well known to Mari, though she had never met him. Her friends had been buzzing with his name for days. This American devil, who spoke fluent colon French and Arabic, had already brought several of her friends to U. S. headquarters for questioning.

"Tell him to wait," Mari told Yvette.

"He says you're to come down at once."

"You heard what I said."

Mari decided to take her time. She sipped her coffee thoughtfully, wondering what attitude to adopt, and was interrupted by Yvette's furious tirade from outside, as the maid tried to stop Hansen from entering. There came an imperative rapping on the door and a curt deep voice said, "Put something on, I'm coming in."

"Enter," she said.

He came in softly and swiftly. In spite of his size and power his tread was light.

He dragged one of her petit-point chairs to the bedside and began to fire questions at her—sharp shrewd questions that made her realize in a few seconds that he knew nearly all there was to be known about her. She had to snap her mind into alertness, covering up, playing for time.

She was amazed that he could be so forceful, for his face was sallow with strain, making the strong shape of his nose and eyebrows stand out in contrast; the sensual lips were dried and cracked, and his dark glittering eyes were stained beneath by fatigue.

She tried to deflect his thoughts by pouring out a cup of coffee and leaning over to give it to him. He flicked his eyes over her bare shoulders and the Alençon lace that made peeping parentheses over her bosom. "Don't try your cow eyes on me," he said.

"Are these the manners of the American Army that we have heard so much about?"

"I'm not the American Army these days, I'm just a sewer worker. I've had six days now in the nasty little moral stink of your friends, and I want to get this over."

Mari took a perverse pleasure in making him show his

power. "You would not insult me," she said, "if I were not a widow, all alone, without anyone to defend me."

He laughed, and the deep sound had a ragged edge to it. "You're about as helpless as a rattlesnake," he said. Against his drawn skin, his teeth showed startlingly white and sharp, especially the incisors.

Their wills seemed to be almost tangible forces, electric on the air of the bedroom. As he looked down at her, his hard, strained face was not softened by the delicate glow of the lamp shade. For the first time in her memory she grew afraid.

"I don't care what you do to me," she burst out, "but nobody can say I've ever been a traitor."

"You and Laval both," he replied coldly. "Now give me the plain truth this time. Why did you go to Paris last July?"

"I was one of a deputation of colons who demanded better protection of our interests."

"But why did you go to Paris? Why not Vichy?"

"To see friends in Paris."

"You met high German officers there?"

"They were everywhere, one could not help it."

"You could not help finding one in your suite at the Crillon Hotel?"

"The Boche forced himself on me," she said, thinking, "This Hansen is inhuman, he knows everything."

Hansen kept up the sharp questions, thrusting incisively into the hurried defenses that her tongue tried to erect. At first, she stared him straight in the eyes, but the black steadiness of his pupils flurried her; they were metallic, and Hansen hardly ever seemed to blink. She began to keep her glance away from his for longer intervals. So it was with his questions; she answered them brusquely at first, but he was never satisfied and probed ever deeper. In the end, numbed by fatique and helplessness, she gave in, and answered badly, not reckoning how the answers would stack against her.

He finished abruptly and said, "You've been smart. You've told the truth. Most of what you say ties in with the reports from our agents in France."

"I have nothing to hide."

"Only what goes on inside that head of yours. I know your kind—sitting on top of the pile, and willing to sell your soul to make sure you stay there."

She gasped as if he had hit her. "I've done a lot of rotten things in my life," she said, "but I've never helped the *sales*

Boches. I was brought up in the slums where you had to stab in the back first to stay healthy, but I've never betrayed my country."

He held her gaze, and his black pupils seemed to expand, as if he were coming out of the light into darkness. "I wouldn't bet on you if the Germans came here instead of us," he said.

The contempt in his voice lashed her into a fury. She began screaming all the wounding insults she could drag up from the recesses of her memory, in the waterfront argot of those early years before she had first met Henri Lander.

She was surprised to see the hard planes of his face relax. "I thought you were tougher," he said almost gently. "There's no need to be frightened. You'll be safe if you play along with me."

This pity was the final stamp to her ignominy, and she felt too floating and spent to be aware of anything but her subservience. He had done with her as he willed; it was almost as if he had possessed her physically.

"You're going to tell us what we want to know," he said in a quiet voice.

And she had from then on. In the days that followed she had bared the whole truth about the people she knew. She explained the setup in the separatist veteran's organization, about the members of the fascist Croix de Feu; she gave the names of the businessmen who had made furtive visits to Count Falken, undercover Nazi agent in Algiers, hoping to get favors from the Germans they expected to become their masters.

Day after day it had gone on; Mari poured out everything she knew, not caring what happened.

Yvette had tried to plead with her, but Mari was like a fanatic, thinking of nothing but her goal of proving herself to Hansen. In the end Yvette had helped her, fearfully, but catching something of her mistress's driving urge.

A jeep called for Mari nearly every night, under the cover of darkness, and she would be taken to the small heavily guarded villa on the Rue Thuillier, where the Counter-Intelligence Corps had its headquarters. American and British officers would cross-examine her about the latest information she had been able to glean.

One night she was fired at from the bushes as she returned to her house, and she suffered a flesh wound in the right arm.

She knew the French Fascists were trying to get revenge. She exulted in it. She drove back to Counter-Intelligence Headquarters, filled with a masochistic pleasure, and showed Hansen her wound, which she had not attempted to tend. She watched his face eagerly, hoping that this proof of what she had suffered for him would affect him.

"I can't put you in for a Purple Heart," he said, in cold sarcasm. "You'd better stay indoors. We'll send for you when we need you."

She waited two days in a maddening monotony, longing for him to come, baring her need for him shamelessly to Yvette, aching to see him, to be hurt by him, even despised, so long as he came.

And then, when her nerves were in shreds, he arrived late at night, and something inside her seemed to split and burst out a hot tide from wells she never knew were in her. He was haggard and unshaven, his eyes were dark craters, and his limbs moved as if they were under water.

"You know Admiral Darlan's been murdered?" he demanded.

She shrugged this aside, and pushed him down into an armchair. She fetched him a stiff brandy, which he drank in one gulp, and as his eyeballs caught the light she saw they were bloodshot. A surge of fierce tenderness welled up in her and she tried to fuss over him, but he cut her short. "Darlan's been assassinated," he said, "the net is out to bring in every suspect. You'll have to watch every step you make."

"You've driven yourself too hard," she said.

"This can upset the whole works."

"How can I help you? I'll do anything, anything." Her longing to comfort him made her add, anticlimatically, "Are you hungry?"

"Yes, I've been on this for fourteen hours straight."

"I'll get you something."

She went into the kitchen, moving feverishly so as to get back to him as soon as possible, and when she hurried back he was fast asleep, his head sagging to one side.

Mari sat on the arm of the chair and bent over him. She touched the stubble on his chin and, wonderingly, the strong clump of his eyebrows, and his coarse black hair.

His eyes opened slowly and fixed on her blankly, as if he did not recognize her. In that moment he seemed completely defenseless, and the pounding inside her swelled up into her eardrums so that she could feel each pulse of her veins.

"Why did you come to warn me?" she asked.

"You're in danger."

"You came—just for me?"

His mouth widened in a tired smile.

"Why?" she asked.

"You and I are the same sort of people."

Her face was only a few inches from his, but she felt they were touching, for a current flowed between them, a diapason of desire.

He pulled her down across his knees, and she could not hold him hard enough, and her long need was still not met. At first she trembled, as if she had come in from a great coldness, but then their warmth stole through to each other, and she tried with her mouth and her clutching hands to give herself up to him, but she and Hansen were still not one, except in their hunger. He thrust his arms beneath her thighs and her body and lifted her up as he rose, and took her over to the divan.

When she came to, her body felt drained. Even the motion of opening her eyes needed a conscious effort. Her lids were heavy. She forced herself to open her eyes fully and turn her head. The light came from the windows, where a pale glow of dawn spread rosily. Mari thought to herself, "We must have lain here for hours."

Hansen was lying spread-eagled beside her. At the sight of him her torpor vanished. As she looked down a wave of tenderness for him filled her. His great body now seemed so defenseless. She ran her hand very softly over the bristly stubble on his chin. She was fearful of waking him, but realized as soon as her skin touched his that his was a stupor of complete oblivion.

She rose and fetched blankets to cover them. She stretched out beside him, getting as close to him as she could. There, sprawled across him in the cocoon of blankets, feeling his warmth, nuzzling her lips along the strong planes of his face, she savored the pleasure of belonging. She had been possessed by him, she was his, she was part of him. But the best was yet to come, she thought drowsily. For when he awoke and his strength returned, they would be able to take their time, to experience with each other the sensual deliberation only possible now that their primal need had been met. They would explore with deep caresses the last and utter delights of one another.

But no! She jolted into wakefulness. The danger! Blair had come here to warn her. When he awoke he would go from her again. They would be driven apart. Panic flooded her at the thought of losing him. The unseen forces which had been gathering around her these last few days, during Blair's absence, seemed swiftly to close in on her, stifling with the fear of the unknown.

In spite of Blair's closeness she felt cut off from him. He looked so alien now, withdrawn in the remoteness of fatigue. In her fright she moved convulsively, and Hansen awoke with suddenness.

"Blair!" she cried, "I'm frightened!"

He smiled. "Take it easy."

His voice broke her self-control. She sank her head on his chest, sobbing, her breasts heaving against the lean fall of his belly. She was overwhelmed by the fear that they had only a little while longer together.

"Hey, now, listen," came his bass voice. He shook her gently. His grip steadied her and she buried her face in his neck, gaining confidence from the strength of his body. Under the disheveled clothing she could feel the hard leanness of his thigh muscles, the sweeping power of his chest. Her need for him began to stir again and she could tell that he, too, was roused.

She leaned over him and joined her mouth fiercely to his, running her fingers over him exploringly. Though she felt his mounting need, Hansen lay heavy and lethargic, still half sunk in his exhaustion.

There were lines of his face she had never seen before. She felt an extraordinary mixture of tenderness and excitement. She knew she should leave him alone, let his body restore itself. But the feel of his cracked lips on hers, the stubble of his beard, the drawn look of his face muscles, made her loving pity and her desire grow in a hunger that could only be assuaged by utter possession of him.

And so it was she who became the aggressor. She rose swiftly, stripped herself naked, and removed his clothing piece by piece with fingers that trembled in their haste. When there was nothing left to hamper her she abandoned herself to the swelling tide of her lust.

She had no need for his power now. Her own mounting

ecstasy caught them both. It became her delight to be the taker, the possessor. While Hansen struggled against his exhaustion Mari felt her whole being thunder as the curve of her fulfillment soared. But even as her wildest transports came, she could not close out from her consciousness the fear which was greater than need.

When at last she lay beside him, spent, the first words she gasped were, "They mustn't take you away! They mustn't!"

The door of the bedroom swung open and Hansen walked in. His heavy brows were knotted in anger. "Get out," he said. His tall bulk moved toward her with surprising lightness.

"You'll have to throw me out," she said. "I won't go till I've proved to you what a terrible mistake you made."

"Don't let's have any hysterics. We had our fun, but that was eight years ago. The party's over."

"You never gave me a chance! I could have explained! You went away. I kept trying to see you right up to the time your unit went to Italy. I pulled every string trying to follow you. I wrote to you for months."

"I got the letters. In fact, I even read them, till they began to repeat."

"I never had anything to do with Martello, I swear it. I've got letters I want to show you, letters from Martello. They prove what I say." She picked up her handbag and fumbled with the clasp, but Hansen thrust out his hand and covered the bag. "Don't waste time on alibis," he said.

The sensation of his fingers on her knuckles was so acute that she felt that she could have no control over her face muscles. She kept her head down, looking at the bag, trying to get to the letters on which she had pinned her hopes, but his long fingers restrained her; she was acutely conscious of their power.

She looked up at him pleadingly, and then she realized that the current of emotion in her, from their contact, was in him too. His black brows were tight in anger, but he could not disguise his eyes, and she knew that he wanted her.

Strength came back to her. "I never cheated you, Blair," she said. "I swear by God. And I can prove it."

He turned away, thrusting his hands into his pockets. "Let's get it over," he said.

Chapter Six

H ANSEN PRESSED his long lips together and unfolded the first letter. He began to read, and Mari watched his eyes as they flicked across each line. His high-boned cheeks, sloping to the sharp squareness of his chin, made her think of the outline of a coffin.

"This letter," she explained, "is the first one Martello sent me after he posted you away out of Algiers."

"To have you to himself," he said, his eyes on the page.

She waited anxiously for any change of expression in his face, but his heavy brows and the muscles of his cheeks seemed to be set in a mold. A dark dread began to seep up from the recesses of her mind—dread that the letter would not convince him.

"I never saw Martello alone, not once!" she said urgently. "After he posted you away I refused to see him. He had to send a jeep and four men to bring me down to headquarters. He questioned me for hours, trying to frighten me, but I just swore at him. That great ape—I told him I'd kill him."

Hansen kept reading. Mari thought of Martello's powerful body, with the shirt strained over his muscle-breasted chest, revealing between the buttons the black fur of hair which covered him. She remembered, with a hate polished and hardened with the years, Martello's brown eyes rolling over her, his ridiculous Bronx accent, his pointed white teeth.

Hansen was thinking: This is Martello's writing, sure enough, bold and blunt. But the words were not anything like Hansen could imagine coming out of that primal, tigerish personality. They were—in turn—pleading, wistful, anguished:

Am I unclean, or something? Can't you imagine what torture it is to me, when you avoid me as if I'm a leper?

Hansen remembered Martello's favorite story, which he invariably bellowed out with his great chest heaving in laughter—the one about the spinster, a regular listener to the Nazi radio, who heard that the American Army was landing, and

41

beamed hopefully, "When does the bestiality commence?" Martello had always identified himself with that conception of a soldier—roistering, concupiscent; but now . . .

Can't you give me just one ray of hope? I'll wait a year, two years, five, if you'll only give me hope . . .

This letter had been written after the unit had left Algiers. Could it really be true that Mari didn't play around with Martello? She hadn't always been so particular. If this letter wasn't a forgery, it looked as if Mari were telling the truth.

A stream of cold blood seemed to pump into Hansen's heart. He was painfully aware that Mari was altering her position, crossing one thigh over the other to lean toward him, and he could hear the whisper of her stockings against each other.

Lust for her rose up in him. In that surging moment he felt his muscles jerk in some primitive reflex which would strike her down just as he had that Delilah in his hotel room the other night. In a split second the whole act flashed through his mind; he saw himself silence those lying lips with his fist, grasp that revealing gown at the V-shaped décolletage, rip the material till it fell from her. He imagined her revealed in her usual black half-bra with the fancy' French garter belt; he could almost feel her own impatience with his own constraining clothes—just like their last week-end together. . . .

Hansen choked off the tumult in his mind. He made himself think of Martello.

"You're lying," he said thickly. "That last night we met, you asked to be left alone with Martello."

"Yes, but I could have handled him easily!" she said. "I had him eating out of my hand. I could have kept him hoping he'd get what he wanted. I'd have made him keep you in the city, instead of sending you away. I could have done it. You must believe me."

Hansen glared at her, trying to hold onto his hate.

"He was crawling to me, I tell you!" Mari cried. "Martello was crazy over me. If I'd handled him my own way I could have stopped him from sending you away."

"But you didn't!"

"You wouldn't listen to me. You just rushed out."

The expression on her face made words mere air in the

way of the current of desire which flowed between them. Hansen had to look down at the letter again, to control himself. The words in the letter were jumbled in his focus:

Why are you so bitter? It's not my fault you quarreled with Hansen. You say you've always been in love with him, and it's my fault you two busted up. Why? If he chose to believe anything about you, it was nothing to do with me. That's a poor sort of love he had for you. Why don't you give my love a chance? Sure I'll pass on your letters to Hansen, as you ask, but . . .

Hansen could not pretend to concentrate on the letters any more. The blood was pumping a sharp rhythm in his wound, so powerfully that he felt as though the bandage was being pulled away, and with it all the bitterness and hardness that had become part of him. "Is this really true?" he asked.

"You know it's true."

He dropped the letters on to the bed and grasped her by the shoulders, "If you're lying to me, by God, I'll kill you."

His grasp made the blood pound a drumbeat in her veins. She smiled up at him. "Go on," she said, "kill me." She let her head tip back slowly, looking up at him, waiting for his mouth. He pulled her to him, and their lips crossed the years of waiting.

His fingers clasped her tight down her bare back, and he could feel the smooth arch of her body straining close to him.

And then, from far away, Hansen heard a bell ringing. He realized it was the phone. He put out his hand and picked up the receiver.

His right hand was still grasping the smoothness of her back. She pressed against him voluptuously as the alien voice in the telephone burbled some explanation and Hansen said impatiently, "Cab I ordered? Send it away!" He slammed down the instrument.

Mari's face lit up with gratitude.

"Oh Blair," she cried. "Thank you. Thank you. Now take me, take me quickly."

Mari raised both her hands and clawed at the pins in her hair. It fell loose in a black rippling mass. Mari's letting down her hair had usually marked the start of their ritual of love in the old days. Now, it rolled back the years. He grasped her to him and the rich ripeness of her mouth was his, deeply joining.

Even as his scorching need seared him he knew this would be just like their very first time. And so it was. Their desire was so great that they could not wait to savor all the delights of each other. Nothing could dam their want. Mari's urgent body demanded to be possessed, and his was so ruthless that he saw her eyes roll in an agony of bliss. He tried to hold himself in check for a moment, to experience with all his senses the actuality of possession. He even managed to raise himself on his elbows, in spite of her gasp of impatience, he let his eyes run over her waves of hair spread over the coverlet, over her breasts, at the bold sweep of her flanks. But then his long-pent need was too much for him and they clung together, swept by the final flood of culmination.

After a while, as his drained faculties slowly restored themselves, Hansen was able to be free momentarily from the stimulus of her body. He was able to think of that night, eight years ago, when they had last been together. The knowledge came to him that nothing had changed. Mari had all the same magnificent grace and litheness, her body had lost none of its wonder. Every familiar taste of her, every surge of her urgent being, every fragrance, had wiped out the vacant years. It was as if nothing had happened in between.

As if prompted by the same thought, Mari murmured, "Oh, *cheri*, it's just the same. Just as wonderful. Eight years. I've dreamed of this for eight long years."

"Remember that first time?" he asked. She made a husky sound of assent.

Then they repeated the pattern of their love. Hansen felt Mari stir and begin to make it her pleasure, as on that first night, to take the initiative. She was leaning over him, nuzzling him tenderly. He felt her mass of luxuriant hair fall across him and her smooth perfection join him.

And so the years finally rolled back, with Mari again sealing their love. He felt the drumming beat of his need meet hers, but this time, as on that first night so long ago, they were able to taste to the full their delight in each other before the floodgates of desire finally gave way and they were swept out into boundless satisfaction.

Chapter Seven

THE MINT TEA tickled Céleste's nose and made her giggle.
"And to think," said Spenser Boward, "that when I met
you on the plane I thought you were the haughty type."
"Oh, I was tired."
"You were very frosty to me at first. You seemed to be
more interested in that other man—the dark, crazy-looking
one in the front seat who kept looking daggers at me."
"Oh, you mean George. He's always like that."
"George?"
"His name is really Djoj." She spelled it out, D-j-o-j.
"That's pronounced almost the same as our George. He's
an Arab, you know."
"You looked like your mother when you said that—sort
of mocking." He looked at her quizzically. The bar of
creamy sunlight that sloped into the Arab café accentuated
the boyishness of her hair and the way she sat with her
legs apart. Was it because she was so obviously a virgin that
he was stuck on her? Even while incredulity at himself grew,
the strange atmosphere keyed his senses more sharply to her
nearness. Here in this bazaar quarter, the shuffling crowd
outside, and the breathless air, scrubbed raw as if by sand,
seemed charged with fecundity. It was pulsing in everything
around him, not only in the pregnant women who walked
outthrust, proud of their fulfillment, the gaudy bluebottle
flies that buzzed over the beggars' sores, but also in the very
hum of chatter; each word seemed to break off and mate
with others in the crowd, breeding new streams of noise.

Boward felt a sense of self-derision at his own urgency
for Céleste. "I'm part of it," he thought, "I'm part of the
same farm-yard. What about her? Is she rarin' to go, beneath all this boyishness, this blah about the Arabs?"

A prick of jealousy came to him as he thought of Céleste's
Arab friend, George.

"What's George to you?" he asked, and his unlined face
formed into a frown that drew the neat eyebrows together.
He was wearing a white linen suit that had neither spot nor
wrinkle, and it made his bright pink sunburn—which went

45

inevitably with his reddish-yellow hair and pale-blue eyes—seem even more inflamed.

"You Americans, always so blunt!" Céleste smiled. "You ought to be very flattered that I allowed you to talk to me on the plane. French girls are brought up very strictly, you know. That's why I told Mari we had been introduced."

"You still haven't explained about George."

"*Explained*, M'sieur Boward?" she said sharply.

"I beg your pardon." The pink on his face darkened to a deep red. "Sorry, that slipped out—it's the way I feel about you, I guess. I'm jealous of everybody else."

"I've known George for a long time," said Céleste. "He is in several of my classes at the Sorbonne."

"Oh." Boward framed his lips as if to speak again, but when his eyes met Céleste's he bent his head to sip at the tea. There was a little depression on the bridge of his nose where his spectacles usually rested, a mark that was pale against the pink skin, and this caught the light as he lowered his head. Céleste studied him while his tawny eyelashes were turned down to the cup. There was a gentle wave in his hair that made evenly spaced troughs of reddish shadow, and the hair ended in neat geometrical lines where the barber had shaped him.

"I suppose you can't, er, see much of George now you're in Algiers?" he asked.

"The segregation, you mean?"

"Yes, it must be a problem. We have the same thing in the Southern States."

"Not quite the same. An American Negro won the Nobel Prize, you have Negro scientists, millionaires—"

"Now, wait a minute. France is more liberal on racial questions than any other nation on earth."

"The French in France, but not here," said Céleste. "Since the war we've massacred literally thousands of Arabs with tanks and machine guns, because they agitated for freedom."

"What can you expect? You're swamping Algeria with more Arabs, through better medical services and social conditions."

Céleste tried to cut in angrily, but Boward was firmly launched in his exposition. He flung facts and figures at her, and only stopped when Céleste forgot her anger and began to giggle again.

"What's the matter?" he asked, nettled.

"You. You're all intellect and no emotion. I just *feel* it's wrong for us to crush the Arabs. I don't need statistics to tell me."

"No emotion?" Boward swallowed, and his prominent Adam's apple made a swift flex. "*You tell me that!* You think I'm a stuffed shirt, don't you?"

"Frankly, yes. But I think you're curable."

They both laughed. "You want emotion?" he asked. "I'll give you plenty. Ever since I met you—"

"That's enough emotion," she smiled. "I think I prefer you as the cynical statistician."

The warmth of her glance made everything seem sharper and more alive. He looked around. Standing by the hearth of multicolored porcelain stood the *caouadji* of the café, like a priest at a ritual. A *tabouka* player squatted in the doorway, his rubbery fingers bringing out a mesmeric slide of notes. Boward let his mind fasten on the music, so that he was carried along by its insistence.

Boward looked back at Céleste and was surprised to see that she was staring at him tight-faced, as if trying to conceal her feelings. "You're thinking it's all very picturesque," she said.

"No, no." He sensed her annoyance. "Just that—"

"Or you're calculating how much it would cost to make this all nice and sanitary and American."

"You're being very rude. Why are you so bitter with me? None of this is my fault, nor America's."

"I'm sorry, please forgive me." Instantly, she was friendly again, smiling at him coaxingly. She put out her hand and covered his. "It's because I can say what I feel to you." Boward held her hand and she made no attempt to withdraw it. He saw her eyes were fixed on the crowd outside.

Boward twisted round and saw a tall lean man in a loose-fitting drill suit, who was walking slowly with the surge of the crowd. The sun caught his untidy black hair and accentuated his rather sunken cheeks.

"That's Blair Hansen," said Céleste. "What's he doing here?"

"Hansen?"

Céleste flushed. "He's an old flame of my mother's. She had a great affair with him during the war. I wasn't supposed to know. I was only twelve. She's in a great dither now he's come back."

Céleste pulled away her hand from his.

"What's the matter? You look annoyed."

"Hansen. He's a vicious brute."

With a sardonic sense of detachment, Boward realized that his supreme need was to get hold of Céleste's hand again. What more could he say about the damned Arabs? "If we could only make them great again," he began, "they could give so much to the world—"

Céleste breathed out jerkily. "Listen," she said in one breath, "I'd like to show you what it means to be an Arab here. Would you like to see the Casbah, after all?"

"Would I?" He made a stroking caress of her hand, and she did not resist.

Chapter Eight

CÉLESTE AND BOWARD entered the Casbah from the top, after leaving their car by the stone fortress that dominated the hill. The chauffeur kept close behind them as they stepped down into the first alleyway.

"Does Michel have to shadow us?" whispered Boward.

She nodded. "Mari's orders. There can be trouble in here." She lifted her face closer to his, to make herself heard above the shrill clatter of Arab cries.

After the sun's dry heat, the gloom of the Casbah pressed on them like a dank breath. The alleyway was barely an arm span in breadth, and was so jammed with people that Céleste and Boward had to shuffle forward in zigzag steps. Every few feet the cobblestoned paving dropped in shallow stairs, in irregular depths, so they had to feel with their soles all the time; they were too jammed in the crush to be able to look where they were treading. For the first few minutes Boward held on to Céleste's arm and tried to fend off the surging mass of white-robed bodies, but he had to let go of her, for no amount of elbow-digging or shouldering had any effect on the crowd.

At first, everything seemed to be in monotones of gray and brown, but as his eyes grew accustomed to the gloom, he was able to pick out the red fezzes, the blue and white of signs in French and Arabic, which marked each cross alley.

He kept as close as he could to Céleste, whose yellow hair glowed among the kaffiyeh headdresses of the Arabs.

On each side of the alleyways the tan-colored walls reared up, blank except for slitted windows, and an occasional inset balcony. Far above, the white of the sky was burning, outlined in a serrated pattern like jagged teeth, formed by the gutters of the buildings. Boward felt he was trapped, with a mass of other victims, on the tongue of a monster, being sucked down into a cavernous stomach for mastication. This sensation strengthened when a sickly stench hit him. This odor changed, as they descended the twisting steps, but it was always there, the immutable rancidity of the Casbah.

The surging of the crowd kept threatening to snatch Boward and Céleste apart, and they had to grip hands to keep together. A monkeylike porter, who carried on his back a bale that was stuffed with camel leather, caused a great wave of disturbance, for the crowd pushed at the bale from every side to avoid being crushed. The porter's burden was secured round his neck and forehead by leather thongs, and as he thrust forward patiently, his neck muscles stood out like varnished cord.

The descent began to get steeper, to twist and turn, and Boward soon lost all sense of direction. He became aware that the alleys spilled in and out of each other, in a mass of confusion. Some reared up like ladders, and others sank down into what looked like cellars, except when a blur of light at the bottom indicated they passed under houses and joined alleys below. The tiers doubled and twisted on each other, through tunnels, steps, and ladderlike covered passages, in a seething honeycomb worn smooth by the mass of humanity.

"Let's go this way," called Céleste, and tugged Boward into a side alley that went in sharp steps upward and then twisted down. It was less crowded, and they were able for the first time to stand and look around them. He wondered whether to put on his glasses, but he remembered that Céleste had never seen him wearing them, and he decided not to.

"Mam'selle!" called Michel, catching up to them. "Your mother instructed me that we were to keep to the Rue du Casbah!" His face was puckered in alarm, and in the dim light looked as if it had been boiled for a long time, so that all the vital juices, and even the expression in the eyes, had been extracted. "We shall get lost," he said.

"I know every *ruelle*," Céleste replied without looking at him. "If you are afraid, you have my permission to go back."

Michel pursed his lips, exasperated, but he stayed.

The houses at this point bulged out over the alleyway on each side, shutting out the light except for a thin ribbon far above. The projecting parts of the dwellings were supported by sloping joists of wood, on which were hung washing and strings of drying herbs. In the narrow doorways, which were framed black by handmarks, stood Arab women clad from head to foot in white. As the visitors drew near, each group of women pulled their yashmaks higher, so that their faces were completely covered.

There were swarms of barefooted boys everywhere, scurrying in squealing packs. Most of their skulls were shaven, exposing ulcerous sores, and a few of them had their heads dyed with henna, the Arab remedy for lice. Céleste gripped Boward's arm and he followed her gaze. A blind child of about five was stumbling down the cobbled steps, teetering over the humps of garbage, feeling the wall with one hand and keeping the other in front of him to ward off any collision. His eyes were sockets of pus.

"Trachoma," said Céleste, "it's very common here."

The alley veered sharply again and they entered an evil tunnel that reeked of human feces and the sickly sweet stench of rotting vegetables. The exit was at right angles to the way they had come in, and as they moved forward into the light the white robes of the crowd ahead were outlined by a shaft of sunlight, each person collecting a blurred halo of incandescence.

Boward and Céleste blinked in the glare, and the hot press of the sun seemed to be something more than light; it was an antiseptic healer, bleaching the putrescence with its rays. It brought out myriad details Boward had not observed before; animal ordures that encrusted the foot of each building, green-gray slime covering the cobbles, and the prismatic brilliance of flies' wings.

"Look!" cried Céleste. She pointed up to a fluttering ragged banner—half green, half white. "The forbidden flag!" she cried, "the flag of the independence movement."

"The rebels?" he asked, "Messali's men?"

"Yes. It's against the law to fly it."

Céleste's face caught the sun glare, and her gray eyes were points of light. Her expression was ecstatic.

While she squinted up at the flag, shading her eyes against the sun, Boward noticed that many of the Arabs around were watching closely, and the shouts and cries of the crowd muted slightly. The black eyes seemed to be unblinking, and the faces shadowed in the creamy burnooses were expressionless.

Céleste looked around and became aware of her audience. She called out something in Arabic, and instantly the watching figures loosened up and the black eyes grew friendly.

"What did you say to them?" asked Boward.

She hesitated, and then jutted out her small-boned chin. "Long live Messali Hadj," she said and looked at her wrist watch. "Come on, we're late, there's a lot to see yet."

Céleste walked ahead of him, for the passageway was too narrow for them to walk abreast without treading in the long piles of garbage. He noticed that her white shoes were stained by streaks of slime, and some of the muck had even spattered up above her fragile ankles. He looked down and saw that his own trousers were dirtied.

"You'd think they'd clean this up," he said.

"Oh, they try." She pointed to a spindly shanked donkey that was standing nearby, bearing two great panniers. A man who was clad only in a sack appeared out of a doorway, bearing a shovel full of steaming filth, and dumped it into the nearest pannier. He shouted "Balik! Balik!" and the donkey stepped daintily to the next doorway to wait for the man to fetch another load.

Céleste looked over her shoulder at Boward and motioned with her head at the rotting garbage that carpeted the alley. "Hundreds of Arabs have to sleep on that every night," she said. She seemed to pay no regard to the muck on her feet, but walked sturdily ahead.

Boward wondered whether Michel, who was close behind them, understood Arabic, and if so, whether he would report to her mother Céleste's outburst about Messali.

What made Céleste so keen on the natives? He began looking into the shadows of the Arabs' hoods to see what sort of people they concealed. Most of them were sallow and pudgy, the city type, but occasionally lean taut faces would come into view, their skin like mahogany; these were the faces of outdoor men—hard and sun crinkled.

"They vary a lot," he said to Céleste, and she eagerly pointed out the various types as they passed by. There were slit-eyed Bedouins from the Sahara oases; a brown-haired Berber whose eyes were almost as gray as Céleste's; some Diyabs in jackal-fur costumes; and a Gnaoua, a Negro Moslem.

Céleste led the way through several alleys that were shaded by a lattice of reeds, making a prison-bar checker of shade on the ground. During every lull in the babble of Arab cries, the buzzing of the flies could be heard, implacable and monotonous.

Boward noticed that both sides of one alley were pocked with little grottoes that opened out to the cobbles; each of them was a shop.

"This is the *souk* of the jewelers," Céleste explained.

Inside each shop, men were crouched over trestles, and in the darkest recesses small boys of six or seven were busy, their pipestem arms angular in the ocherous light. Boward peered at the boys and saw their faces were prematurely lined.

In front of each shop was a tray of the jewelry made by the workers in the grottoes. The bangles and the brooches, earrings and charms gleamed with a sinister brightness amid the decay of the alley. Céleste pointed out some elaborate rings of agate and moonstone. "Religious amulets from the Yemen," she said. "Women wear them so that they will bear more babies."

"*More?*" he echoed.

"Oh, yes, some women pray all day for fertility. They kneel in the Mosque Mohammed Ech Cherif, a few alleys higher up."

He tried to conceal his disgust at the filth and spawning. "It always happens in slums," he said. "It's an instinct to beat death and disease."

Their glances met for a fleeting second, and for the first time he saw a depth of expression in her eyes, which seemed to be personal to him. She pressed his arm. "Come on," she said, "we're late."

Under a patched awning was a fruiterer with a rainbow piled around him—green of fresh peppers, vermilion of chilies, yellow of onions, pink of sliced melon—and a rosary of garlic suspended over him.

A few of the dwellings that they passed had bronze knockers of curious shape. When Boward asked Céleste the meaning of these, she explained, "They're symbols of fertility—

phallic designs." She spoke casually, and Boward was annoyed by her detachment. He longed to shock her into acknowledging the potentialities between them.

He heard Céleste make a tsk of annoyance. She was looking at a middle-aged couple, obviously Americans, who listened, with the blank gape of tourists, to their French guide. ". . . and near this spot, m'sieur, 'dame," the guide was saying, "the captives of the Barbary pirates were auctioned off to the highest bidder. Thousands of men and women were sold into slavery. Pardon? Oh, yes, many Americans. Often the women were bought for the harem of the dey himself." He gestured to the fortress at the top of the hill. "Then the American Navy was sent here, with the U.S. Marines. Boumboum. No more slave market."

The woman tourist clasped her wrists, through the handle of her carryall, with an air of satisfaction.

Boward noticed a group of women who wore no veils—their skins were wrinkled like nutmegs, and their noses were broader than most of the Arabs he had seen. "Berbers, said Céleste, "they were the main race here before the Arabs came six hundred years ago."

They passed a side alley, which rose in a rapidly diminishing width till it apparently vanished into a building. Near the intersection was a group of women who were ranting at each other. There was a buxom Negress whose breasts seemed to be about to burst out of a calico blouse; a henna-haired young woman in a sleazy red dress; an Arab girl who seemed handsome till the sun caught her gap-toothed smile; and several diminutive pale blondes. Boward was surprised to see that they were all unveiled.

"Are they Berbers, too?" he asked.

Céleste looked at him sharply. "No," she said.

An urchin ran up to Boward, his little claw tugging at Boward's sleeve. "Tu veux belle fille?" he shrilled, "belle fille?"

Boward felt annoyed at his own innocent lack of perception.

"They're all over this section," said Céleste. "There are hundreds of them. At night they all shout out for customers. Their main place is called the Rue Kataroudjil. Whoever named it had a sense of humor—Kataroudjil was a terrible Barbary pirate who raped thousands of women here in the Casbah."

She looked at her watch once more. "We're late, we must hurry," she said.

"What's the rush? We've got all day."

Céleste made no reply, but led the way at a rapid pace down a series of sharp slopes. Boward's curiosity grew. Where was she going? Late—for what? They passed through several ruelles and tunnels, shouldering hard against the swaying crowd, and in a few minutes emerged into the broadest alley he had seen, one that was almost wide enough for a car to drive in. Here were herds of goats tethered to staples, their yellow eyes gleaming fanatically.

Céleste hurried through, climbed sure-footed down a stone stairway that was almost as steep as a ladder, and at the bottom they found themselves on the arcaded Rue Gambetta, with taxis honking, Europeans clustered round the crowded stalls, and bright sunlight that made them blink.

Céleste turned to Michel, who caught up with them, his small face tight in a sulk. "We'll wait here," she told the chauffeur. "Take a taxi round the hill and bring our car back here." She took a pile of crumpled bills out of her bag and gave them to the chauffeur without counting. "Hurry!" she ordered, "we're very late."

Michel sullenly hailed a cab and jumped in.

"Couldn't we have gone with him?" asked Boward. "That would have saved a lot of time, if you're in such a great hurry."

"I wanted to speak to you without Michel listening," she said. "He's an old sneak, he'll tell Mari everything that happens. He adores my mother, he'd do anything for her. He's worked for her ever since she married my father."

She looked up into Boward's face and flicked her tongue over her lips nervously. "I thought you'd like to go out to the seashore for lunch," she said.

"Fine."

"There's just one thing." She laid her hand on his arm. "Would you mind very much if I slipped away for half an hour after lunch?" she asked.

"Slip away?"

"It's like this. Mother hates the Arabs, you know .that, don't you? I have several old friends here who are Arabs, and I want to meet them without Mari hearing about it. I know a way to get away after lunch without Michel seeing me."

"But, listen," he said, "you're a grown girl. If you want to see any of your friends—"

"It's best this way, believe me. You won't mind, will you? It's a lovely place, you'll be able to sit by the sea."

"No, I don't mind." A suspicion leaped in his mind. "These Arab friends of yours—is that jealous guy on the plane one of them?"

"George! Oh, no. I don't think he'll be there." She pressed his hand. "Thank you, I shan't be away long."

Her warm look made an upsurge of happiness flood him, then a reaction followed.

"By God," he thought, "one smile from her and I feel as if I'd made her. Biology is trapping me. Unless I'm careful I'll be hearing wedding bells."

Chapter Nine

THE SUN-DRUGGED STUPOR of the streets increased Hansen's impatience. All the morning gone, and still he'd not managed to make contact with Messali's men. The city had changed so much; nearly every one of his old contacts seemed to have disappeared.

He considered whether to leave the city and go out to Bouzarea, where Messali was rumored to be directing the whole network of the Arab underground resistance movement. No, the French Security Brigade would be tailing Messali day and night, and they'd make life unpleasant for anybody trying to contact the Arab leader.

His last chance left was the Café Ech Haraj, in the Arab quarter. The rebel leaders had occasionally met there during the war; maybe they still did, if the French hadn't got wise.

Hansen lengthened his stride to the limit of his long legs and went along the Boulevard de la République, keeping close to the railings that guarded the steep drop down to the quays beneath. A faint breeze from the sea flattened the loose-fitting drill suit against his lean figure.

"Hi, Joe!" A barefooted little urchin was bobbing beside Hansen, giving the same shrill cry with which the gamins used to coax candy out of the GIs. The boy's head was shaven, encrusted with the familiar ringworm scabs, and his mouth had a circle of dirt round it, like a bulls-eye. "*Bak-sheesh*," he wailed, "alms for the love of Allah."

Hansen threw him a bill and said in Arabic, "Run to the *hamaam* and wash yourself. You offend my nose."

The smell of the boy stirred up a vivid, almost painful, memory of the war years.

Something seemed to have gone out of the European quarter these days. It was soft and flabby, back once more in the Oriental lethargy that had always irritated him. He missed the hard, masculine alertness of wartime, when the streets were jammed with cocky GIs; he missed the vicious snarl of the jeeps and the male thunder of the planes that swung low overhead. Now, everywhere you went, you saw glossy little Frenchmen talking softly and rather sadly, describing their amours with expressive wiggles of their manicured hands. And in Posquet's, where the Yanks and limeys had often got into bloody brawls—usually ending up with beer all round—the homosexuals now sipped their *limonade Abdullah* and ogled each other.

By a lime-washed wall, two Arab boys sat with their feet hidden beneath their voluminous *kashabias* and giggled at him as he passed by. They kept lifting their little *chechias* from their shaven heads and lowering them again, in mockery of the infidel's habit of hat raising. Their black eyes were dancing with malice, and after he had gone by they spat on the ground.

He turned. "*Ulad el harram*," he grinned at them, "Children of that which is forbidden." Their swarthy faces gaped in surprise, and they began chattering to each other like birds.

Hansen reached the arcade that bordered the Arab quarter. The crowd grew thicker, and he had to edge his way among Arabs who looked up at his great height curiously, their skins wet bronze in the hot light.

The press of the crowd slowed him down to a shuffle. He kept running his eyes over the faces of the crowd, hoping for the sight of somebody he remembered from the war years, but none of the throng, nor the idlers in the café who sipped mint tea and played *tauleh*, struck chords in his memory.

He saw Céleste's blonde head and kept his eyes away from her; he had no time for polite conversation. Besides, she was with a man.

The air was so dry and hot that Hansen had to keep pluck-ing at his shirt collar with his long bony fingers. At last he came to the small open space at the end of the arcade, and here the ground, exposed to the full power of the sun, was covered with a fine layer of bleached dust, sparkling like powdered sugar in the light.

The Café Ech Haraj was still there. As Hansen walked toward it he noticed an urchin darting across his path with a pile of papers under his arm. He was selling the rebels' daily, *Independence,* which Messali's men had been bringing out for eight years, in spite of constant police raids and banishment of its printers to the French Congo.

Hansen bought one of the papers and sat down in the café, opening the paper so that its title could clearly be seen. When the *caouadji* came for his order, and the two men looked into each other's faces, a dim measure of recognition flick-ered between them. Hansen vaguely remembered this sallow, white-stubbled man with the wide-flared nostrils; he had been here during the war years.

"*Marhaba,*" said the Arab, "Welcome."

Hansen decided to play this straight, in the formal Arab style. "I hope there is health?" he asked.

"Thanks be to Allah and the prayer, there is no ill. And you?"

"My eyes are gladdened to see this great Moslem city again. It is eight years since I was here, fighting, with my Arab comrades against the *roumi*"—he used *Christian,* the Arab's word of supreme contempt for the French. "It is good to see a fighter for the cause. I remember you well."

"Your face is well known to me," said the Arab cautiously.

"I hope to meet some of my old comrades," said Hansen. Neither of them said any more. Hansen knew the Arab mind; to probe for information would be fatal. This would take time, but he had made a start.

He sat, sipping mint tea, for half an hour. He kept the paper up in front of him, pretending to read it. He became aware, out of the corner of his eye, that a group of men were whispering and looking in his direction. He hoped that some of them would remember he had arrested many of the French Fascists during the war. Several times men passed very close to him, obviously inspecting him at close range. Hansen did not take his eyes from the paper.

After a long wait a shadow fell between Hansen and the

arched door of the café. He looked up and saw a tall slender figure in native robes; his scarlet agal holding his headkerchief picked out the light.

Hansen was startled into a grunt of surprise. It was the younger of the two men with whom he had fought two nights previously. Hansen recognized him by his high-arched brows and the bruise along his jaw.

"Why are you here?" asked the young man. He sat down at the table.

"I tried to convince you the other night. I'm on your side, and I want to help you."

"You're not the sort of man who'd help us because he's sentimental about the Arabs. You are working for Kuhn, who has contacts with the French and the Arab traitor, Bel-Safarte. Suppose you are trying to betray us?"

"I can only show you by my deeds. I can do much for your movement, as I did during the war, when I removed many of your enemies."

"How can you help us?"

"I want to explain that to Messali. Kuhn is prepared to pay large sums to ensure peace up in the mountains, where he wants to open up mining developments."

The youth gestured impatiently. "Messali Hadj would never speak to you—he is too busy. Anyway, he is out of the country."

"Are you his deputy?"

"Me! I'm only a junior novice. What exactly does Kuhn want from us?"

"He has bought a concession to open up an iron-ore development in the El Hazy Bloug valley."

"Right in the heart of rebel territory! So you want to bribe us to let you exploit our country? The more riches you Americans discover in our land, the harder the French will fight to keep control. You are hindering us in our work."

"Are the Arabs so timid that they wish to stay poor, for fear stronger men will take what little they have from them?"

The youth flushed, and Hansen followed up swiftly. "I wish to speak to your committee today. I have an important proposal for them."

"It's no use trying to buy us. We may be slaves, but we are not for sale. We are going to win freedom without help from foreigners."

"Those of you who live to tell the tale. You'll plunge all

North Africa into bloody rioting and finally take over a country that is devastated."

"Did you Americans do better? It took a terrible civil war to free your slaves after two hundred years of captivity. We Arabs have been slaves for only eighty years—it took the French twenty-five years to subdue us—and already our night of captivity is nearing the end."

"But you can win without firing a shot."

The young man frowned, and the bruise on his cheek made his face look strangely puckered. "How?" he asked.

"By using modern public-relations technique, lobbying and influence. You haven't made the slightest attempt to win over the people of France to your viewpoint. They're intelligent, democratic people—"

"I know that. I was educated in Paris. None of your ideas would help us with the French colons here—like your friend Madame Lander."

Hansen concealed his irritated surprise; that Arab grapevine again that made Bell Telephone look sick! "The colons are the least important," said Hansen. "Put them on the defensive against world opinion."

"There's nothing I want more than a peaceful solution."

Hansen was surprised, for usually the young Arabs were hotheads.

"Let me talk to your committee," Hansen asked. "I'd like to suggest how it can be done."

"Well, I'll ask the committee," said the young man slowly. "I'll tell you what. Come here tomorrow night, and I'll let you know whether they'll see you. No. You'd better not come here. Go to Wazzareb, the salt plain by the sea. You know the old fort?"

"Yes."

"Be there at nine o'clock. Come alone. If you bring anybody, or are trailed by the French, we shall not contact you."

Chapter Ten

MARI LANDER leaned over the stepped edge of her square bath. "Yvette!" she called. "What time is it?"

Her personal maid's sharp old voice answered acidly from

the corridor: "Don't worry, madame, I'll make sure you are ready in time."

Mari sank back into the froth of winking bubbles, and her limbs became beaded with the iridescence from essence of sandalwood oil. The sense of urgency would not leave her; there was so much to do and Hansen would be here soon. She rose, dripping, and dried herself hurriedly with a fleecy towel. She slipped into an ice-blue peignoir and silver kid mules, and walked through the bedroom. It calmed her nervousness, with its spacious white and gold *décor*, draperies of burnished brocade, the delicate love seat, and the small Correggio original over the lace-covered bed. When she came to the robe room she stood for a moment, savoring the whisper of the fountain in the courtyard below, and the fragrance of the bitter-orange shrubs.

She sat at the dressing table, and the rows of crystal and silver backed brushes caught the translucency that always gave her confidence. The draperies diffused the sun glare into a limpid web of light that glowed on the off-white walls and softened her reflection in the great mirror. She sighed, in this last moment of repose, and then switched on the two powerful fluorescent bulbs, which flooded her in a relentless daylight glare. The whole room seemed to alter; every shadow sharpened, making black and white angles on the graceful *bonheur du jour* and the Louis Quinze chaise longue. One arc of the beveled mirror refracted a prismatic rainbow, and the two long rows of mirror-fronted closets behind made double images of her in the glass.

Her black hair, and the dark wings of her brows, seemed wet under the fierce light, and when she leaned forward, patting the skin beneath her eyes in a critical inspection, the long nails caught a cruel red lucency.

She thrust her face resolutely up into the glare, turning from side to side to examine the skin. In this harsh light, the smoothness of the skin ended short of the great eyes and the ends of the mouth, and instead there was a faint tracery that did not have the same firm texture as the rest.

She busied herself on her make-up, and soon became so absorbed that she forgot the passing time. Later, when Yvette leaned round the door and said, "He'll be here in half an hour," Mari put her hand up to her throat and said, "But I've hardly started! Come, help me." She jumped up and went to the chaise longue, where she stretched out with the back of her neck against the headrest. "Do my hair," she said, "and ring for Jeanne."

"Jeanne is finishing downstairs," Yvette replied. "Be calm, madame, there is plenty of time. I can manage."

Yvette fetched the manicure box, a small treasure of alabaster covered with Moorish filigree. Mari laid it on her knees and set to work with the polish remover.

"Your hands are shaking," said Yvette; "perhaps Jeanne had better do your nails for you after all."

"No, she has plenty to do down there."

Yvette's long face, with its attenuated nose and vertical lines flanking the mouth, made her look like a skeptical camel.

"Don't look at me like that," said Mari, "you're sneering at me, I know you."

"We know each other, madame. Fifteen years together is a long time."

"If you're trying to remind me of my age, you don't have to." Mari pulled her peignoir tighter round her.

"You know I'm not," said Yvette, and her hand rested momentarily on Mari's shoulder. "I'm afraid for you, that's all. I remember how much misery this m'sieur caused you before."

Mari drew a sharp breath, about to flare up with an angry reproof, but instead she twisted onto her hip and looked up at the maid curiously. "Can't you understand?" she asked. "Hasn't this ever happened to you?"

Yvette moved to the back and began taking out the pins from her mistress's hair. "Yes," she said slowly, "once I was tempted as you are now, but I managed to cast him out."

Yvette meant the Devil. She always talked of him as if he were a neighbor with whom she often quarreled.

There came a silence from which grew overtones of restraint, and then Yvette said, "I don't want you to feel the same as I did—when that happened."

The maid took out the last pins and the long mass of hair fell in ripples, beyond the backrest, and its full weight pulled on Mari's scalp, giving her a pleasurable feeling of femaleness. She stretched felinely, and the peignoir moved its softness over her, making a clinging pull over each curve.

"This time," said Mari, "it will be different."

"That day, you looked just as you look now."

They both knew she meant the day when Hansen had flung

Mari aside and left her with bruised wrists, alternately sobbing and swearing, on the great ottoman downstairs.

"This is a bad love," said Yvette.

"Bad? Don't be a sanctimonious fool. You aren't in the confessional now. You're my oldest friend, Yvette, but sometimes you madden me with your smugness."

Yvette made no reply, but swept the brushes down through the snakes of hair, and the black shine made a great crackling, as if it were on fire.

At length Yvette said, "It's eight years. You've both changed. Don't count on this man too much."

"We haven't changed," said Mari. "I know we haven't."

The phone began ringing on the bedroom extension. Yvette went to answer it and her voice seemed to Mari—who was already back in her reverie—to come from far away: "It's for you. It is M'sieur Hansen."

Mari scrambled up from the chaise longue, her mind fumbling back into alertness. She rushed into the bedroom, her robe streaming out loose behind her. One of her mules fell off and she went lop-footed to the phone.

"Yes, yes?" she said eagerly.

"Listen, bad news," said Hansen. He sounded as if he were in a hurry. "I can't make it. I've got to go meet some Arabs."

"Let me go with you."

"You! You're poison to the Arabs."

"You're not contacting any of the rebels?"

"No. Just a business meeting. I won't be back till very late tonight—"

"Even so, wouldn't you like to—" She broke off. Instinct told her she must not throw herself at him. "Oh, Blair, must you go?" she asked instead. She tried to keep the desolate note out of her voice. She could tell that his mind was not on her at all. He would only be irritated by any demonstrativeness.

"I'll phone you when I get back," he said. "Got to rush now."

The phone clicked at the other end, and the old familiar feeling of worried waiting flooded through her. Mari shivered and she did not know whether it was because of her nakedness against the lace bedspread or from her premonitory fear.

She looked up and saw that Yvette's face was grim and disapproving.

Chapter Eleven

Boward decided not to put on his glasses, because he knew he looked owlish in them. Instead, he avoided reading the menu by asking Céleste to pick out the best dishes.

He could see the sun curving in her hair, but the finer shades of her expression were lost to him. His blurred focus made her softer, almost dreamlike, and her gray eyes appeared to be enormous.

"Well," he thought, "women always look better this way."

Céleste had transformed from the shy, abstracted girl he had met on the plane. Now, she was gay and excited, arguing with him about her damned Arabs.

They were sitting under a striped awning on a terrace poised over the Mediterranean. In front of them the waves were undulating in fronds of crystal. On each side of the restaurant the steep slope from the highway down to the water's edge had been skillfully landscaped, and a luxuriant mass of green shone from the boxwoods and cypresses, with a spectrum of color interspersing it—the red of hibiscus, purple of bougainvillaea, the brilliant hue of plumbago. Each color was a jewel clean on the blanket of light.

"What a waste of time, all this chatter," Boward raged inside. "She and I ought to be down there in the shrubbery. Instead, we're still fumbling around this ridiculous mutual awareness. *Homo Americanus* in the rutting season. Instead of me leaping on her we lock clichés. Like those first times necking in the old jalopy—the girl and I each pretending that the wrestling was good clean fun."

Céleste took some grapes from the tall taboret beside their table and rose to feed the lovebirds which chirped in a cage by the balustrade. Boward noticed that she was not looking at the birds, but at the woods below, then she glanced at her wrist watch.

"You want to get away from me!" he accused. "You want to rush away to those Arab friends of yours."

"Oh, no! I love every minute of it with you." She came back to the table full of vivacity. He leaned across the table to bring her closer into his range of vision, and saw that her face was alight with happiness, and there was a curlicue of laughter at each end of her boyish mouth.

The waiter brought a spirit lamp to the table and made coffee for them. Céleste explained that the little white pod that the waiter dropped in was a cardamon seed, to give it extra kick.

Boward gave a mental leer: Aphrodisiac?

He decide to get back to her favorite subject. "Now take Arab literature," he said. "It's fossilized. It's still in the same pattern as five hundred years ago—just like Arab architecture, food, and customs. They haven't even discovered romantic love yet—"

"Oh, you're so wrong! Ben Bahaj and Jadji Douad wrote some of the most fiery love poetry I've ever read."

"To hell with all this," he thought. "Supposing I just lean across to her and say 'Pardon me, Miss, do you mind if we go to bed?' "

He grinned at the idea, and saw her puzzled glance.

He mastered his self-mockery and said, "Arab poets are mechanistic. They give long anatomical descriptions of a woman, the shape of each of her parts, but they never mention emotion or romance. It's like reading a Sears Roebuck catalogue written by an old roué."

"You're a fine one to talk," she burst out. "You Americans are the least gentle lovers in the world. You expect to buy romance like you do everything else in your materialistic country—I'm sorry." She patted his hand. "I shouldn't have said that."

"We're getting somewhere," he thought. "An intellectual striptease."

Céleste pushed back her chair. "Are you ready? I'm afraid I'll have to leave you now."

"Oh, er, your friends are here?"

"Not far away. Shall we go?" She dropped her voice to a whisper as the waiter came onto the terrace. "Let's go down into the garden—there's an arbor down there where you can wait."

"Okay." He felt confused by the realization that she was about to leave him. He beckoned the waiter for the bill, but Céleste said, "Oh, no, I've already signed for that. Mari has an account here."

Boward protested vigorously, but she said in a tone of finality, "Let's not argue, please. Mari insists that I bring my friends here—Arabs are not allowed. Why should you pay for her idiosyncrasies?"

Céleste gathered up her things and led the way down a twisting wooden stairway that was open slatted, so that the vivid colors of the garden below could be seen below their feet.

Boward followed, exasperated. "Shall you be long?" he asked. "I'm going to miss you." She twisted round sharply and looked up at him with a finger on her lips.

He followed her, silently, down to the gravel path. They walked abreast through a riotous burst of flowering shrubs. The fragrance filled him sensually—the heady sweetness of heliotrope, the tobacco odor of mimosa, and the female scent of oleanders.

Céleste seemed to be the focus of all loveliness. She turned and said to him, still in that crisp voice of decision, "Michel will be back with the car to collect us at three-thirty. If he should come down here—he ought not to, but he may want to spy on us—tell him to go back and sit in the car and that I'm picking flowers, or something."

"This is crazy," said Boward, "having to organize a conspiracy to meet your friends."

They came to the arbor, which was in the Roman style, with stone columns thickly interlaced by wisteria and bougainvillaea. For the first time, Céleste seemed to lose her calm poise. She looked at her wrist watch and then repeated the action, as if she had forgotten to look the first time. She asked him to step inside the arbor with her, and they moved into the scented dimness cut off entirely from everything, except a narrow view out onto the sea.

"You won't go away?" she said. "You won't go back to the restaurant? You don't mind waiting?"

"I'd wait for you all day," he replied.

"You're sweet." She fumbled in her handbag and pulled out a little paper-covered book. "Here's a new collection of short stories," she said. "They're in English."

"You think of everything," he said. He could tell that she was nervous. He wondered whether to risk everything and grab hold of her. He took her hand and said, "Don't be long. I'll miss you. Céleste, today was fun. Let's meet every day—"

To his amazement, she tiptoed, with her arms thrust out behind her, and gave him a kiss full on the lips. He grabbed her and sought awkwardly for her lips again, and she yielded, moving her mouth against his sensuously. A blaze of images shot across his mind.

Céleste leaned back against his encircling arms, and looked up at him with her lips still full from the kiss. "Every day?" she smiled. "Very well, if you wish. Every day."

He pulled her head toward him again, and she said, her lips against his, "And you won't mind if I see my Arab friends while I'm with you—like today?"

She disengaged herself and waited for his answer.

"No, of course not," he said.

She stepped out into the sunshine and he followed. He watched her move lithely along the path that led toward the wood. She soon became blurred in his vision, then vanished into the powder yellow and downy gray of the wood.

Boward went back into the arbor and picked up the book she had left. There was part of her still with it, a faint per-fume stealing out from the leaves.

Chapter Twelve

Céleste reached the cover of the wood, and took out a handkerchief. She rubbed furiously at her lips to free them from any reminder of Boward, then looked at the cambric carefully, as if expecting to see something on it, though today she had remembered to wear no lipstick.

The ground soon became so rough, as she moved forward through the cypress and terebinth trees, that she had to hold out both arms to steady herself. Checkered sunlight fell de-ceptively on sharp ridges of rock, and several times Céleste slipped, but she scrambled forward without bothering to ex-amine her grazes. Soon she was in a saffron twilight, where a latticework of branches plucked at her. She pressed on till the wood began to thin out and the fluted arches of the trees let through a hint of the blue sea. She came in sight of a massive boulder that threw a wedge of shadow far down the slope; then broke into a slipping, sliding run, careless of the scratching tendrils. There was a painful pumping inside her chest.

Yes, he was there. She scrambled forward and they went into each other's arms in a straining grasp. Not a word was spoken. Her breath was so spent that she could only hold on to him, letting him take her weight.

"You're late!" he said. "I've been going mad."

"I tried . . . so hard." She spoke with each rapid intake of breath. "Mari watches me . . . like a hawk."

"But you took hours over lunch I watched you both— you and that red-headed American."

She leaned back against his encircling arm and looked up at him. "You haven't had your wound seen to! You promised me you would. The bruise is worse." She put up her fingers to his mouth, which was puffed and split.

"It's nothing," he said. "I've been busy."

"I knew there'd be trouble if you got mixed up with Messali."

His face tightened in irritation, and she stopped his words of protest with her lips. When they looked at each other again Céleste noticed that blood from scratches on her cheeks had streaked his mouth. She began to wipe it away, but he held her fingers. "No," he said, "that joins us." She could feel the salt taste of the blood on her tongue.

He made her sit down on one of the outcroppings of rock, and he tended the scratches on her arms and legs, dabbing them with her handkerchief.

"I hate having to meet like this," he said, "like criminals on the run."

"I know. Last night was awful. Hansen nearly saw us."

"Have you found out any more about him?" he asked.

"No. Why are you so interested in him?"

"Anything that Kuhn does affects our organization. Hansen is Kuhn's man."

A tracery of sunlight, which filtered down through the leaves, picked out his tanned skin molded closely to the high cheekbones. Céleste ran her fingers through his black hair and said, "It was crazy for us to leave Paris. Are you still determined not to go back?"

He nodded. "The Arabs' revolt is nearer than I thought. There's trouble blowing up, serious trouble."

Céleste fought down her impatience. "You'll stay here in Algiers? You won't go back to college in the new term?"

He rose and straddled the rock, so that he could hold her. "Don't let's argue today," he said. "Isn't it enough that we're together?"

"We'll be together for two months, till I have to go back

to Paris. But what then?" She saw the worry draining into
his face, and instantly was contrite. "Oh, all right," she said,
and changed the subject by leaning back and inspecting his
khaki shirt and trousers. "I've never seen you dressed in
those," she said.

"My old Army issue," he replied bitterly. "I got them
defending your country."

She smiled and said, "Remember how you were dressed
when we first met?"

His face loosened, and while they held each other, her mind
went back to their first meeting in Paris.

During that freezing Parisian winter, with no heating in
their draughty rooms, the students had packed together
every evening in the cellar clubs on the Left Bank—dancing,
smoking, arguing—so jammed together that even the stairs
leading down to the clubs were a solid mass of young people,
who had to peer at their companions through the acrid
haze from cheap cigarettes.

Céleste had gone to La Vie Libre, one of the larger clubs,
and huddled in a corner among a group of ten or more
students who were jammed round a little table. She could
not move her limbs, for she was crammed in too tightly. Her
feet were itching from chilblains, and she was dizzy from the
overbreathed air, but she resolved to stay until fatigue drove
her out into the vicious frost.

Then she saw him. He looked bizarre even in that gathering of many types—"and many sexes," as he grinned at her
later. He wore a turtle-neck sweater, a woolen cap, and
round his neck and head he had wound many lengths of a
thick scarf.

"Your weather!" he shivered. "The only thing you French
have left to us Arabs in Algeria is the sunlight, and you'd
steal that if you could."

He and Céleste began arguing furiously over French im-
perialism in Algeria.

When he was warm enough he took off his muffler and
wool cap, and she saw the fine sweep of his jaw line and
his thick black hair.

She found her mind wandering from his arguments, for
she was cramped and weary, but she held on to one resolve—
she would not tell him who she was, for Mari Lander was
well known in Algiers as an anti-Arab colon.

When they finally left at three in the morning and walked down to the Pont Neuf and stood on the bridge watching the beauty of the lights on the Seine, it never occurred to either of them that they were cold, nor did they even think of going home that night. Instead, they wandered slowly over the cobbles, where the frost glowed blue in the moonlight, to Les Halles, the great vegetable market. There, in a little all-night café, they ate bowls of onion soup, and talked eagerly about themselves till dawn pierced the steam-covered windows.

Finally, she had watched his face anxiously and blurted out her identity, and to her amazement he flashed a smile. "I know," he said, "you were pointed out to me. I decided to convert you."

Her chagrin was so deep that at first she was angry, but then she saw the funny side of it, and they laughed together till the burly porters in the café looked at them and made rude gestures with their hands, signifying that the young people were crazy.

"What's your name?" she asked at length. "George what?"

"It's not really George. It's Djoj." He spelled it out. "It's pronounced like George."

"Don't tell me how to pronounce Arabic, I bet I speak it as well as you do." She asked him, in Arabic, "What is the name of your fathers?"

"Warouk. We're the only family in Algeria that doesn't claim descent from the Prophet or one of his generals. We have no money, our land is merely a few miserable acres that even the goats despise. In other words, we just have what you French foreigners have left us."

"Nonsense. My father was poor when he emigrated to Algeria, but he worked his firm up to be one of the most prosperous in the country."

"On Arab sweated labor."

But they soon forgot about politics, in the wonder of getting to know each other. . . .

If they kept absolutely still, here in the hush of the wood, they could feel each other's hearts beating through their thin clothing. Céleste strained closer to George and made a whispered laugh. "That stupid American was lecturing me all through lunch on how little the Arabs know about love," she giggled. "I nearly burst! He said the Arabs regard women as cattle."

George's eyes, the color of dark sherry, narrowed in anger. "This American, Boward, will see more of you than I will."

"But this is your own idea, to come back to Algiers," she burst out, but when she saw the jealous cloud on his face she tried to turn his mind to themselves. "That Boward is crazy," she said. "What does he know about love? Oh, *cheri*, do you remember our first spring together?"

Céleste and George had soon drifted off into a world of their own. They rarely went to any of the students' haunts, except for meals, for they were too absorbed in each other. They took the Bateau Mouche steamer on its trips along the Seine, they sat in the gallery at the Marigny Repertory oblivious of what was going on down on the stage, and they searched out every undubbed American movie, so that George could improve his English, which he was studying with great intensity. Sometimes they sat through the whole show twice, so that George could memorize whole passages of Metro-Goldwyn-Mayer or R.K.O., and afterward they would often horseplay, striking exaggerated imitations of the scenes, acting out pieces which they remembered from the movie.

Whenever the *météo* forecast fine week ends they would cycle along the poplar-lined roads that led out to lonely woods and meadows, star-sprinkled with buttercups and daisies, and here they rambled in solitude. The hedgerows that buttoned up the breasts of the hills were preening with new colors, and the clouds swayed crazily, trying to scrub the sky an even cleaner blue, and Céleste and George were so happy that it was almost painful. They had an overflowing feeling that they must hold on to every sound and scent and image before it was taken from them.

Céleste, especially, felt this, for she had a secret worry. She gradually came to perceive that though all her waking and dreaming thoughts were devoted to George, his love for her was not his entire motivation; it was an important part of him, but only a part.

This became increasingly apparent as the spring mounted in high summer. Céleste lost most of her interest in studies, missing many classes, and she became what the other students called a *flâneuse*, a loafer who did just enough to escape severe censure. But George concentrated on his studies, and as examinations drew near he spent all his time over his books, with Céleste acting as interrogator and researcher.

She tried to conceal her utter dependence on him, but it was a losing effort. She wanted to please him too much to keep back any shreds of her independence. She stopped using lipstick, which he disliked, she left off seeing any other men, she took a deepening interest in Arab affairs.

Her greatest pleasure, next to the times when he put aside his books and took her on his knees, was to sit silent, watching the candlelight flicker over him while he worked. Then his lean, spare face would look to her as if it were carved from the finest grained wood, and the guttering light threw sharp shadows that accentuated his high-bridged nose and the almost feminine sweep of his long lashes.

When the term ended, George had to stay in Paris, because he could not afford the fare home, and Céleste made elaborate excuses by phone to Mari in Algiers, so that she could stay with him. This poverty of George was one of several invisible barriers between them. Céleste had plenty of money but she took care to conceal this, down to the most minute detail, for George had a hard pride, which would never let him accept any form of help from her. She pretended that she had a very meager allowance from her mother, she put her jewelry in a safe deposit and her fur coat in storage, and wore her oldest clothes. Céleste's generous allowance from Mari piled up at the bank and she watched it grow with a miserly pride, telling herself, "One day that will be for both of us."

George managed to earn a few francs by writing occasional articles for the agricultural magazines and the small political weeklies, and each of the checks that resulted was the signal for a joyful celebration, in which all barriers between them —of nationality, politics, and money—were melted away, and anything seemed possible.

The fall term began. A violet haze over the boulevards at the sunset hour, which grew steadily earlier, and the mournful whisper of dead leaves crimping in the gutters, kept reminding them that winter was coming again.

As they held each other, in this shell of quiet amid the trees, they could feel the warmth where their skins touched, and a deep pleasure filled Céleste at the contact.

"We wouldn't be separated if we were in Paris," she said. "We wouldn't have to sneak and pretend."

"I know." He said it with a soft groan.

The rock was cutting into their flesh, so they rose and lay full length on the stony ground, moving into each other's arms again as if their minds and bodies were one.

"Then let's go back," she whispered. "That's our world. Let's go back before it's too late."

She felt him tense and the worries that had fretted them for months clouded their minds again. . . .

The realization had come to her gradually, as the winter dragged by, that there were unspoken things between them. They made no mention of what they would do when they graduated, and they avoided talking of Algeria or their people back home.

Then one morning, the springs of their tension suddenly burst. The papers carried cables from Algiers, describing a riot in Kabylie, and among the Arabs reported shot by French soldiers was George's own uncle. "He was a man of peace," said George, white and shaken. "He was no rioter."

"It was an accident, I'm sure it was!" she cried.

"Maybe, but this settles it. I can't turn my back on what's going on in Algeria. It may be my father next, or my sister. I'd be a miserable coward to hide here."

"What are you going to do?" Her fear made her voice go off key.

"What most of my people are doing. Work for Arab independence in Algeria."

"But you can do that much better here!" she cried. "The Government's in Paris. You're an educated man, a writer. You can influence them much better here. I can help you. We'll work together on propaganda, agitation—"

"While my relatives get shot?"

She stormed at him, pleaded with him, but he had made up his mind that he would leave the Sorbonne at the end of the summer term, without graduating.

George became torn by the stress between his desires and his duties. It grew worse when his father heard his intention to quit the Sorbonne, and ordered his son to finish his tuition. The elder Warouk wrote to his son, "You will be far more use to Algeria as an expert farmer than an amateur soldier."

The weeks dragged by, in growing anxiety and unspoken things between George and Céleste. They were still in that suspended state of uncertainty when they flew to Algiers at the end of the term. On that trip they could not sit together. "Mari Lander's daughter mustn't have her name linked to mine," he said, and added grimly, "I may be notorious before very long."

She brought her face tenderly against his bruised cheek. "Let's go back to Paris," she urged softly. "Fighting will never get freedom for the Arabs—what can you do against tanks? You must get the French people on your side—that can only be done in Paris."

"We've tried that long enough," he said. There was a pause, in which only the high hum of cicadas could be heard.

"There's going to be fighting," he said at length. "We can't avoid it. They've driven us apart. There's no future for you and me."

Céleste heard herself say in a flat voice, "You want to get rid of me."

She felt numbed. She knew that very soon she would be filled with fear or bitterness, but now her mind was frozen.

George sat up and leaned over her. His bruised face seemed to be strangely lopsided, with his expression of misery. "You know that's not true," he said.

"Don't pretend. You want us to part."

"My dearest wish, ever since I met you, has been to marry you—"

"Oh, why haven't you said so before?" The numbness melted out of her mind and she sat up to face him. "Oh, you dear sweet fool. Why have you taken so long to tell me that? Don't you know that's all I've ever lived for?"

"But how can I ask you to marry me? I can't drag you into this trouble. There's going to be fighting—"

"We've always known that. All the more reason not to wait. Let's take our happiness now."

"You don't know how serious this trouble is. It's not going to be local fighting, but civil war. I've only been back here three days, but I've learned enough to know that the whole of North Africa is going up in flames. We've got arms now, great piles of them from the American dumps, and the central committee plans to use them."

"Well, I can learn to use a rifle."

He stared at her in surprise. "You realize what you're saying? You'd fight your own country?"

"Of course not. The French people would never send an army to fight Algeria. You've only got to fight these colon Fascists."

"But your own mother! She's one of the leading colons."

"Not any more. Hansen is her only interest."

"Then the American is in love with her? He has come back for that—not anything else?"

"Don't let's waste time talking about him. Darling, don't you see how crazy you are to keep us apart. We—"

"This Hansen. He is not mixed up with the colons, then?"

"Let's talk of us. Your own leader, Messali Hadj, has a French wife. Why shouldn't you?"

"That's different. They married years ago, when nobody dreamed there would be civil war."

"She suffered exile with him, years of poverty, she's been on the run, fought in the underground—"

"I won't ask you to do that, I won't. I love you too much."

"Listen." She held his wrists and brought her face closer to his. "Don't let's wait any more. I'm almost twenty-one, don't let's waste any more of our lives apart."

"There is one chance," he said.

"What?"

"Messali Hadj is away on a very important mission. The central committee is very optimistic about it. They hope we may get our freedom without fighting."

"He'll manage, I'm sure he will." A growing excitement mirrored in her face, and he found himself being caught up by her hope. Here in the peace of the wood, with her love so resolute, his uncertainty melted.

"Anyway, we have two months together," he said.

"Don't be silly. It's not just two months. I'll never go back to Paris without you."

Chapter Thirteen

THE MOON BATHED the great salt marsh in a luminous glow of decay, as if the entire expanse between the sea and the inland hills were a long-drowned giant finally washed up by the waves.

Hansen shivered as a breeze searched through his clothes.

He looked at his wrist watch and saw that nine o'clock had long passed. Never on time, these Arabs. Or perhaps he had been shadowed here by French agents? If so, the Arabs wouldn't come near him.

A high squeaking noise came from the rough track which led to the main road, and he saw a white shape floating through the air toward him. Hansen crouched down in the shadow of the fort, then he realized that somebody was riding a bicycle toward him. It was a white-robed figure holding a bundle. Hansen froze, tense, till he recognized the young Arab who had promised to meet him.

"Hurry, we're late," said the youth. "Here, put these on." He thrust the bundle at Hansen. It was a *gallabiah*, the coarse homespun robe of a peasant, complete with headdress and binding cloth.

"This is too damn melodramatic," said Hansen.

"Either wear it or don't come. We've got enough trouble ahead tonight, without risking more."

Hansen did as he was told. The youth said, "Sit on behind," and waited impatiently for Hansen to straddle his legs over the cycle's back carrier. The Arab pedaled away vigorously across the marsh toward the coast road. The machine squeaked and rattled, and every time it hit a bump a barb of pain shot into Hansen's shoulder wound.

"What's your name?" asked Hansen.

"You'd better call me George."

"Ah, a party name. You're a real conspirator."

"You probably think it's amusing, but we can't trust anybody, even in our own band. We have to hide our identities if we can." George was panting with the effort of pedaling. "We have found many agents of the French, the Communists, and the traitor Bel-Safarte in our organization."

George stood up on the pedals, pressing harder as the slope increased, then they got off, and George thrust the machine under a shrub of thorns. He motioned Hansen to move cautiously, and led the way up through a belt of thistles to the road, which glistened like black oil under the moon. They could see right across the salt marsh to the farther side, where the land curved round in a crescent. The great riblike pattern of the water runnels held an eerie glow of phosphorescence.

"The others will soon be along," said George.

While they waited, Hansen drew him out with casual questions, to find out his background, and George readily told him about his agricultural studies at the Sorbonne. After a few minutes quavering headlights came into view, and an ancient truck lumbered up and came to a slow squeaking halt.

"Jump on!" called George, and climbed over the tail-board. Hansen found himself being helped up by many straining hands. The truck started off again, and the dozen or so Arabs who were in the open back, sank down again once more, so that they were invisible from the roadway.

"This is the American," said George to the others. They turned their faces toward him curiously, and touched their foreheads in greeting. In the moonlight their faces looked chocolate against the white robes, except for their eyeballs, which caught a glow. One of them, who had the high nasal voice highly thought of among Arabs, began a traditional chant, but he was quickly hushed by the others.

Hansen observed that the truck was traveling toward Algiers, and he realized where the meeting was to be held. He whispered to George, "So we're going to the Casbah?"

George nodded. "All our meetings are held there—it's the one spot where we're safe from the French—they rarely enter it at night."

Hansen saw that some of the Arabs wore sweet-smelling *raham*, tucked into the edges of their turbans. They were all young. Most of them spoke in the camel-driver dialect, the Arabic of the poorest class. Hansen's sense of wasting time was increased—these weren't men of a revolution, they were like any gang of country louts joyriding in a borrowed truck.

As if reading his thoughts, George whispered to him, in English. "Most of these are raw recruits," he said.

Hansen noticed once again that George had a strong American accent.

The lights of the seashore roadhouses, then the gaudy fairground, and lamp-lined suburbs began to throw yellow lances of brightness into the back of the truck, and the Arabs crouched lower.

The winking red light on top of the Naval Observatory pylon came in sight, and the truck took the curving road that led up to the *medina*, the Arab quarter.

The Arabs left the vehicle in a side street, then split up into pairs and made their way to the nearest alley of the Casbah.

The bracket lamps set high on the peeling walls threw

cones of light down over the main alleys. The smaller ruelles were in pitch darkness, and in each of these, Hansen knew, there were the *mumfa'*, the homeless outcasts, huddled together for warmth in the only bed they knew—the slime of the Casbah cobbles. The harsh pools of light made sharp contrasts between the white robes of the bustling crowds, and the darkness of side alleys, so that the scene was all black and white.

A wild repetitive wail of *haki* music slid on sixteenth tones, drowning out the noise of the packed crowd, and the sole relief from the sound was an occasional flute, high pitched and monotonous. The only doors open to the teeming night were the cafés, which were so crowded that each one belched out foul air into the narrow alleys.

Hansen had to keep close behind his companions, who darted through the crowd exuberantly, now they were free from discovery. They kept taking short cuts through the side alleys. Finally their progress became so tortuous that in the darker alleys Hansen had to hold on to George's shoulders and try to gauge from the motion of the youth's body when to step up or down, where to feel with his soletips for the recumbent forms of the *mumfa'*.

Often, when they crossed one of the lighted alleys, he saw the green-and-white flag of the underground stuck into sloping joists of buildings, and each time one of these came in view his companions gave whoops of excitement. At last they came to an alley that was so small that two men could hardly pass abreast in it; they descended a spiral of slippery steps, and one of the party knocked on a door.

After a muttered exchange they were let in one by one, under the scrutiny of armed guards, and they found themselves in a long, greasy-walled passage.

George went ahead, explaining about Hansen, and a great argument flared up. George shouted, "But it's all arranged with the Deputy!"

The guards, men with obstinate peasant faces, took no notice, and their leader ordered George and Hansen to remain by the door while instructions were sought. After a wait of several minutes one of the guards returned with a long strip of black coth.

"The order is that he must be blindfolded," said the guard.

Hansen protested, because the cloth looked filthy, but the guard insisted. The man wound the material tightly round

Hansen's head, so that his eyes were completely covered.

Hansen was led up a twisting flight of stone stairs, along several passages, and then into a room that was full of raucous noise. He figured it was fairly large, for he could tell from the number of voices that there were at least twenty men present.

"Sit down here," whispered George, and Hansen squatted on what felt like coarse matting. As he did so there came a sag in the medley of angry talk, and Hansen guessed that the rest of the gathering had only just noticed his entrance. Then the dispute flared up again, and Hansen realized they were arguing about him.

"Quiet!" shouted an elderly voice, apparently that of the chairman. "Is the stranger to think that Arabs quarrel like women?"

"He should not be here!" called a voice from the far end of the room. "He may be a spy." A babble of other voices supported the speaker, and Hansen heard Mari Lander's name shouted by several men.

The mention of Mari made anger coil inside Hansen.

"Why is this American always with the Lander woman?" demanded a fresh voice belligerently. There was a wave of growls at this, and Hansen tautened, ready to make a fight for it. These Arabs were all unstable, they could flare up suddenly. This looked ugly. Before he knew it there would be a kangaroo court and then tomorrow he'd be found in a gutter with his throat cut. He wouldn't be the first one to end up like that in the Casbah, not by a thousand.

George's voice made itself heard above the hostile voices. "This American and the Lander woman are infatuated with each other. She no longer has any interest in the colon movement!"

The angry dispute broke out again, and Hansen had a vivid mental image of the swarthy faces turned toward him menacingly. He raised his arms in a gesture to command silence. "You Arabs have long memories, isn't that so?" he demanded. He made his voice dominate the falling noise. "Are there any of you here who were working for this organization when the American Army landed?"

A babble of confused noise broke out.

"If so," said Hansen, "you can tell the others you remember me when I was Captain Hansen in the American Army, how I worked with your leaders to trap the colon pigs, how

I put thirty of them in prison, how I sent one of them, Léon Fougasse, to the firing squad."

A pause of complete silence, then a few voices spoke. "Yes, there was a Captain Hansen"; "It is true that the dog Fougasse was shot."

Hansen waited, outwardly calm, for this to sink in.

The eager voices slowly climbed in pitch. They were all for him now.

"Take the cloth from his eyes!" came several cries.

A flash of inspiration came to Hansen. He held up both hands to secure silence, and shouted, "No, keep me blindfolded, then if ever I am captured by the Security Brigade I shall not be able to identify any of you, however much they torture me!"

A roar of applause greeted him.

An excited man yelled, "The Brigade got my brother last week—they took away his manhood!"

George whispered to Hansen—again in the queer American accent—"Don't believe it, that's something like your third degree. The Security Brigade often gives an electric shock to Arab prisoner's genitals. It doesn't do any harm, but many Arabs believe it takes away manhood."

The elderly chairman was trying to bring order, but a babble of excited comments were flying concerning the dreaded Brigade. Hansen could sense that emotion was boiling up, in one of the irrational spurts typical of Arabs.

The confusion increased and Hansen tried to let his disgust be apparent. God help Algeria, if these men were to be its leaders. No wonder the Arab world was weak.

The voices dropped away, apparently for no reason, and Hansen strained his ears. Then a voice that he had not heard before spoke. It had bass tones—very unusual in an Arab— and seemed to come from above. Hansen figured that the man was standing up among the squatting figures, who knew and respected him and were anxious to hear every word he said.

"You are prattling like children," came the bass voice. "Our people are starving while the French gorge themselves on our produce, we try to cultivate the hillsides while the invaders seize our valleys. We are full of disease, but they cure their horses before tending us. Who among you has not had the blindness of trachoma somewhere in his family?"

There was a dead silence.

"They make sure we get poor education. Who among you can read or write his own language?"

A soft crowd-noise of shuffling.

"Ah! Only one." Hansen guessed that was George putting his hand up.

"And so we live like cowardly slaves, dust on the feet of the invaders." The bass voice had a power in it that made the base of Hansen's spine prickle. "Yet what do we do? We bleat like sheep. Are there no men here?"

Only an uneasy mumbling answered him.

"No? Then I speak as a man to you children of the city. We in the hills will not wait any more. We are sick of meetings and talk and phone calls. We have arms now, and we shall use them."

The chairman plucked up his courage and butted in, "Messali Hadj knows better than any of us what to do. We must not spoil his plans—"

"Messali, Messali, that's all I hear. The Hadj is a great politician, but he is no warrior. This is a task for men of the saddle and the rifle!"

Hansen whispered, "Who's the man with the deep voice?"

Softly, George replied, "He's the leader of the Berbers. They call him Chef-Chauen, that's Berber for The Devil."

"If that's not typical," thought Hansen, "these characters wrap up everything like a musical comedy."

Chef-Chauen bellowed out, "They fear us, I tell you. Every mountain pass in my territory is thick with French troops."

"They may fear us in the mountains," retorted the chairman, "but not here in the cities."

At that moment there came a shout from outside the room, then another, repeated nearer. The room grew quiet, and the noise of running feet could be heard.

"The French!" came the voices. "The French are coming!"

Hansen heard the feet burst into the room, and the rapid gasping breaths of several men out of wind. "They're all round the Casbah!" cried one voice, and another gasped, "We're surrounded!"

Chef-Chauen overbore the clamor that broke out and questioned the newcomers sharply. "Are they troops or the Security Brigade?"

"All of them—troops, the Brigade, and armed police!"

Chef-Chauen demanded, "How many are there?"

"Hundreds!"

"Are they coming into the Casbah?"

"They may. It looks as if they're waiting for us."

"Silence!" roared Chef-Chauen. "What does it matter if the French are somewhere near? Haven't we lived our lives under their guns? Are we going to slink away like carrion dogs because they are here now? Let us finish our council, like men, but this time let us talk war."

Chef-Chauen took over the meeting, dominating it with his powerful voice. But Hansen could sense the taut nerves and the side glances. He whispered to George, "Why are the French waiting so openly? I think they're setting a trap for us."

Chapter Fourteen

KUHN LEANED FORWARD on the low chair, naked, and thrust his head into the steam that rose from the bowl. He sniffed up the pungency, and it made him so dizzy that he had to grasp his thighs.

In occasional glimpses through the steam, he could see the liquid in the bowl bubbling darker and darker. This was Kuhn's latest remedy for his asthma—breathing fumes from infused herbs prescribed for him by an Arab physician.

Here in his bedroom, with the windows closed tight against the danger of dust or pollen, the heat was so great that sweat and condensed steam were running down his jowls, dribbling down into the gullies and creases of his slack flesh.

His heart was pounding with the effort of stooping. Just at the moment when he believed the constriction inside his skull was about to yield and give him back the benison of normal breathing, he heard the phone ring.

Kuhn swore and took his head out of the steam. He grabbed the phone and barked, "Who is it?"

"This is Bel-Safarte."

"Well," said Kuhn, "what do you want?" He tried to keep the distrust out of his voice, for the renegade Arab leader, who was collaborating with the French, had often helped him.

"Big news," said Bel-Safarte. "At this very moment a great roundup of my enemies is taking place in the Casbah."

The soft cautious voice carried more charge than an excited shout. Kuhn's mind sharpened into alertness. "The rebels are being caught?" he asked.

"All except Messali—he is out of the country. Special plans are being laid for him."

"I suppose the French tipped you off?"

Bel-Safarte ignored this. "I think perhaps you would like to see me again?" he said. "This will change the whole political picture."

"Yes," said Kuhn slowly. "Maybe we'd better meet."

"Good. I'm sure that this will cement our relations."

The phone clicked off, and Kuhn slumped back onto the bed. Alarm gradually took hold of him. Hansen had said he planned to meet Messali's men tonight.

Alarm merged into angry rage. "The fool!" he mouthed out loud. "The blundering fool! I hire him to fix things with the Arabs and he gets into this mess. My name will get dragged into it. This will set me back years in my plans."

Kuhn breathed heavily, trying to control his rage.

This roundup meant that the rebels were finished. Mari Lander had been right—they were a miserable lot. Mari— She'd be very interested to know that Messali was finished. He could break the news to her.

He could not see the phone for his eyes were still brimming, but his groping hand found it.

Mari turned down the radio and with her other hand picked up the phone. As she did so, she was surprised to notice her daughter spring up and look anxiously at the instrument.

"Are you in, if it's your young American?" asked Mari, her hand over the mouthpiece. "Have you quarreled with him? You're very nervous tonight."

Céleste nodded rapidly: "Yes, I'm in."

"Oh, good evening, *Mr. Kuhn.*" Mari emphasized the name to let Céleste know.

Kuhn's voice sounded labored over the phone, as if he had been running. "I have big news for you," he said. He repeated what Bel-Safarte had told him.

Mari was silent, as the news sank into her mind. "This is

wonderful," she said at length. "You're sure of this? There are always so many rumors."

"I'm positive. The raid is taking place this minute in the Casbah."

Mari could sense that Kuhn was hoping for a long talk, but a dark pattern was forming with her subconscious, and she felt a compulsive need to be alone, so she could think. She thanked Kuhn swiftly and rang off.

"What's the matter?" asked Céleste.

"Oh, nothing. Old Kuhn says there's a big roundup taking place in the Casbah." She spoke absently. "The leaders of the Arab rebels are being arrested."

Even as she said it, the submerged pattern blazed up in Mari's mind. Blair Hansen's mission! Suppose he had gone to meet the rebels? She remembered his words on the phone, "I've got to see some Arabs." At dinner the other night, Kuhn had seemed keen on the idea of contacting Messali—till she had been rude to him. No, the old man wouldn't have sent Blair to see the rebels, unless—a stab seemed to pierce her—unless Kuhn had deliberately sent Blair into a trap. Maybe the old man had noticed something between her and Blair at dinner the other night. God knows she had felt so delirious at being with Blair again—she must have shown it in her face. Maybe old Kuhn had decided to get Blair out of the way. How could she find out?

She must be alone to think this over. Mari tried to mask her face with a smile, and went over to her daughter. "I'll run up to bed," she said. "I'm tired."

She gave Céleste a perfunctory kiss and hurried out. She was too caught up by her growing anxiety to notice that Céleste's head and body were set rigidly, as if clamped in a cast.

Céleste went out into the darkness of the courtyard to escape the prying look of Yvette, who was fussily moving round, emptying ash trays and smoothing cushions.

Was George safe? Had he been caught in the Casbah raid? If only she could warn him, or was it too late? Surely the police had not gone into the Casbah—they never dared to do that at night. Perhaps it was just another rumor. She must find out.

She hurried back into the room and through into the hall.

"Where are you going, mam'selle?" mumbled Yvette, who always treated Céleste as a child.

"Out for some fresh air." Céleste flung open the front door and ran across the gravel drive. Sharp pains shot into her feet, for she was still wearing her slippers and the stones cut through them. She opened the side door of the garage and felt her way in the darkness to the sliding door, which she unlocked and rolled back. At that moment the thought came to her that the underground leaders would never give up without a fight.

She never remembered getting into the car, nor driving it down the hill into the city. She was filled with a blind urgent haste. The first thing that registered in her brain was a traffic policeman's whistle at the intersection with the Avenue Franklin D. Roosevelt; she ignored the officer's furious signals and skidded across, tires screeching.

"They mustn't fight," she kept saying to herself. "I hope they'll arrest George, then he'll be safe."

Her anxiety seized on this hope. Yes, George must be arrested, then he'd be safe. They mustn't start shooting, they mustn't.

The tree-lined streets rushed by. She jolted over the tram tracks onto the Rue Chasseloup and flung the car down the last half mile to the Place de la Gouvernement.

The cones of the headlights picked out a glitter of bayonets. Oh, God! These were troops! Her grip on the wheel became rigid with fear, and she almost ran into the curbstone.

Céleste swerved into a side street and braked to a grinding halt. She scrambled out of the car and ran to the Rue Sambetta, the dark arcades of which formed the foot of the Casbah. She tried to slip across the street, through the steel-helmeted troops who stood at ease along its entire length. The yellow street lamps flickered on their long bayonets, and made their faces look lime colored. She was waved back by a young lieutenant who wore the navy blue uniform and breeches of the Security Brigade. Oh, Blessed Mother, the Brigade! Please save George.

"This side of the street is closed, mam'selle," said the lieutenant. He was young, and gave her a respectful ogle.

"*Je m'en fous,*" she replied.

He looked startled at her oath, and peered closer. She fought down her panic and thrust out one hip and smoothed her dress from hip to thigh, copying the way she had seen

Parisian whores bargain with clients. There came a short
burst of snickers from the group of Security Brigade men.
    The lieutenant made one swift glance over his shoulder
and the snickers flicked off. "Mon Dieu," he said. "You are
the most elegant *fleur du trottoir* I've ever seen. Why do you
stick in this hole?"

"You have a better idea for me?"

"But, yes, *mignonne*, I have many ideas."

His pale lashes caught the yellow of the street lamps as he
leaned closer to stare at her. She could see the Brigade insig-
nia, of a metal flame, gleaming on his left sleeve.

"What's the trouble?" she asked, looking past him at the
troops. She was trying to gauge, in her mind's eye, the nearest entrance to the Casbah.

"We're waiting to round up a few terrorists in there," said
the lieutenant, jerking his head toward the Casbah.

"Waiting," she thought. "That means George is still safe."

"Why don't you go in there after them?" she jeered, trying to draw him out. "All you brave poilus—what are you
waiting for?"

"Oh, we're going in, when the time comes." He made the
guillotine sign. "We've been hanging round for hours, waiting for the signal. I was bored—till you came along."

"Me, too," she said.

Céleste glanced fearfully at the uneven line of steel-helmeted troops. Terror closed her throat. George and the others
were trapped, unless—she looked calculatingly across to the
forbidden side of the street, at the arcade that was an elaborate façade for the mounting warren of the Casbah. In the
shadows of that arcade, the bazaar fronts were shuttered
against the night, and there were thick pools of darkness
behind each buttress.

"What are you here for?" asked the lieutenant.

"To meet a friend. We arranged a rendezvous over in the
arcade and—"

"He isn't here. We're keeping everybody out of that side of
the street. What sort of a man would make you meet him
here?" He held his nose in an expressive gesture. He added
sharply, "You weren't meeting one of those Arab animals?
You're not one of those in there?" He jerked his head con-
temptuously, but she knew he meant the brothels of the
Casbah.

"Do I look like that?"

"No, no, don't be angry. Don't worry about your friend—I can be very friendly." He put out an exploring hand, his body shielding the motion from the troops, and she did not flinch from his touch.

"I don't like the light," she said. "I thought officers had finesse." She leaned nearer to him, and when his hand went out to her again she motioned with her eyes to the darkness of the arcade. She edged away, keeping her eyes on him and moved to the nearest shadows. She held her breath, fearing he would call her back, for she was now on the forbidden side of the street. He followed, and grabbed her clumsily in the dimness.

One of the troops out in the street began to hum a ditty, and the others took up the bawdy words, which were obviously meant for the lieutenant. He took no notice, but she saw his teeth show in a nervous smile. He breathed hard as he pulled her round to face him. She could tell he was excited.

Céleste resisted his fumbling hands, and stared over his shoulder along the deserted arcade, which was patterned with crescents of yellow light from street lamps set under each arch. The Casbah spilled alleys into the arcade at several places near here—but where?

While she held the lieutenant's arms, to restrain his eager, hurting fingers, she was trying to visualize the bazaars in the daytime, to remember the closest entrance to the Casbah.

"You make me work," said the lieutenant. He was trying to be blasé.

The solution snapped into her brain. The nearest entrance was right next to the Bazaar El-Khoumi, about thirty feet away.

Thirty feet.

The lieutenant swore, then tried to recover his *sangfroid*. *"Tu s'exaspere aux désirs de l'amour,"* he said in a tight urgent voice. "When can—we meet?"

She had an inspiration. "Have you no control over your men?" she demanded. "Make them stop insulting us with that song."

His pride was pricked, as she hoped. He moved into the open and bawled at the men, ordering them to be quiet.

Céleste ran toward the entrance, and she was almost there before some of the soldiers saw her and yelled. There was a great shouting, but she kept her eyes on the dark fronts of the shuttered bazaars, which were barely distinguishable in the shadows.

"Catch her!" yelled the lieutenant. She heard the hobnailed boots of the soldiers pounding on the sidewalk, and the roar of the men's voices magnified as they burst into the echoing arcade. She reached the Bazaar El-Khoumi and clawed frantically at the darkness that lay beside it. She moved into the black hole as fast as she could, and her groping fingers met nothing. She gave a sob of relief when she realized that her guess was right—this was an alleyway.

Céleste stumbled forward, her arms outstretched, her feet feeling for each step. Her soft slippers struck something and she realized that it was a sleeping body, one of the countless *mumfa'*. As she stepped over the man she snatched a backward glance and saw that the slit of the alley entrance was half filled by the black silhouette of the troops jostling in after her. Their noise filled the confined space like an angry beast.

A whistle blew, and the roar died away. "Come back!" shouted an authoritative voice, which echoed through the arcade. "It's a trap!"

But one of the soldiers was right behind her. She could hear his nailed boots loud on the cobbles. She felt his fingers clawing on her shoulder. She twisted round and buried her teeth in his hand. The man swore in pain and let go.

Céleste threw herself forward on all fours and scrambled to get away from the soldier.

The whistle blew again, and the noise subsided. She crawled in an agony of panic, then rose and felt her way again, tripping over bodies, grazing her hands on the walls, and she stumbled against a flight of steps. She groped her way up, her breath coming in painful bursts. She missed the top step and lay full length on the slimy coldness of the cobbles. She lay dazed for a few seconds, and could hear the voice of the lieutenant, fantastically distorted by the close-pressed walls, "Back to your ranks, men, she's only a whore!"

She heard the nailed boots moving away, and she lay still till her exhausted muscles could summon strength once more. The slime seeped through to her skin, all down her front. Céleste felt sick with terror; there was a sharp taste of bile in her mouth.

In front of her, at the top of a slope, was a rectangular patch of yellow. She knew that meant it was one of the main alleys, the only ones that were lighted at night. Around her, in the dimness, she could hear the excited gabble of many voices. She dragged herself to her feet and moved forward.

Chapter Fifteen

HANSEN HEARD the chairman's voice cut into Chef-Chauen's fiery speech. "This is a time for cunning," said the old man, "not for brave words. We must think why the French are surrounding us. Are they coming in?"

"They never do," retorted Chef-Chauen. "Not at night, anyway. That is why we always meet here."

"Troops have sometimes come in, when there were plenty of them." The chairman's voice had the high pitch of old age.

There was a pause of absolute silence, then a shrill babble of alarm broke out among the Arabs. Hansen took a deep breath and shouted, "I think the French are coming in to capture us!"

The noise snuffed out.

"You have been betrayed," Hansen continued. "You must all get out of here. Hide among the *mumfa'* in the gutters, or up on the roofs. Separate—each one go to a separate place."

"No!" roared Chef-Chauen, "we're on our own ground now. I say, kill the French if they come in!"

"Foolish talk," said the chairman. "They would start shooting, and many innocent people would be killed. Remember Sétif. We don't want another French massacre of the Arabs."

"Haven't any of you been weaned?" cried Chef-Chauen. "Follow me, those who want to fight!"

There was a noise of sandaled feet hurrying out of the room. The Arabs who remained argued whether to go up on the roof or follow Chef-Chauen down into the alleys. Gradually the voices grew less in number, as more Arabs left, till finally Hansen sensed that he and George were alone. He wrenched away the cloth from his eyes and saw that he was in a long greasy-walled room that had a blue-tiled frieze.

"Let's go up on the roof," suggested George, and led the way out of the arched doorway. They went along a corridor and turned into a stair well that was thick with sleeping bodies. They groped up a series of flights of stairs, trying to pick their way between the bodies by the indirect light from rooms leading off each landing.

"We're almost there," said George and pointed up to a door on the next flight, which gave out onto the roof. They walked out into the moonlight. The air was sweet and clean after the sourness inside. The flat roof was filled with white-robed figures of Arabs, some standing in groups, chattering furiously, others sleeping Bedouin-style with burnooses drawn up over their heads.

The flat roofs were terraced, mounting with the incline of the hill. Most of the buildings had ladders or stairways to join them with their neighbors. Jumbled among the roofs were scores of lean-tos and other temporary dwellings, in which the crowded Arabs had tried to make homes. Under the eye of the moon the Casbah was a black-and-white escarpment. Stark against the cold light was the great onion-shaped dome of the Mosque Mohammed Ech-Cherif.

George led the way across the roofs, lithely clambering up the stairs that connected the various levels. Hansen found it increasingly tiring to follow the younger man, for his bandaged shoulder was a lattice of pain.

They had just descended to one of the lower roofs when a great glare burst in their eyes. For one instant Hansen steeled himself for the expected shock wave, thinking it was a bursting shell, but then he realized it was a searchlight. No, there were two of them.

"That's the French signal!" said George.

They clambered back up the ladder and raised their heads cautiously into the fierce beams, which coned down from the top of the hill, centering on the rooftop of the Messali headquarters.

All around, there mounted a growing tide of noise as sleepers awoke and joined the excited chorus.

"We were nearly caught," said George. "A traitor must have told the French where we were meeting. Those searchlights were planned to pinpoint the building where we met. We got out just in time."

The glare was too blinding for them to see what was happening on the roof of the Messali headquarters. Both beams came from the top of the hill—one from the fortress of the Casbah, and the other from somewhere over on the right. Here and there, isolated figures were standing up on the

roofs, shielding their eyes against the glare, or waving de-
fiantly, but most of the Arabs were crouching in the shallow
shadows of the parapets, as if the sudden light were a weapon from which they had to shield. Down in the alleyways
the crowd-noise was growing. Hansen looked over a parapet
and saw that a mass of white-robed figures was growing
denser as more people poured out of the dwellings.

Abruptly, the noise of the crowd below changed from a
murmuring buzz to a great moaning growl, like a wounded
beast.

"They're coming in!" cried Hansen. "The troops are coming in!"

Céleste's bare feet slipped on the slimy cobbles every time
she came to an incline. She had lost her slippers when she
scrambled away from the soldier, and her dress was stained
all the way down with the nameless ooze of the alleys. Each
time she slipped, the slime covered her cut knees.

Now that her first panic had passed, her mind slowly
poised to an icy calm. She knew she was in great danger
from the men who eyed her curiously, but she hoped that
her bedraggled appearance was some protection. She closed
her mind to everything but the need to find George and warn
him. She knew she had to move quickly, for the troops might
enter the Casbah at any moment. She headed toward the
mosque. In there, she figured, lay her only hope. Some holy
man in the mosque might believe her story and send a warning to Messali's men. Nobody else would be likely to listen
to her, in fact if they heard her French-accented Arabic
they would probably attack her, thinking she were a French
spy.

Céleste scrambled up through the honeycombed tiers of
alleys, in desperate haste. She had to keep to the lighted passages, for the ones in darkness were too jammed with sleeping bodies and too dangerous.

The alleys, which she knew so well by day, now looked
strangely different, and she had to keep on checking with
the neat little name plates—the French authorities' attempt
to bring order and identity to the swarming rat's nest. Every
ruelle was labeled with prim solemnity, even those which
were little more than garbage dumps at the bottom of blank-
walled shafts.

She was getting nearer now; the Rue Annibal, the Rue

Desaix; here was the short cut up to the *souk* of the saddlers, then the Rue Barbarousse. By this time, Céleste's heart was pumping so hard that it seemed to be in her neck, stifling her breathing.

Even in her frantic haste she could sense an unusual air of excitement among the Arabs. She could hear them calling out rumors about the French troops.

She came to the high covered steps that formed the only outlet from the Rue Odéon, and as she entered the blackness a hand grasped at her thigh. She wrenched herself away but her attacker, who had been sprawled out by the foot of the steps, lunged out and caught her ankle. Céleste lost her balance and fell backward, landing on the man. Instantly, he grasped his arms round her and pulled her round to face him, gripping her with ferocious strength. She caught the cloying, sickly sweet smell of hashish on his panting breath, and she gave a piercing scream. She fought wildly, but the power of the drug-crazed man was overwhelming. She shrieked again and he rolled over on top of her, ripping at the front of her dress. Then miraculously, Céleste felt the man being lifted off her bodily, and she saw him flung hard against the wall. Still dazed with terror, she had a confused impression of somebody, who was immense and black, helping her up.

She found herself sobbing with relief, clasped against a tremendous bosom that reeked of violent perfume. For the next few minutes her mind was still so confused that she had no clear awareness of mounting the steps, nor of reaching an alley, which, alone of all those in the Casbah, was full of light from open doors. As her thoughts cleared she realized that this was the Rue Kataroudjil, the street of the brothels, and her savior—a six-foot, heavily built Negress —belonged here. The dark dress of the woman was superfluous on her great frame, which thrust out boldly against concealment. She was a magnificent powerhouse of blackness.

"You new here? Don't you know you shouldn't leave this alley?" demanded the Negress in a voice that was almost a bass. Her Arabic had the soft slurred accent of the southern tundra, and her voice made the words sound soothing.

"I got lost," said Céleste.

The black woman pressed her arm closer round Céleste's shoulder. "I'd better fix you up," she said. "You look terrible."

Céleste realized that her dress was ripped down to her middle. Her skin showed through in a long triangle, gray from the slime.

The Negress guided Céleste past the bright doorways, in front of which women were lounging in every stage of undress. Some were European women, in slatternly underwear; there were a couple of Berbers whose eyelids, stained black with kohl, contrasted violently with their peroxided hair. Céleste saw a Spanish woman wearing nothing but a mantilla, and behind her, in the cubicle, a cracked phonograph was whining out a *seguidilla;* nearby was an Arab who still wore her yashmak, though her tattooed body was all exposed. Céleste saw an aged harridan in a stained ankle-length dress, which held her like a shroud round a skeleton; and there were a couple of girls of about twelve, still nub-breasted, who were naked to the waist.

A party of swarthy Egyptian sailors was reeling from doorway to doorway, shouting drunkenly, while the harpies bickered in ragged bursts, and shoved at each other, trying to entice the men to enter.

Some of the women called out bawdy greetings to the giant Negress and she shouted back at them gruffly. Even in her terror and exhaustion, Céleste wondered what sort of man could ever dare to hire this vast creature. The Negress reached her own doorway, but Céleste resisted the pressure of the woman's friendly arm and said, "No, you're kind, but I've got to go."

"Go?· Where? It's not safe to leave here."

"To the mosque. I must hurry."

The Negress looked down at her. The whites of the black woman's eyes were shot with weaving lines, like marble, and her cavernous mouth was hanging open, exposing the teeth.

"Tell me," she demanded. "Who are you? Where's your place?" The great shovel hands grasped Céleste's shoulders. "You must clean yourself," she said, "you must rest."

Céleste was about to blurt out her story when a bright glare shot down into the alley, bathing the face and the arms of the Negress in little daggers of light. The whole alley was bright in the glow reflected from the glare above. A noise that began on a low octave slowly gathered power—the sound of thousands of voices, alarmed and excited.

Céleste fancied she could hear the soldier's whistle blowing again. "They're coming in!" she cried.

She ran to the end of the street of women, out into the Rue Archeron, and became caught up among a great swirling crowd that was yelling cries of panic. She found herself being jostled, with the rest of the throng, in the direction of the great beam that was directed on the center of the Casbah.

The troops came down the main alleys in single file, at a steady trot, their long bayonets swinging, hob-nailed boots clapping, and a loud-speaker voice behind them braying monotonously, "Make way for the troops!"

The Arabs pressed back against the walls to let them pass. Chef-Chauen, from the darkness of the doorway where he was hiding, saw a group of about twenty white-robed figures, who had been squatting near the entrance to the Messali headquarters, suddenly spring up. They produced wicked-looking Bren machine guns from under their voluminous *abeyehs;* then spread out to cover the exit from the head-quarters.

No sooner were they in position than various columns of troops appeared, each converging on the little alley at almost the same moment.

The walls streamed reflections from the searchlights that battened on the roofs above, and the scene was lit starkly. Two grizzled officers in high kepis barked laconic orders, and the man hunt went forward, an old familiar drill. One column of troops entered the headquarters house, headed by a couple of men who held a powerful signal lamp, while two others carried its battery. Chef-Chauen could see the beam appear fragmentarily in the slitted windows, mounting higher and higher as the troops methodically searched the building. In the alley, the officers stood beside an oxlike private who carried a walkie-talkie. Several times they spoke crisply into the mouthpiece of the instrument.

Chef-Chauen saw the reflection of the searchlights glisten-ing on the steel helmets of the troops. A longing for action welled up in him. All he had was his long knife, but the troops had beautiful shining guns. He could almost touch some of the muzzles each time the soldiers moved past the arched doorway in which he crouched. A few Arab voices were shrieking insults at the troops, from the safety of the balconies and slitted windows above.

"Christian pigs!" they yelled. "Filthy roumi!"

This gave Chef-Chauen an idea. He whispered to several

of his companions, telling them to go upstairs and create a diversion by throwing things at the troops.

While he waited, Chef-Chauen saw that several of the soldiers who were clattering into the ruelle, wore the navy-blue uniform of the Brigade. The blue lozenge emblem on their sleeves—the hated sign—made Chef-Chauen's rage leap up in him and he took his knife from its sheath, flicking his thumbnail on its razoredge.

At last it came, the diversion he had asked for. A spattering, splashing sound was followed almost immediately by a roar of rage from a group of soldiers, who edged into the center of the alley, wiping filth from their shoulders and faces; as they did so another load fell on them. Wild shrieks of delight and abuse split the air from above. All the troops turned their heads toward the scene, and Chef-Chauen poised his knife and drove it hilt deep into the back of the nearest soldier. As the man collapsed Chef-Chauen snatched his Bren gun and backed into the shadows.

The other soldiers whirled round and fired from the hip. Chef-Chauen saw the orange spatter of the muzzles as he ducked into the maze of passages. While he ran he fumbled with the beautiful Bren, and when the splitting roar of the soldiers' guns crashed in the enclosed space, he had his weapon ready. He turned, put his finger on the release and emptied the whole chamber at his pursuers in one long burst of revenge.

The shots echoed in menacing cracks from down in the alley, and Hansen shielded his eyes from the glare of the searchlights, trying to make out what was happening below.

"They're fighting," he yelled to George.

"Or there's another massacre."

Hansen felt the pain of excitement clawing at him, stretching up tentacles to whip the raw parts of his brain. He felt himself drawn to the violence that was raging.

The sound of the firing had an electric effect on the packed crowd below. The people scrambled to get out of the way into the safety of the buildings.

Hansen and George could see eddies of humanity struggling round the doorways. There came a fresh burst of firing, then another, and within a few minutes the alleys near the scene of the shooting were practically deserted, but the farther ones were still packed. Hansen could see some of the bolder Arabs in the crowd peer round the corners to see the French. The shouts of the mob drifted up, shrill and excited.

Hansen and George were so absorbed in watching that they did not realize troops were right behind them until they heard shouted commands. They turned and saw a column of troops in green berets running across the roofs, springing powerfully up the stairways. The soldiers made no sound.

"Commandos!" said George.

Hansen and George watched the commandos till they were swallowed up in the blinding glare of the searchlights. When they looked down into the alleys once more they were empty, except for some troops who were keeping close to the walls, spread out in street-fighting formation. In the bright reflection from the searchlights the cobbles seemed like tattered strips of lace.

Hansen and George each saw the figure at once. Something tawny glowed, momentarily, in the pool of light thrown by an alley lamp, and moved down the deserted alley toward the area of the shooting.

Hansen strained his eyes. It was a girl, a girl who swayed as if drunk.

"She'll get hit!" he cried.

George grasped his arm in a convulsive grip. "It's Céleste!" he yelled.

"Who?" Hansen peered down, trying to make out the figure.

"Céleste!" George rose to his feet and shouted, "Céleste! Go back, go back! You'll get hurt!"

The girl apparently did not hear. She swayed on.

"I must go to her," said George. He turned to go, but Hansen held his sleeve.

"Don't be a fool," said Hansen. "You can't go down there —you'll be killed!"

"I must get to her." George shouted, and wrenched his arm free, but Hansen grasped him again, this time with both hands, and the youth struggled furiously to free himself.

Hansen tried to hold George, but his wound-stiffened shoulder made it difficult. George ducked and wrenched himself away, then ran agilely over the roofs toward the nearest door. Hansen knew he could never catch him, so he turned back to look over the parapet at the scene below.

He saw the girl fall flat on her face, then he heard some

shouted commands. A file of troops moved toward the girl and picked her up. They all moved away in a close pattern, the tawny hair of the girl among the steel helmets of the troops.

Not till that moment did George's shout of "Céleste" and the tawny hair of the girl, link up in his mind.

"Céleste Lander!" he said.

Chapter Sixteen

SEVERAL RIFLE CRACKS made double echoes in the confined space of the alleys, and each one was followed swiftly by bursts from machine guns. Hansen figured that a few Arabs were firing pot shots at soldiers, who were blazing back.

This could easily turn into another massacre, he thought. All that was needed to set it off would be for a few troops to lose their heads.

What had happened to George? He was probably hanging round the troops, trying to catch a glimpse of Céleste. What was Mari's daughter doing in the Casbah? Was she a member of the Arab underground?

Hansen pushed his way down the nearest stair well. He moved mechanically against the buffeting of the excited figures; his mind was on Mari's dinner party, when Céleste had angrily defended the Arabs. Yes, it was all beginning to tie in. Céleste went to Sorbonne University, and so did George; they had probably met there. Mari would get the shock of her life if she found out that her daughter was carrying on with an Arab rebel.

When Hansen emerged into the alley the packed crowd was buzzing with wild rumors. He could tell from their high-pitched tones and excited gestures that they were on the verge of the mob hysteria that turned Arabs into a howling mob of fanatics. Only one spark was needed.

He kept looking for George, but it was impossible to distinguish faces among the mass of shadowed headcloths. He had to slouch and keep his knees slightly bent, for his height would have made him conspicuous.

He let himself be carried by the surging whirls of the

crowd. This was the best hiding place, he decided, here among the mob. Better not try to get out of the Casbah tonight, there was probably a tight cordon round it.

He tried to imagine himself in the mind of the French. What would they do, now that the night's operation had proved a flop? Hansen figured that the Security Brigade's next move would be to concentrate every man on a roundup. The order would go out—bring in every suspect, make a spot check, all through the Casbah, put every man on the search, do it all night, all week, if necessary, but bring 'em in.

Hansen remembered the search technique with Arabs. You put disguised guards at strategic points, then made a lot of noise, letting a whole section know you were checking up on them. Arab psychology did the rest. The guilty ones blew their top and tried to escape, and if your guards were in the right place you nabbed them. That way, you could find your quarry in a crowd of thousands.

Hansen guessed that heavily armed squads of the Brigade were already spreading out through the Casbah, on spot checks. Several times Hansen caught glimpses of burly figures grouped round doorways and he guessed these were the business end of Brigade traps. Hansen let himself drift with the crowd for half an hour, and then he began to tire from the constant stooping. He longed to sit down somewhere, but the cobbles were too slimy, and he knew that in the bright light of the cafés he might be recognized as a roumi.

He passed the end of the Rue Kataroudjil where the whores were beginning to stop work for the night, and a few alleys lower down he noticed one of the halls of the *danse du ventre*. He decided to kill an hour in there.

The dingy interior stank of human breath and sweat. In former days, when the official French brothels had flanked it, gaudily painted and decorated outside with great plaster nudes, this had been a tourist trap, with chandeliers, pornographic murals, incense, and divans; but now the gross paintings on the walls were peeling, and there were merely rows of wooden forms for patrons. The only links with past days were the ornate caryatids that flanked the dingy stage, and even these stone goddesses were blotched greasily with hand marks.

Hansen seated himself at the side, so that his size would be less noticeable. The place was crowded, in spite of the late hour. "I'm not the only one who wants to lie low till the French have gone," he thought.

Two stomach dancers were in the middle of their act, and the audience was so still that it might have been anesthetized. The women, plump and heavy breasted, in the Arab taste, stood almost directly above the limelight at the front of the stage. They rolled their ventral muscles to every hypnotic slide of the music, which came from a two-chorded guitar and the maddening flute of a *rhaita*, with a tattoo of drums beneath to accentuate the repetitive rhythm.

The women were naked to the hips and they wore baggy *sarrouel* pantaloons down to their bare feet. It looked as if their ponderous bodies contained sinuous reptiles that pulsed out horribly in time to the music, first making their stomachs lift and twirl, then flapping in and out quickly like a sail about to jibe, and finally the serpentine creatures in them seemed to move up to their breasts, making them spin together like wheels, then in opposite rotary directions. All the time, as the beat of the music slowly increased in pace, the women held their fat arms above their heads. Hansen closed his eyes wearily against the nauseous spectacle, and let himself doze off. His mind was floating just within consciousness, so that he was aware of the dance finishing, then the flute took up a solo in a nuance that made Hansen raise his lids. He saw that two boys, clad in the muslin headpiece, slave bangles, and tight robes of those trained from infancy for the profession of homosexuality, were going through a parody of courtship. Hansen closed his eyes but the brittle voices of the boys irritated his nerves. It seemed an hour before the lights went up and the patrons became individuals again, freed from the jell of prurience.

Hansen's neighbor nudged him and grinned. He was an oily little man with waxed mustaches and a red tarboosh; he looked like an Egyptian merchant. The man licked his fleshy lips and said, "*Ah c'est le débauche dans tous ses exotismes!*"

Hansen tautened in alarm. "Why did he speak in French?" he thought. "Is he trying to trap me?"

Hansen did not trust himself to reply, but nodded and grinned. Then he noticed the gleam of his wrist watch. Damn, that's what had given him away. The guy had seen the watch, and naturally thought he was a rich Arab, and had spoken in French to let Hansen know he, too, was top-drawer educated.

"I must be cracking up," thought Hansen. "I might as well hang up a sign. Lucky this guy didn't tumble."

The lights went down again before the Egyptian could make more talk, which he was apparently anxious to do.

The next turn was better. A couple of Spanish-Moroccan girls came on and did a castanet dance. They were young and fairly well shaped, nude except for long black stockings and high-heeled shoes. They twirled and banged the castanets with furious vigor, but their faces were masks of indifference. The tawdry backcloth received distorted shadows of their bodies, slanting their bouncing black hair, their conical breasts, and the castanets into absurd caricatures. They were a relief after the other turns. "Nothing like good old-fashioned sex," thought Hansen.

The rhythm beat faster till the click of the castanets was as continuous as a stick drawn across railings, and when the girls stamped their feet harder, in the frenzy of the climax, long jiggles of blue shadow rippled up out of their black stockings, between the muscles of their thighs and rumps.

The audience tensed itself for the moment when the girls would throw themselves on their backs and perform their final contortions, but an alien sound cut roughly across the herd excitement. It was the heavy clump of soldiers' boots and barked commands. Somebody at the back shouted, "The Brigade!" -

The music faltered away into a few plaintive beats, and the girls stopped, slowly letting their arms droop. The audience twisted round, staring at the entrance.

"Everybody stay where you are," called a brisk voice in the stilted Arabic of a Frenchman.

The audience broke out in a buzz of fright. The two dancers looked at each other uncertainly, panting from their exertions, and their deep breaths projected loops of shadow above their breasts. For the first time their faces betrayed an emotion, and it was fear.

Hansen thought, "The French are taking their time coming in. Must be deliberate. They hope to make him bolt—whoever they're after."

The lights blazed up, and everybody rose, in nervous expectancy. The two girl dancers scurried off stage, holding on to each other. Then the troops came in, and there was a sharp drawing-in of breaths among the Arabs.

Each of the soldiers had a Bren gun, held at the ready, its

ugly snout wavering over the audience. Behind the soldiers came dark figures, the men of the Security Brigade. When the Arabs saw the navy-blue uniforms of the Brigade members, and their grim faces under the shiny caps, an undercurrent of murmurs rolled through the hall—a noise of panic.

An officer entered—a trim gaunt man with the tight ageless face of the professional soldier. Behind him were two tommy gunners who guarded a small white-robed figure. This group passed down the main aisle to the front and turned to face the crowd.

"Sit down all of you!" ordered the officer. The white mass of the audience sank obediently, and then the rows of soldiers with their aimed guns seemed even more threatening.

The small figure who was guarded by soldiers began looking intently at the audience, through a black yashmak that completely obscured the person's face from view.

Hansen realized that this might be a woman or a small man. This was probably the informer trick. You rigged up somebody like this and made your victims fear they were having the finger put on them. It usually worked well, for the guilty ones gave themselves away by their nervousness.

The little figure was moving slowly along the rows, with the tommy gunners pointing their muzzles at each person being studied. The trio was taking its time, letting the tension mount. Several times the informer gestured, and the tommy gunners ordered the individual being scrutinized to show his face and hands.

Hansen felt trapped. When the group reached him they would certainly spot him. If this informer had been present at the rebel's meeting he would put the finger on him as one of those taking part. "Then I'll be lucky to escape prison, or deportation," he thought.

He'd have to kiss good-by to any chance of the big money with Kuhn. The Brigade would make the most of him to offset the flopped raid—he would be the scapegoat, the Brigade would probably build him up as a leader of the rebels. And what about Mari? What would she think?

The little figure was very near. Hansen felt a wild desire for action. If that informer once looked at him he was finished. The small black-masked figure was ordering a man to rise, and when he obeyed, Hansen was surprised to see he was a six-footer, and broad in proportion. One of the tommy gunners asked a question and the big man answered in a deep voice. The idea flashed across Hansen's mind—could this be Chef-Chauen?

In that second all the lights went out. The hall was plunged into complete blackness.

A pandemonium of noise and struggling burst out. There was a deep bellow of *"Y'Allah!"* and some whirling shape knocked Hansen off his balance. He recovered, and flailed out blindly with both his arms, to clear a space for himself.

No use trying to break through the entrance—it was heavily guarded. Maybe he could escape by way of the stage. There was just a chance.

He threw himself forward through the panicking mob. The noise seemed to be magnified by the darkness that was full of clawing arms. He scrambled into the aisle, which was one mass of struggling bodies, and fought his way to the stage.

Somewhere near, the officer's voice yelled, "Sit down! Or we'll fire!"

A blast of shots came from the entrance.

Hansen squirmed his way forward again, using all his weight to shoulder Arabs aside. He made one more heave of his shoulder but met no resistance and fell onto the boards of the stage. He hauled himself up just as a few wavering lines of white from flashlights cut into the gloom.

"Everybody sit down!" screeched the officer.

Several other figures were groping around the stage. Hansen could just make out the paleness of their robes. Hansen thrust past them. He realized that the backdrop of the stage had collapsed. He fumbled his way ahead into the darkness. The noise was less earsplitting now; he guessed that many of the terrified Arabs were cowering underneath the forms in the hall.

The lights went up again, and he saw he was in a narrow space that was littered with junk.

Hansen scrambled over to a passage that led diagonally away from the stage. He heard a scuffling noise behind him. He dodged into a doorway on the right and found himself in what looked like a large clothes closet, half filled with robes hanging from a rack. In it were the two girl dancers, huddled together with their arms round each other.

They looked at him in mute terror.

"How can I get out of here?" he demanded.

The taller of the two naked girls bared her teeth to her gums, like the snarl of a trapped animal, and pushed at him wildly. "Go!" she said. "You'll get us killed!"

The steps of soldiers were approaching. Hansen put his hand on his lips as he edged back into the hanging clothes.

The noise of the approaching boots seemed to be clanging, ominous. As he arranged the rows of clothes to conceal himself Hansen caught a last glimpse of the larger girl staring at him. Then she began to scream.

Hansen knew it was hopeless. He scrambled out to make a last dash for it. He ran almost into the arms of a burly Brigade man, and clutched at his gun to turn the muzzle away from himself. He strained his whole strength against the man, trying to twist the Bren round to the wall. It went off, with a stutter of crashes, and even as the noise burst in his ears he saw a soldier swinging the butt of his rifle at him, but he saw it too late. A great blow fell on his head.

When the mist cleared from his vision he was lying on the floor, amid a forest of black boots and corded breeches, which soared up into the dark tunics of the Brigade. Far above, tight hard faces were staring down at him, and there was a sharp hurting light.

Chapter Seventeen

They all had it in for him, Hansen could see that. The voices in the courtroom, and the eyes of the police *fonctionnaires* were all hard with malice. The fan that stirred the air above the head of the magistrate vibrated maddeningly, plucking on Hansen's nerves.

The pain of his head wound was throbbing inside his skull as if something were imprisoned there, trying to claw its way free. Every now and then the pain blotted out his senses, and he would grip hard to the dock rail to stop himself from falling. The voices in the courtroom would fade away, as if he entered a long dark tunnel, and then slowly he would move out into the light again, able to see and hear once more.

When the guards had marched him in and made him stand in the iron-railed dock of the commissariat, the argument between the presiding *juge d'instruction* and a lawyer apparently defending Hansen had obviously been going on for some time. Hansen could tell that from the exasperated looks on the faces of the magistrate and officials.

The defending lawyer was on his feet again, waving a law book. "The Code is clear," he shouted. "You can give 'provisional liberty' to any accused person, if responsible persons come forward as surety."

"Responsible *persons*," said the magistrate in a thin, bored voice. "You have produced only one person."

One? Hansen's mind slowly gathered round this fact. He tried to close his mind to the voices that cut like a saw into his consciousness. One person? So somebody had come forward for him. Kuhn?

Hansen gripped the dock rail tighter and for the first time peered round at the rows of faces in the courtroom. They merged into the white-tiled walls, forming a pale blur, but then he saw a black gleam of hair and that oval face with the great dark eyes, and he knew that the friend was Mari.

She was keeping her face fixed on the magistrate. Hansen kept staring at her, hoping she would return his glance, but she never changed her position.

"Very well," the magistrate was saying, "if you can get the American Consul to ask for the prisoner's release that will be another matter."

"I've already told you that the Consul is out of the city," said the lawyer.

The magistrate shrugged disagreeably. Hansen could feel the pain clawing inside his skull again and the voices began to fall away. Then, from far away, he heard Mari. His mind clung to her voice, and he forced himself into consciousness.

She was standing up. "You give 'provisional liberty' to murderers," she cried. "Why not to this American citizen?" Her voice was shrill and fierce.

"This foreigner," said the magistrate, "has gravely injured a member of the Security Brigade—"

"I object. That is not proven!" shouted the lawyer.

The magistrate shook his bald head, as if pestered by flies.

The thin-lipped Brigade major intervened. "We have no guarantee that the American will not sneak out of the territory."

"It was an accidental wounding," cried Mari. She went on arguing, but Hansen's pain was closing out the scene again. When he could hear once more he became aware that the noise in the courtroom had doubled in pitch. Everybody seemed to be shouting at once, but Mari overbore them all. "Very well!" she shrieked. "I shall go to the Governor General himself!"

That changed the atmosphere. The voice of the Brigade major took on a new note of conciliation, and the magistrate sounded less obstinate. Hansen realized they all thought Mari had pull up at Government House. They began to weaken, under cover of a bluster of protests. Hansen gave himself up to the pain. He did not care what they did to him so long as they let him sit down. He was only dimly aware of an interminable period of wrangling over guarantees.

The next stimulus he knew was a warm stupefying glow. He realized that he was out in the open sunlight, and Mari was beside him. Her chauffeur, Michel, was helping him into the limousine. He sank back onto the cushions and did not try to resist the pain any more. He saw Mari lean forward and shut the sliding glass panel behind the chauffeur's head, then she turned and sat looking at Hansen, her face set hard.

"Tell me," she said sharply, "tell me the truth."

Hansen forced his mind to grasp her meaning. "The shooting? It was an accident. He shot himself with his own gun while we were struggling."

"Not that. You know what I mean." She was sitting in a strained attitude, bolt upright, her black eyes fixed on him intently.

"What on earth are you talking about?" God, she was steamed up, he knew that look of hers.

He realized that Mari had not attempted to make up her face, after the ordeal in the courtroom. The lipstick on her full red mouth was cracked and smeared, her nose was shiny, and thick tendrils of black hair had loosened from her chignon.

"Céleste, that's who I'm talking about," she said. "What's going on between you two?"

He groaned aloud. This mess was getting more rotten all the time.

"Answer me!" she demanded. She began to storm at him. "So! Just the same as that hussy! Nothing to say! She just shrugged and—"

"Wait," he said. "I haven't the slightest interest in Céleste. I had no idea she was in the Casbah. The only time I ever spoke to her was at your dinner party."

She stared at him, holding her breath, and then said in an anguished voice, "Oh, if only I could believe that."

His irritation vented itself on her. "Don't be stupid. I've had énough to put up with. You know where I've been every minute since I've been in this city."

"Yes, but you could have met her in Paris. You might have been carrying on with her for years."

Across his mind flashed the memory of young George in the Casbah, dashing down into the alleys, to get to Céleste. Should he tell Mari? Hell, no. It would only mean long explanations, a terrible scene between Mari and Céleste.

"I've never seen Céleste, nor thought of her, nor spoken to her," he said, "except at dinner in your house."

"But Céleste herself—she was calling out for you!" The hard note crept back into her voice.

"Me? Impossible."

"When Céleste recovered consciousness after they got her out, she kept screaming, 'He's in there. I must warn him.' The officers told me. The doctor had to give her a sedative."

"She didn't mention my name, surely?"

"No. But who else could it be? You were both in there together."

Hansen realized that Mari was all set for an emotional scene. Oh, God, he couldn't stand that. He burst out with an oath that he made as frightful as he could, swearing by his eyesight and his mother that he was telling the truth.

She was moved; he could see that. His oath was in the French style for high drama. She took a deep breath, but before she could prolong the scene he shut her up by pulling her to him, and covering her lips with his. "You're all I want," he murmured against her mouth.

Why, for Christ's sake, couldn't she relax?

She remained taut for a few seconds, then made a sighing sound and softened herself against him. The side of his head was stinging, now that he had turned to her, for the dressing over the bruise where the soldier had hit him was pressed hard against the seat rest. The pain and his weariness made the touch of her completely without stimulus. All he wanted was a stiff drink and some sleep.

But Mari was getting more ardent. He tried to deflect her by venting the one emotion left in him—rage at the Security Brigade.

"They beat me up," he said. "Those bastards beat me up. I'll get even with them."

Mari made sounds of concern, and began using her hands and lips caressingly.

"What's the matter with you?" he demanded. "Why the hell did you knock yourself out to get me free, if you thought I was two-timing you?"

"I had to find out. I couldn't stand not knowing. I was going crazy. I was so jealous of Céleste that I had to get away from her—I was afraid I might kill her."

She clenched and unclenched her hands and her nostrils became distended. He suddenly felt how alien she was.

"But why did Céleste go down to the Casbah?" she asked. "Who was the man she was calling for?"

He shook his head wearily and closed his eyes.

She began thinking out loud and her voice seemed distant, in his tiredness, as if he heard through a muffling fog: "Surely, it couldn't have been to meet Boward—but who else? Ah, perhaps that is why Boward refused to answer the phone at the Consulate when I was trying to get you free. Yes, he is ashamed. He persuaded her to make that crazy rendezvous in the Casbah. That wretched girl, she's disgraced me! Caught like that, covered with filth and half naked. She's lucky she wasn't killed. I'll make sure the American Consul knows all about that stupid Boward."

She sat up straight and began to paint her lips. The tree-lined streets made alternating light and shadow play across her face.

Hansen closed his eyes wearily, full of bitter self-disgust. What a stinking mess he'd got himself into. There had been no word from Kuhn. The old man had washed his hands of him.

Another thought began jabbing his misery and he voiced it out loud. "They tell me the Brigade man is hurt badly," he said. "If he dies that'll be all I need. Where do they guillotine people in Algeria?"

Mari shook her head. "No," she said. "I know my own people. They're exaggerating to make the affair more exciting. The Brigade man must be dying, to make it dramatic. We love drama, we French."

"That, from you," he thought.

Mari was herself again. She was smiling while she painted her mouth. By the time she'd finished, the car was climbing the hill, and the afternoon sun was sloping in through the windows uninterruptedly. She began fussing over him tenderly. "I'll get my doctor to come round to see you," she said.

Only now did Hansen realize that she was taking him to her own home. Even so, the implications of this were only faint in the recesses of his mind.

"All I need is a stiff drink and some sleep," he said.

"Of course, *chéri.*" She nuzzled her forehead against his.

The tires cracked over the gravel of the driveway and when the car pulled up Hansen felt the full reaction of the long strain hit him. It was a great effort to pull himself out of the car. He was so absorbed in making it that he did not realize, till he reached the door of the mansion, that Céleste was there, talking to her mother. The girl looked scared and nervous, till Mari replied to her, and then Céleste's face cleared.

"But with Boward?" Mari was saying, "I despise that man. He got you into this disgusting business."

Hansen moved out of earshot and he found that Michel, the chauffeur, was holding his arm. Hell, he was more weak than he thought. Then he caught sight of the maid, Yvette. She was looking at him in that fixed mad way of hers.

By the time he had dragged himself to the living room his whole mind was concentrated on the need for a drink. He asked Yvette for one, but she ignored him and went out of the room.

In the doorway he saw Michel, who seemed to be swelling and dwindling, alternately. And then Mari came in and poured him a straight brandy, and everything came back into focus.

Chapter Eighteen

Céleste hurried back from the newsstand to the limousine, her mind blazing with relief that George was safe. The message he had left with her old friend the newsstand proprietor, was in George's own handwriting: "Will wait at our place all evening."

He was safe, they would soon be together again.

Céleste saw Boward staring at her through the limousine

window, his nose slightly flattened against the window, and the absurd distortion of his face acted as a trigger to her bubbling excitement. She laughed out loud. His neat, smooth face puckered up in a frown as she climbed in.

"What's the joke?" he asked.

"I just feel good." She gave him a glance that tried to convey it was because they were together.

"You're up to something," he said. "Why did you phone me to suggest we go out this evening? I don't have any illusions about where I stand with you."

"Silly," she said. "I knew you'd be *sympathique*. I'm so desolated. All this terrible publicity." She pointed to the newspaper she had bought at the stand. The headlines were black with news of the French raid on the Casbah and the critical wounding of the Security Brigade man. Céleste's photo was at the foot of the front page, in a story headed INTREPID TROOPS RESCUE DAUGHTER OF THE WELL-KNOWN MADAME LANDER. The picture showed Céleste with her dress ripped right down the front; the caption writer had punned EXPOSÉ AU CASBAH.

"I bet your mother had to pull strings to save you from being arrested too," said Boward.

She shrugged. "It was obvious that I had been assaulted by the Arabs." .

"What *were* you doing there?"

She hesitated, then looked up at him, giving him the full effect of her eyes.

"I know I can trust you," she said. "I went there to meet some of my Arab friends."

"Alone, at night? That's suicide."

"I went in with friends." She shook her head as he tried to interrupt. "No, they're not members of the underground, I promise you."

Céleste knew that Boward was not convinced. She looked at the neat parting of his red wavy hair, his breast pocket that showed the correct triangle of handkerchief, and she hated herself for having to play up to him.

"You've got your claws out," he said, taking hold of her hand. "You're up to no good, I can feel it. What's going on inside that head of yours? Where are we going?"

"To the seashore restaurant—the one we went to before." She tried to keep out of her voice excitement that the car was taking her nearer to George every minute.

"Uh-huh." Boward made the sound expressive of his skepticism. "And, of course, you're going to meet some of your Arab friends in the shrubbery again?" His mouth was pursed up sardonically.

Céleste felt color flooding up from her neck. "Yes, just for a few minutes, if you don't mind."

Boward laughed, but the sound had a false edge to it. "You're using me. I'm just the stooge who covers up, while you—"

"No, no!"

"Know what I think? You're meeting Hansen. You were in the Casbah with him. Tonight you're going to take up where you left off, and you want to be quite sure that your mother doesn't suspect you of stealing her lover."

Céleste slapped his face hard. "You dare say such a thing!"

At the same moment, fear struck each of them; Boward that he had overreached himself and lost his chance with Céleste; she that he would refuse to cover up for her any more, maybe even tell Mari his suspicions.

"I'm sorry," he said. "I didn't mean it. It's just that I'm so jealous about you." (God above, why was he wasting his time with her? All the well-stacked girls who'd tried to get their hooks into him, yet he messed around with this one. He'd never get anywhere with the conniving little bitch.)

"I'm sorry too," she said. "I know you think I'm acting very strangely. I'll be able to tell you everything very soon. But you can't believe I'd have anything to do with that horrible Hansen?" (Anything, anything, to keep him quiet. After tonight, there would be no need.)

Céleste leaned back close to Boward, in a snuggling movement. "Hansen is in bed at Mari's house," she said. "She has two doctors fussing over him—though they say it's only slight concussion. Mari is clucking like a hen. She's crazy for Hansen." She added boldly, "If you don't believe me I'll introduce you to my Arab friend this evening."

Boward closed his fingers tentatively over her thigh and she made no resistance. "I know you're using me for something," he said. "But so long as it means I'm with you, okay. What's your game?"

"I'll be able to tell you later," she said trying to put intimacy into her voice. She motioned with her head to indicate the chauffeur, Michel. "He snoops on me," she whispered. "He tells Mari everything I do."

When they arrived at the restaurant, Michel sprang out to open the door for them, and Céleste noticed that the chauffeur was looking at her with his ferret eyes bright and inquisitive. A stir of nervous dislike filled her. Michel nosed out all the gossip—suppose he knew that messages could be left at that newsstand? She'd have to be very careful with him.

She joined Boward and forced her expression into softness again. "All this pretending," she raged inside. "I must finish it."

Twilight was falling by the time Céleste and George had gotten through their whispered babble of explanations.

George cupped her chin in his hand and peered down at her in the fading light. "I can't see you properly," he whispered. "It's always the way. Something always seems to come between us."

She pressed harder against him, and he could feel her trembling. "There's nothing between us," she said, "except what you choose. Darling, I'm frightened—you're in such danger now. That informer who betrayed your meeting has probably told the Brigade your name."

George shrugged. "I think he has. The police came to the house asking for me this afternoon, though it may have been one of their routine Gestapo checks. The police know I work for Messali anyway. They watch his headquarters day and night. I'm going to keep out of sight for a week or so, till I know definitely whether they're after me."

"Oh, darling, I'm frightened."

"Don't worry, the organization is lying low. We shan't have another meeting till Messali gets back. By then everything may be all right."

"There's another thing," she said softly. "Mari will soon find out from Hansen that it wasn't him I was planning to meet there. Hansen will be able to convince her, because she wants to be convinced."

"And then your mother won't let you out of her sight," said George in a hopeless tone.

"I might be able to persuade Boward to say I was going to meet *him*, but I don't think so. He, too, thinks I was there to meet Hansen."

George remained silent, while the misery and hopelessness grew in him. He became aware, as clearly as if she had shouted her thoughts, that Céleste and he were each thinking the same thing: This might be their last meeting.

"No, no," he said, stroking her soothingly. "We won't be parted."

"Let me go with you," she asked. "I don't want to go back home, not ever."

"That's impossible. Your mother would turn Algeria inside out to find you. I'd be charged with abduction, or whatever it is."

"I'm nearly twenty-one," she said. "When I am she won't be able to do anything."

"Even then it would be hopeless," he said. "What could I offer you? What could we live on?"

"Live on?" She loosened her embrace and leaned back to peer up at him. "Don't talk like an old aunt. Do you really think we couldn't earn a living?"

"I couldn't. Not while I was working for the movement. It wouldn't be fair to you. Suppose I ended up with French bullets in me, like my uncle?"

"Don't even say_that." Her nails dug into his arms.

She was silent for a moment and when she spoke again her whole tone had changed. "What are we being gloomy about?" she asked. "We have tomorrow, at least. Let's be together all day. We'll meet early and drive out somewhere —I don't care what happens so long as we can be together. And who knows—Messali may have arranged something important, so there won't be any more killing. Maybe there'll be peace, and we'll be able to go back to Paris, where we belong. Oh, darling, let's have tomorrow!"

"I don't think you ought to be seen with me," he said slowly. His whole being was crying out, wanting to be swept up by her eagerness.

"We'll go right out of the city, then they won't be able to see us." She was bubbling over with excitement. "I know!" she cried. "We'll go to my mother's cottage up in the mountains. It's wonderful there—with a waterfall and trees, and not a soul for miles."

He hesitated. Céleste tiptoed, moving her lips against his, caressing him.

George felt her mood taking hold of him, and nothing seemed to matter but this one last chance to be together.

"All right, let's do it," he said, cupping her face in his hands, and then they were happy again.

Boward lit another cigarette from the butt of his last. The arbor felt stifling, now that the sundown breeze had died away, so he went over to the entrance, Tendrils of wisteria jogged against him teasingly. Why was Céleste taking so long, what crazy thing was she doing this time? Then he heard steps crunching on the gravel path. He straightened up, peering eagerly toward the wood, but soon he realized that the steps were coming from behind the arbor. He remained rooted, his alarm increasing as the steps grew louder. He made out a small figure in a peaked cap. It was Michel, the chauffeur.

"I regret to bother you, m'sieur," said Michel, "but they will soon be closing the restaurant."

Boward could not find words. His mind was jammed by indecision.

"I thought you would like to know, m'sieur." Michel spoke in an interrogatory tone. The chauffeur changed his position, his shiny peaked cap catching the starlight as he twisted his head; he was obviously trying to peer into the dark interior of the arbor, to see what Céleste was doing.

"Yes," said Boward. "Yes, we must go back."

Still the man didn't move, and panic made Boward say sharply, "All right, you go back to the car. We'll be up in a minute."

"Very good, m'sieur."

The man's voice seemed derisive. What did he think was going on? If this got around—Boward suddenly remembered Céleste saying that Michel spied on her and reported back to her mother. Michel may have seen Céleste slip away into the wood. There'd be a terrible row if Madame Lander found out.

"What a fool," he thought, "letting that little bitch use me. I must get her back to the car quickly."

He waited till Michel's steps had died away, then he crept stealthily to the wood, making his footfalls as light as possible in case Michel were listening.

The gloom under the trees made it hard for Boward to see. He stooped forward, arms groping so that he could feel the treacherous outcroppings of rock that reared every few feet out of the underbrush of dead thistles. Then he heard voices ahead.

Boward dared not call out, for fear Michel might hear. He straightened up and peered ahead. His eyes had now grown accustomed to the gloom, and he could make out a figure who stood silhouetted against the pale starlight that filtered through the trees. There was still a faint amber glow from sunset at the west end of the wood, and this made the figure slightly more distinct. No, it was two people, a man and—somebody with fair hair. Céleste. She was in the man's arms.

Boward stood absolutely still, his will paralyzed. He heard their voices murmuring—the deep tones of the man, the softer cadence of Céleste.

Boward shouted out to her, and his voice seemed to come from another person. "Céleste!"

He heard her make a sharp cry, then call out, "Who is that?"

Before he could answer there came the noise of underbrush being trampled, as if somebody were running away.

Boward made a few steps forward, his feet slipping on the rocks. He saw the lightness of a dress materialize out of the shadows and he knew that it was Céleste. She stumbled up to him.

"Oh, it *was* you!" she cried. She was catching her breath, as if she were scared.

He was too choked with fury to say anything.

"What's the matter?" she asked.

"You tramp. You've been using me. I saw you both."

"What are you talking about? Why didn't you let me introduce you to him?"

"And break up your love-making?"

"Are you crazy? He's old enough to be my grandfather." Céleste's words tumbled out frantically.

"He's running away very quickly for a grandfather. I can hear him."

Loud in the stillness came the crackling of the man moving away through the woods.

"He's an old man," Céleste burst out. "I've known him since I was a child. We have to meet secretly because the police are after him."

"Don't try to bluff it out. I'm not a fool." But doubt was clouding his mind. The light was very deceptive.

"He wasn't an Arab," he said. "He looked like a tall white man to me. Are you sure Hansen is in bed?"

"Phone the house, ask Mari. Oh, you're so wrong. Listen to me." She felt for his lapels in the dimness and held them, moving herself against him. "I give you my solemn word you're wrong. I can take you back to my friend, you can see him yourself. He's only running away because he thinks you're the police."

She was so close to him that he could feel her breath. Abruptly, she let go of him and put her face in her hands. "You think I'm lying, you spied on me."

He felt his anger melting into indecision. "I wasn't spying," he said. "Michel came to tell me that they're closing the restaurant and—"

"Please believe me, darling." She had never called him that before. The eager pleading in her voice stirred him, but some detached part of his brain was aware of the fact.

"Let's run after my friend," she bluffed. "We can catch him up if we hurry. He can't go very fast—he's so old. I daren't call out to him—Michel would hear me. If you don't believe me, let's run after my friend."

He hesitated, and then she flung her arms round him. Her mouth sought for his, and she squirmed her body against his. "Please believe me," she gasped against his lips, "I'll die if you think I'm cheating you."

His lips joined to the pressure of hers, but his mind was still resisting, and he was aware that the noise of running had died away in the distance.

"Why were you—" he began, but she stopped his words with her mouth, and then everything dropped out of his awareness but the soft searching of her tongue. She seemed to be frenzied. He ran his hands down her, and his desire for her melted the insistent press of his disbelief.

"Damn you, you bitch," he thought. "I'm going to have you."

"We'd better go back," she said at length.

They grasped hands and stumbled back together over the rough ground, out of the wood and up toward the restaurant. Once, she slipped, and he grasped her in time to stop her falling, then he turned the clasp into an embrace and she clung to him wildly, sensuously, without any reserve. His hands ran freely down her, and he pulled up her dress and his fingers thrust into her skin. Her submissiveness excited him, and he pulled her toward the arbor but at last she resisted. "No, no, darling," she gasped. "Later. Michel will be coming again."

She moved away toward the restaurant, and he followed.

and all he was conscious of was the female smell of the oleanders and his need.

When they reached the light he saw there was a high color in her cheeks, and her eyes seemed to share the same eagerness that filled him.

As soon as they were in the car she turned to him and went into his arms. "Why didn't you do this to me before?" she whispered.

His mind was so inflamed that he could not speak. Excitement leaped up in him, and as the car moved off, swaying them closer together, his hands could not fondle her enough.

"You do believe me, don't you?" she asked softly. He tried to ignore the question, but she held his wrists.

"Of course," he said thickly.

She released his wrists, and he slid his hand down into her dress.

"I'd do anything to make you believe," she whispered. "Would you do anything for me?"

All the desire that he had been suppressing was afire. His hand was running over one breast, exploring the small nub, pressing its firmness.

"Darling," she said, in a tight urgent voice, "you must do something for me if you want to see me again. Will you tell Mari that I went to meet you in the Casbah last evening?"

"What!"

"Otherwise she won't let me out any more. Oh, I do want to see you again. Will you tell her? It's not much to ask. If she thought I'd gone to meet Arabs she would never let me out again. Don't you want to see me any more?"

Even in the heat of his excitement, some part of his brain recoiled. These damned Arabs of hers again. He would get into trouble if he told Madame Lander he'd been mixed up in that Casbah business. Suppose it got back to the Consulate?

"Will you?" she asked, and he felt her body stiffen as if to resist him.

Oh, hell, he must put off saying anything to her mother, he must think of some other way round it.

"Not tonight," he said. "I couldn't talk to her convincingly tonight—not after this."

"But you will!"

She relaxed completely, passive under his hand, and his new-found sense of power over her had to be vented. He felt a wish to hurt her, and his fingers grasped her more roughly.

Chapter Nineteen

THE DAWN was still low, and eucalyptus trees bathed the whole length of the highway in cool shadows, but the old truck that George had borrowed for the day's outing was already overheated. Jets of steam began to whistle out of the cracked radiator cap, and each time these spurted up George and Céleste cowered in mock fear. The solid tires of the vehicle were shredded by age, and made a continuous whipping sound.

"She'll never be able to make it up to the mountains," said George.

"Yes, she will." Céleste was full of a calm happiness.

They came to a small rivulet that bubbled over bleached pebbles, bringing out a shimmer of garnet and coral colors.

"We'd better fill her up," said George. The truck slowed down with a grinding squeal, and they sprang down and scooped water into an old can. When the water was poured into the radiator, a great plume of steam billowed up.

Céleste took off her silk cowled *chadur*, which she had put on to face the chilly dawn when she crept out of the house. Her fair hair shone like lacquer in the sunlight.

"Know what this stream is called?" said George. "Oued Saada, the River of Happiness."

"Oh!" Céleste grew excited. "Let's make it our river!" She raised some of the water in her cupped hands, and drank from it, and so did George, and then they kissed, their lips cold and wet.

Céleste looked east, at the quiet wings of the morning. She said, "We're all alone, they haven't followed us."

"Don't count on that. Your mother will raise hell when she finds you're gone. Why didn't you leave a note to say you'd be back tonight?"

She made a slow smile. "Maybe I won't," she said.

George glanced at her, puzzled. "Oh, yes, you will," he said. "Come on, let's hurry. I'm hungry. I think we'll be able to get breakfast with an old friend of mine in Djouma. That's the next town."

They climbed back into the truck and began to shout student choruses, beating their arms to the rhythm.

They went through Djouma, a white straggling town which sheltered inside thick medieval walls. The shade trees were wilting under the scorching sun and scrawny dogs lay stupefied by the heat. A concrete minaret reared up, in fantastic modernity, out of the Biblical huddle of dwellings.

On the other side of the town, beyond the keyhole-shaped main gate, George turned into the dusty courtyard of a house in which carpets were hanging out of each window to air.

George's friend appeared in the doorway. He was an elderly Arab with a nut-brown face so deeply lined that it might have been scoured by a wire brush. He kept giving the greeting of warm friendship: *"Ahlan wa sahalan!"* The two men went off into a flood of Arabic so fast that Céleste could not follow it.

As custom demanded, the Arab took no notice of Céleste until George introduced her, and then she could see the flicker of disquiet in the man's eyes. She knew that he was perturbed at his old friend traveling with a Frenchwoman, but he concealed his feelings behind the strict ceremonial of hospitality. He kept begging them to eat with him, and when they at last agreed, after the three refusals that etiquette demanded, the host went to give instructions to his womenfolk. He came back beaming, and they all sat cross-legged on gaily colored mats of plaited straw.

Céleste gradually began to feel that she was an intruder, in spite of the way the older man kept gracefully bringing her into the conversation. She felt worse when she realized that she was probably the first unveiled woman ever to enter this house, certainly the first Frenchwoman. She hoped that George was not aware of the overtones that were gathering.

George suddenly asked if he might see his friend's crops, and they walked out into the harsh sunlight, which by this time was like a fire near the skin.

George gave a cry of delight and pointed to an irrigation trough, made of cement, in which ran a thin dribble of water. "So you have a well now!" he exclaimed.

"Yes, there's an artesian over by that clump of young trees. The Service de la Colonisation arranged it. It was Thuillier, of course. If only all the French officials were like Thuillier!"

"Yes, he's a great man. We can learn much from him. Think of it—all this valley could be covered with artesians."

"No, my land is right on the edge of the *chott*, the salt marsh. You can't do anything with that soil."

"But, yes! The scientists have plans for that. Do you know that they hope to irrigate the Chott Ech Chergui, and bring one hundred thousand more hectares under the plow?"

"More land for the French, I suppose."

They changed the subject again and began to examine the seedling olives that had been planted near the irrigation trough. "These are far too close to each other," said George. "They ought to be at least twenty meters apart from each other—the roots spread out very wide."

The host shrugged. "I have not enough land. The colons have taken land from us, so I have to take it from my olives."

"Oh, but the Service is giving olive trees to many of the peasants, and the *paysannats* are giving us more land."

It hurt Céleste to hear George having to defend the French; she knew it was because she was there.

"We don't get the good land," said the older man mildly.

Once more George broke off the subject. This time he picked up a handful of earth and put it in his mouth. He cocked his head to one side, grinning at Céleste's exclamation of disgust, and then spat out the soil. "You're right," he said, "this is far too calcareous, you'll never get fine trees on this soil."

"How do you know?" asked Céleste.

"By the taste."

There was an awkward pause, and Céleste knew that if she were not there, the two men would have burst out in angry abuse of the French. She was stabbed suddenly by the old wish—if only she could absorb herself completely into Arab ways, so that George wouldn't have to think of any barriers between them.

"I won't let him be embarrassed because of me," she thought. "I'm going to buy a burnoose, I'm going to speak Arabic always." She smiled to herself as she realized that she was thinking as if they were married already, and then she frowned, in case her companions noticed the smile and misunderstood.

The tension lessened when the host showed them his diminutive garden, in which were a few fig trees, and rusting stalks of papyrus.

A steaming bowl of couscous was ready when they returned. The womenfolk, who had laid out the meal on the huge round *saniya* of beaten copper had, by Arab custom, already retired out of sight into the *harim*.

Céleste grew uncomfortably aware, as she crossed her legs, of the host's glances at her bare limbs and thin blouse. "What must he think?" she asked herself; his own womenfolk were not even allowed to show themselves to visitors.

They ate the couscous hungrily, in the Arab style, with the first three fingers of their hands. The dish consisted of rolled semolina with currants, a hot peppery sauce, and lumps of camel's meat; and afterward they had fruit, with flat bread, sheep's butter, and honey.

There was no need for much talk till the meal was over. Céleste was grateful for the long periods of silence. When they had finished, unspoken thoughts began once more to weigh heavily in the air. Céleste tried to break the tension caused by her presence; she began to identify herself passionately with the Arab cause by speaking acidly of the French administration and the brutalities of the Security Brigade. She soon stopped, for her words appeared hollow even to herself, and she realized that her Arabic must sound comical—Europeans always did when they tried to pronounce the difficult consonants.

It was no use; she and George would have to leave. Their host was probably offended at George for bringing a Frenchwoman, an unveiled infidel, into the house. Poor George, she mustn't let him get into a situation like this again.

George rose and said he and Céleste would have to continue their journey. The host made fervent expressions of sadness, repeating the *"Hafath-kum Allah"*—"God guard you"—but Céleste sensed that he was not really sorry to see them go.

As soon as they had started off in the truck, Céleste turned to George and poured out all the worries that filled her. "That was awful," she said. "I don't want it ever to happen again. I refuse to be different from you! I'm going to get myself Arab dress. I want us to speak Arabic forever. I'll change my name to Arabic—"

George turned his gaze from the road and smiled at her, but there was a worried gully between his brows. "That wouldn't work," he said, "they'd still distrust you, they'd still know you were French."

"But Madame Messali, the wife of your leader—everybody loves her, and she's French."

He patted her knee. "I won't let you get mixed up with me till this is all cleared up."

"You mean—you want us to wait till the Arabs have taken control?" She knew he meant that, but she made a great show of sounding aghast.

"Yes, I can't drag you into misery and danger and hatred. That's all you'd ever get out of marrying me now."

Céleste stared up at the firm line of his profile, etched finely against the almost molten light of the sun. She tried to will him to look at her, so that he would see the unhappiness on her face, but he kept looking ahead.

"I'll make you change your mind," she vowed to herself. "I'll make you."

She found it difficut to keep up the miserable look, for slowly, as the solitude of the countryside was borne in on her mind, her intimacy and oneness with George was emphasized. All their problems seemed far away. Nothing could come between them, the idea was absurd.

She noticed that his body was vibrating in the shuddering progress of the truck, and every time it hit a bump George would jerk up in a ridiculous manner. She laughed, and her mood keyed itself to a growing optimism. The lines of a Paris music-hall ditty flashed into her mind, and she began forming the words silently, and jiggled her rump muscles in the cadence of the song:

> *You don't know it but your number's up,*
> *For I've got my hooks in you.*

She giggled at the thought of what George would say if she sang the words out loud. He raised his eyebrows at her interrogatively, but she said, "Nothing, I just feel good."

They had reached the head of the valley by this time, leaving behind them the last of the *douars*—clusters of lonely little mud huts, the color of coffee. The gorge swallowed them into its shadowed mouth, and the note of the engine changed into a high-pitched groan as the gradient grew steeper. It took nearly an hour of corkscrew driving before they finally emerged up on the tumbling expanse of the *gouban*, the burned plain, which lay parched under the sun.

They seemed to be all alone in a world that was completely barren and forbidding, except for the purple mountains ahead, but George grew taut with interest. Several times he stopped the truck to examine the brown parched earth.

"It could be fertile!" he cried, his tanned face shining in the heavy light. "All it needs is water."

He waved his arms to take in the whole plateau. "If we had the capital we could sink wells all over this, and produce enough food to fill every empty belly in Algeria. Just think of it—thousands of hectares of olives and figs, tomatoes, wheat—"

"One day you'll help to do it," she said, trying to make him happy. "Oh, darling, you ought to be farming, instead of fighting. You could do so much, and I could help you."

He was too absorbed to hear her. "All that it needs is capital," he said, "the soil is good."

"Perhaps Kuhn isn't such a bad man after all—that's all he ever talks about, raising millions of dollars to develop the country."

He shrugged. "Dollars? Then we'd be slaves of the Americans instead of the French."

"You don't really believe that yourself."

"Imperialists are all the same."

As he climbed back into the truck Céleste caught her breath, for above their heads, as if nailed to a thin streak of cloud, were several black blasphemous crucifixes. "Vultures!" she cried.

"Talk of the devil!" he grinned.

The heat from the tortured engine grew so great, as the truck groaned across the plateau, that their legs felt burned. A shimmering veil of heat rose over the hood so that their view ahead was as if looking through water. The range of mountains they were approaching was backed by another, much taller, and behind these again, looming ephemerally at the limit of their vision, was the main spine of the Atlas Mountains. In the vibrating haze, the stairs of the mountains ahead looked like a moving escalator up to the sky.

"We should be there by twelve," said George, "if the engine doesn't fail."

"I'm so thirsty—the minute we arrive I'm going to drink the waterfall dry. Then I'm going to make you a meal. I'll send the caretaker home."

"It was crazy to come out so far—suppose the truck breaks down?"

"I don't care."

"One thing, it's downhill nearly all the way back."

Céleste smiled slyly and hugged her knees. "If we come back," she said. George ignored the remark.

The plateau began to tilt up toward the mountains. Great boulders, like misshapen eggs of monsters, threw oval shadows, and the sand slowly changed to the color of pepper. After a few more miles they came to the entrance to a wide valley, which was scored by a vast *oued*.

"In winter that's a cataract," she said, "and after the rains the whole valley becomes alive with flowers."

Now there were only a few stunted ilb trees and cacti. They climbed till the air, to Céleste's excited imagination, seemed to be growing more rare and heady every moment. The pavement had been gouged by the torrents of winter and powdered by the sun, and their progress became one series of shuddering bumps.

The sun was nearly overhead when they reached the side road that led up to the bungalow. At the intersection there was a *douar* of mud huts, which was without life except for a few chickens that flapped out of the way, squawking.

The truck floundered over the potholes of the track, jarring their spines so much that George and Céleste each had to take the wheel while the other ran alongside to get relief. They could see the yellow ribbon of the truck zigzagging up the sharp slope, and halfway from the summit was the belt of trees that concealed the cottage. Céleste and George grew so eager to arrive that each time one of them got out they would push hard at the back of the truck to help it along. The accelerator had to be kept down flat on the floorboard to keep the ancient vehicle moving.

When at last they reached the trees, their faces and limbs were caked brown with dust, which sweat had gullied into grotesque lines. They passed the thick belt of protecting thorns, then plunged into the cool shadows of pines and terebinths—and there was the cottage before them. They turned off the engine, but even then it continued to squeak and groan. Laughing at its noise, they ran across to the waterfall, which tumbled down into the garden. As they ran they pulled off their clothes, letting them drop in the dust. It became a game to see who could escape from their garments first. They wrenched off the last as they reached the water and stood under it. They gasped at the shock of its coolness on their skins. They turned up their faces into the splashing drops, scooping up the liquid with their mouths, so that when they came together, with the fall enveloping them, their lips were cold and pristine.

Chapter Twenty

THE CARETAKER was still scratching his head in bewilderment as he rode his donkey down the steep slope to the valley. He clutched a thick roll of bills that Céleste had given to him.

The clop of the donkey's hoofs died away, and the only sounds left were the noise of a golden oriole singing high in the trees and the patter of the waterfall.

Céleste and George lay on the grass, sleepy after their meal. The cottage lay on a green shelf of the mountain, bowered in oleanders. The wood around it filtered the press of the sun on all sides except the front, where the picture windows, crowned with broad awnings, looked over the valley to the mountains on the other side. Farther down the slope were great clumps of scarlet *mihirs*, and a magnificent *sabarac* tree lifted its arms over a carpet of wild flowers.

George was stripped except for his shorts, and Céleste was wearing one of her old sun suits, which she had discovered in the cottage. It was now too small for her, and although she had undone the straps, the long question mark formed by the outline of her bosom and flat stomach was sharply pronounced. He was close enough to her to see the delicate pulse of her throat, and the minute shadows cast over the point of each breast. She lay with her thick lashes upturned to the arch of trees. He dozed off, and when he awoke she was still in the same position. He pulled her to him, to bring her from the daydream that he was not sharing.

"What are you thinking?" he asked, his lips nuzzling her ear.

"In a little while the caretaker will be out of the valley—then we'll be completely alone. We've never been really alone before."

There came a sudden flicker of movement across the ground as a little *gecko* house lizard, of flaming orange, flicked across the desiccated earth. It stood still for a mo-

ment, its prehistoric head rearing, its eyes beady, then Céleste flung herself sideways to catch it, but the reptile darted
out of reach. She raised herself on her elbows, and as she
did so she held up the sun suit over her breasts. She looked
back at George, laughing, and in that moment, George had
an acute awareness of her; every detail was pressed in his
memory, and he knew that he would always remember this
moment—her hands covering herself with the tight cloth,
the dampened gold of her hair making thick curves, a little
red tattoo all down her bare back from the press of the
ground, and fragments of soil still clinging to the swell of
her thighs.

He tried to get back to the safety of words. "Yes, it's
lonely," he said. "Why did your mother choose this place
to have her cottage?"

"Oh, she had to be absolutely private," Céleste frowned.
"She used to come here with friends. I wasn't supposed to
know anything about it. Darling, don't let's think about her.
I want this to be our day—don't spoil it."

He stroked her gently. "Nothing can stop it being our day,
we're together."

She rolled over on her side, and pressed herself against
him. "I meant what I said earlier on—about wanting to be
an Arab, I mean."

"Sweet, that's impossible."

"Not if I try hard enough. Don't call me 'sweet,' call me
sidi. I like the Arabic much better."

"*Sidi*, you're crazy and I love you."

"You're trying to put me off. I'm serious."

"Don't make it hard for me. I want to be with you always
—you know that—but we must wait till this trouble is over.
I can't expose you to danger."

"But the suffering you'd make me go through, if I were
away from you, I'd go mad."

He gave a groan, almost of physical pain. Her love seemed
to close him in, stifling his judgment; the contact of his
fingers with her bare back seemed to be more real than all
the resolves that he had forced into his mind. The swell of
her breathing moved against him and made his nerves tingle.

Suddenly her mood changed and she sat up. "I keep thinking about us getting married," she said. "I try to imagine
it. How do your people get married? What is an Arab wedding like?"

"Oh, it's quite a big affair, even for the poor."

"Tell me what it's like. I want to imagine what it would be like for us."

He felt relieved by the change of subject. "The people prepare for weeks beforehand," he said, "and when the day comes it's a holiday for the whole village. There is a great feast to which everybody is invited, even our enemies. We eat pigeons covered with sugared layers of thin pastry, and we boil whole sides of lamb in saffron. There are dancers, wearing brightly colored brocades and velvet and ornaments, with ribbons fluttering, and they leap and sing for hours, till everybody gets excited and joins in."

"But what about the bride and bridegroom? Imagine it's our wedding—what are we doing while everybody is feasting and dancing?"

"Well, I'd be getting ready in ceremonial robes—the finest I could get, perhaps a gold agal head cord, and a silk kaffiyeh, and a ceremonial dagger."

"You'd look so tall and handsome. Oh, *sidi,* I want it so much. Go on, what then?"

"I would be inside my father's house. The music would grow louder from goatskin drums, and bamboo flutes and the *rhaitas,* and the people would begin to chant."

"But I? Where would I be?"

"In your parents' house. When the excitement is at its peak I come out of my house with my father beside me, and all my relatives behind, and I walk very slowly—very slowly, mind you—to your house. Like this."

He sprang up and drew himself to his full height, put out one foot slowly, then the other, in a motion that was so retarded that every one of the long muscles on his thighs and body was emphasized by a play of slow shadows on the golden skin.

He came back to her and sat cross-legged. "Finally I reach your house." He broke off and laughed bitterly. "I can just see your mother waiting at her door to welcome a lot of howling Arabs."

"Forget Mari," said Céleste sharply. "What then?"

"I come into your courtyard which is all prepared with special rugs and hangings. I exchange ceremonial words with your parents and the *muta'awah,* the holy man, and then —I go in to you, where you're waiting all by yourself."

"You mean we meet in private, there are no staring peo-

ple. Oh, that's wonderful." Tears welled into her large
eyes.

The emotion in her face made him uneasy and he tried to
make her mood lighter. "It's a big moment for both of them,"
he grinned, "very often it's the first time they've ever seen
each other. Even today, marriages are often fixed up by the
parents."

She was still in her rapture. "So it's as simple as that,"
she said, "the two of us alone together, and no prying eyes.
What am I dressed in—when you come to me, I mean?"

"Oh, you're wearing a beautiful robe that you have been
embroidering for months. You wear a lot of make-up. You
have your eyebrows painted very dark, and sort of exaggerated. There is a lot of kohl on your eyelids, and your lips
and cheeks are very red. You're painted so much that you
look like a doll. You hold your hands like this"—he put his
palms together before him in a suppliant position—"and you
sit cross-legged on a dais."

"Let's do it!" she cried. "Let's pretend it's us."

"Oh, let's stay here." He tried to draw her to him, but she
sprang up eagerly and said, "You wait here, I'll call you
when I'm ready."

She hurried into the bungalow, ignoring his call, and he
sank back on the grass, wondering at the strange mood that
had come over her. He looked up at the sun anxiously. The
line of shadow had moved steadily higher up the trees, and
now there were only a few scattered patches of light on the
eastern side of the hollow. This was a preview of twilight.
Soon it would be the sacred moment of *mughrib*, the setting
of the sun, and he would have to go back to Algiers with Céleste.

Abruptly, in the stillness, broke the sound of Arabic music,
a wild flute to which a woman was chanting a traditional
tune. George sat up, astonished, till he realized that Céleste
must have switched on the battery radio, and tuned in to
the Arabic program from Algiers.

He lay there listening, and gave himself up to the simple
primitive melody, and the others that followed. He drummed
his fingers on the grass to keep time.

George called out to Céleste but there was no answer.
Curious, he rose to his feet and went over to the patio, and
peered through the picture window. The reflection of the
sky was on the glass, so that he could not see in. He heard

her call out, "You've come too soon—go back!" George laughed and pulled open the door.

The music filled his ears more loudly. Céleste was standing over by· the mirror, in an ankle-length gown of white silk, and over her head was the hood of her *chadur,* so that only her face and hands were visible.

"What's that you're wearing?" he asked. "One of your mother's?"

"Oh, *sidi,* you shouldn't have come in yet, I wanted it to be the real thing." She hurried over to a *serir,* a low couch of bamboo, which was piled with fat cushions, and seated herself on it cross-legged. She held her palms together, in the position he had shown her.

He stared at her anxiously, trying to gauge her mood. He sensed that to her this was not a game; her face was set in solemnity. He saw that she had made up her face; the lips were bright, the curves accentuated almost liquidly, and she had emphasized the size of her eyes with mascara and something bluish on the lids. She looked up at him, and her only motion was the rapid rise and fall of her breathing.

He went over to her, and tried to speak lightly. "You make a wonderful bride," he said. "How did you make that thing fit you?" She kept looking at him silently, and he felt the blood pounding in his forehead, a heavy weight that fogged his mind till he was conscious only of his yearning for her.

He sat down on the *serir* facing her and took hold of her hands.

"*Sidi,*" he said, "you shouldn't do this."

"Why? This seems so right and beautiful."

He tried to speak again, but his throat seemed to have thickened. He lifted her hands and kissed them, so that he could find a focus for his eyes away from hers, for there was no mistaking the message in them. She lifted her hands higher and passed her arms round his neck, and the faint scent from her stole to him, and the accentuated femininity of her face seemed to belong to some new person,· infinitely more desirable than he had ever known before. Their lips met, and he passed his arms round her, and he knew at once that beneath the thin robe she wore nothing. The touch of her through the silk blurred the last shreds of his resistance. He ran his hands over her caressingly, and she relaxed completely. Their bodies already seemed to be fused, beating with one blood, one love, one urge. He lowered her back, full length, onto the cushions, and then he pressed himself to her.

Chapter Twenty-One

THE SURGEON-COLONEL buttoned his tunic over his pajamas as he entered the ward. His jaw distorted with the effort to suppress a yawn, but he still managed to look imperious.

"Well?" he barked, blinking his sleep-puckered eyes. "Why didn't you call me sooner?"

This was the stock opening of all consultations in the Medical Corps; it provided a foolproof alibi, with witnesses, for anything that might happen afterward. Invariably it went right down the chain of authority; the surgeon-commandant had already said it to the surgeon-captain, who in turn had sent it vehemently on its way down toward the last irreducible culprit, the frightened night nurse.

"But, *mon colonel*," said the surgeon-commandant, "the hemorrhage took place only four minutes ago."

The colonel took one look at the patient who lay, waxen and still in the half light of the oxygen tent. "Ah, the one who was shot by the American."

"Yes, *mon colonel*, that is why we bothered you. In view of the political importance of the case—"

"Show me the X-rays," snapped the colonel. The commandant held them up against the light and pointed out the shadow of the bullet. "It must have ricocheted from the wall, then glanced off that rib," he said, delicately pointing with his little finger. "It's lodged in the pharynx by the lower border of the cricoid cartilage. When we tried to remove it this afternoon the constricted musculature prevented us—"

The colonel silenced him with a glance, and flipped through the notations concerning the first operation. The sour taste of sleep was in his mouth. His annoyance grew, for he knew that the commandant's respectful pose concealed deep relief that responsibility had now passed to the colonel.

After a series of curt questions about the patient's heart, his dehydration, and the blood transfusions, the colonel decided swiftly. "We must operate at once," he announced. "Oesophagoscopy under general anesthesia. Alert the operating room." He glanced distrustingly at the elderly commandant, whose white beard stubble was glinting as he gazed up at his superior. "I don't want any further delay," said the colonel. "Make sure everything is ready. I shall require a thiopentone induction."

"No delay—you hear?" said the commandant to the captain, and turned back to the colonel. "You are hopeful, *mon colonel?* You think you will succeed?"

"There is always danger on the operating table," said the colonel. Words quivered unspoken on the air, "Especially with your delay."

Hansen felt stifled by the heat of the bedroom. It was well past midnight but the room still seemed pervaded by the press of the sun. Delicate perfume lingered on the air from Mari.

He felt sticky, and wondered whether to take another shower but he could not summon the energy. He kicked back the single sheet that covered him, and wriggled to the far edge of the double bed, so that his clammy skin felt cooler. He looked at the metallic stillness of the draperies, wishing for a breeze, however slight.

Where was Mari? It was at least half an hour since she had got up and gone downstairs. She'd been in a queer mood all day—one minute she couldn't do too much for him, and the next she was jumpy and nervous, especially when night had begun to draw on. Probably because of Céleste—where on earth had the girl disappeared to?

Hansen knew that he would not be able to sleep any more tonight. He had dozed off at intervals all day, in between Mari's visits. His body was satiated but his mind was burning with a mass of disordered thoughts. He tossed his head irritably, longing for escape from the worries that filled him. "If that Security Brigade man dies, I'll be sent to prison," he told himself. "Even if the guy recovers, I'm washed up with Kuhn. I'll have to clear out of Algeria and start over, somewhere else."

But what about Mari? She was full of wild talk about never leaving him, but when the novelty of having him back had worn off, she would see there was no future for them. It was impossible, anyway. Now he was broke, with no job, and serious charges hung over him because of the wounded Brigade man. Kuhn would try to disown him when the case came up, that was obvious. Kuhn would swear he knew nothing about Hansen contacting the rebels.

Hansen was too long for the bed, and his feet were pressed uncomfortably against the posts at the bottom. He twisted so that he lay diagonally across the bed. Even this slight movement made the pain stab again at his shoulder, in savage little bites.

Mari and her damned doctors had fussed over him all day. There was nothing really wrong with him, he knew that.

Where the hell was Mari? Maybe she was having a set-to with that crazy maid. He had heard Mari going on at Yvette during the afternoon, her voice raised in furious anger, and the maid seemed to be answering back. Yvette had probably made some snide remark about him; she hated him, she always had, even back in the old days.

Yvette must have been given the afternoon off, after the row with Mari, for soon afterward Mari had come back to the bedroom, looking relieved, and then for an hour or so there had been nobody in the world but the two of them. She abandoned herself to her passion, as if she was trying to crowd all the wasted years into these moments. And while she was with him nothing seemed to matter, he was able to blot out from his mind the whole rotten mess.

He was still amazed at how little she had changed. Many times that afternoon, and as the hot languorous night drew on—with her firm white body joined to his, and her fervent whispers of endearment, and the shining look in her eyes —he had had the sensation that time had slipped a cog, and they were back again in this very room eight years ago.

Where was Mari? She had gotten up and left at least half an hour ago.

Hansen reached out to the side table and picked up his wrist watch. Three o'clock in the morning. Hell! What was she doing? Would she leave him alone for the rest of the night, or would she come back for more?

He was shocked to realize that he'd had enough. For the time being, anyway. "Brother," he thought, "I wouldn't have believed this possible a few nights ago. Maybe I'm getting past it. Or more likely she's turned nympho. Enough is enough."

He heard her footsteps, and irritably he propped himself on his elbows. When she pushed open the door her peignoir of thin nylon outlined the firm curves of her body. He sighed in resignation, knowing that he'd soon be worked up again.

"Oh, you're awake," she said.

"Of course. Where've you been?"

Mari closed the door carefully. "It's Céleste," she said softly, "she still isn't back."

"Don't look so tragic. She's all right. She probably has some big romance."

"No, it's not that." Mari came over to the bed and sat stoop shouldered, her face slack with dejection. "There's something awful happening. I can feel it. I know Céleste's in trouble."

Her black hair was loose, falling in long ripples over her shoulders, emphasizing the whiteness of her skin. "Céleste is in trouble again," she said, "I'm certain of it. If she disgraces me again I couldn't stand it."

"Oh, she's probably out with Boward."

"No, I've just been talking to Boward—I got his number from the night operator at the American Consulate. Boward swears he hasn't seen or spoken to Céleste all day! When I told him off about arranging to meet Céleste in the Casbah, he sounded queer. He was very evasive, till I said I was going to complain to the Consul, and then he blurted it all out. He said he didn't arrange to meet her there at all—Céleste asked him to say he had. Then he told me something that happened when he took Céleste to dinner the other night. He said she slipped away on some pretext, and when he went to search for her he discovered her in a man's arms. A big man, he said. *Chéri*, I thought I'd die—for one moment I thought the big man was you!"

"Me?"

"I know, I'm crazy. It's clear what happened. Céleste has been using Boward as a cover. God knows what she's up to."

"Listen," he said. "Céleste is grown up now. You can't stop her seeing anybody she wants to. She's probably infatuated with some guy. Don't drag the police in—she'll only be in all the papers again if you do. Whatever she's doing, it's of her own accord."

"But she is my daughter. She may be in danger. She's still only a child."

"Everybody's crazy when they're her age. She's used to staying out half the night in Paris. She left here of her own accord, she wasn't kidnaped, she'll soon be back. Come to bed."

"No. If she's not back in half an hour I must call the police. God knows what might have happened to her. I'll never forgive her if she's all right."

"What?" He tried unsuccessfully to grasp her feminine logic.

"If she were still in Paris, everything would be so wonderful."

Hansen felt irritated by this new worry, on top of all the others. He tried to soothe her by drawing her gently to him and stroking her hands. "Please wait till morning, before you call the police," he said; "there's probably nothing to worry about."

Her hands were startlingly cold against the heat of his palms. He tried to make her forget. He pulled down the peignoir from her shoulders and caressed her breasts, cupping them gently as he whispered in her ear.

Mari went to pieces suddenly. She clasped her arms around him and broke into dry sobs. "We're fated," she managed to say, "something always goes wrong."

"There, there." The touch of her curves stirred him, and even in his growing desire some detached part of his thoughts marveled at the pull of her sexuality; every time she was near him she was like a burning glass focusing all his maleness.

But that was all—any attractive woman would have the same effect. In spite of being aroused by her, Hansen felt a mordant sense of self-derision. He didn't get the big bang out of this he used to, not with Mari anyway. Now that he knew he had her where he wanted, that he could do with her what he wished, it didn't seem the same. Nor was it easy to fake ecstasy.

She began to breathe more rapidly under his touch. Here we go again, he thought, and took her swiftly and ruthlessly enough to satisfy her. But he was relieved when it was over, and he could relax again.

Chapter Twenty-Two

KUHN WOKE as the rope began to tighten round his neck. He lingered for a moment in stupor, not knowing whether he had been dreaming or not, and he had to feel his neck to make sure he was safe. Then his painful breathing made him realize that once more his asthma had forced him through the familiar nightmare, which so often had jerked him into consciousness gasping for air.

Suppose the Security Brigade man died? Hansen would be charged with manslaughter. "Then I'll be dragged into it," he said out loud. "My name will be in all the papers."

The press was already asking awkward questions—such as why Hansen had been in the Casbah, why he was disguised, why he resisted arrest. Some papers were already calling Hansen an agent of the Arab underground. "I'll be linked with them, too," muttered Kuhn.

What a fool he had been to hire Hansen. "All I wanted was peace and order," he told himself. He kept repeating this, as if it were a mnemonic that could save him. Then, "I thought Hansen could fix it for me with the Arabs. Now he's got me in this mess."

He twisted his head from side to side on the pillow. He felt old and helpless. If only there were somebody here to help him, but he couldn't trust anybody. That damned Hansen hadn't even been near him. Just as well, perhaps.

Kuhn blinked his eyes to free them from their waking moisture, and looked at the comparatively small part that his frame occupied in the great bed. If only he were not alone.

Madame Lander! His imagination blazed up with thoughts of her here beside him.

But she wouldn't. She was acting very queerly. Why had she persuaded the magistrate to let Hansen have bail? Why was she so interested in Hansen? What was going on between those two?

"Hansen's no more use to me," he thought. "Even if everything turns out all right. It'll take me a long time to live down this business. Probably months. The French authorities will always be suspicious of me after this. It's all due to that damned Hansen. Here I am with my plans ruined and he hasn't even been in touch with me. He's fast asleep, right here in this hotel."

A mental image of Hansen's sleeping peacefully while he, Kuhn, lay in pain, made helpless rage course through him.

On an impulse, Kuhn reached out and grasped the phone. He asked the operator for Hansen's suite. He listened to the thin bzz-bzz with satisfaction, visualizing Hansen being woken up.

The operator cut in, sleepily, "Sorry, m'sieur, I've just remembered. M'sieur Hansen has not been in for three days."

Kuhn stared at the phone morosely, and slowly replaced it on the hook. *Gott!*—Madame Lander! Hansen was with Madame Lander.

He cursed with rage and groped his way out of bed to the dressing room.

A chorus of birds woke George. He opened his lids slightly, and minuscules of rainbow danced between the lashes. He felt suspended in a cool, airy lightness. His senses had awakened, but not his mind. He moved his arms, and became aware that Céleste was in them, with her back to him. He was breathing the scent of her hair.

He opened his eyes slowly and saw her tumbled hair gleaming in the level rays of the dawnlight that was pouring in through the picture window. Many of the strands in her hair were pure gold. He could see one pale freckle on her shoulder and there were a few others, following the curve down her back, till the shadows of the sheets made a mystery of her body. The birds were fluting as if their hearts would burst; he could pick out the high insistent tune of lapwings.

George raised himself cautiously on his elbow to see Céleste's face. He did not wish to break the spell of this moment. The clear light that streamed in the room, almost horizontally, made her face glow, and her lips were slightly pouted like a little girl's. Into his right arm, which was around her, flowed the pulse of her breathing, the gentleness of her breast rising and falling; this seemed to make them one, joined together by the coursing of their blood.

She looked innocent and defenseless. A poignant rend of tenderness struck him. And then, as he awakened fully, the meaning of what had happened forced worry into his mind.

He should never have done this. He must have been crazy. He knew that this would always be the peak, there could be nothing beyond this, for him.

He looked down at her, and her eyes opened wide, the gray irises catching gold flecks in the dawnlight. There was a smile on her face that did not part her lips. She stretched up her arms and pulled him down to her.

She murmured, against his cheek, "Oh, dearest, we really are married now, we really are."

He tried to resist the tide of belonging that had caught him up. "But you must go back," he said.

"We can't ever be parted now," she said. She twisted round to face him and they pressed against each other, straining as if afraid that somebody would try to tear them apart.

"Promise me," she whispered in his ear, "promise me we'll always be married."

The Security Brigade man's face seemed to have changed back into a small boy's; it was smooth and unshaped, and one lock of his hair had fallen over his chalk-white brow. Now that they had taken the intratracheal tube from his mouth, and smoothed the bedclothes into a rigid respectfulness, it was as if he had been tucked up for the night. But the dawnlight was climbing steeper, making the lamps more pale; the sky framed in the window was growing more opaline every minute. The last flicker of life in the young man was so dim that the surgeon-commandant, bending with his stethoscope, had to listen intently to know that this was still a sentient being.

The priest's robes rustled as he moved around in his ritual, the Host in a silver pyx 'round his neck. He took the holy oil of chrism and anointed the dying man, cleansing him of the sins of sense. He muttered the words in a flat sad monotone: ". . . in the name of thrones and dominions, in the name of principalities and powers; in the name of virtue, cherubim and seraphim. . . ."

He paused, his lips close to the young man's ears, but there was only silence. The thin-lipped Brigade major responded for the soldier, "Lord Jesus, receive my soul."

The priest continued while the light mounted, filling the sterile ward with the promise of a new beginning.

The Brigade major glanced out of the window, forming

words silently between his tongue and the roof of his mouth.
". . . in the name of principalities and powers . . ." So
young to die. This morning he would have to write to the
boy's parents. The same old letter: this was just like the war
again. *Mort pour la France*—in the name of principalities
and powers. This was a strange way to die for France—shot
by an American in a bawdy house. Still this American was
an enemy of France, he was in league with the Arab rebels.
The minute that the boy died, Hansen would be *pincé*. He
wouldn't be able to escape, Madame Lander or no Madame
Lander. The Brigade must get hold of Hansen first—that
was important, there were many comrades of the dead man
who would ask for the privilege. And afterward, when that
necessity had been seen to, Hansen would be handed over
for trial. This would be an example to the foreigners,
this might teach them to keep their noses out of Algeria.

The surgeon-commandant straightened up and took off
his stethoscope. "It is all over," he said.

The major crossed himself, and so did the others, then he
crossed hurriedly to the door and beckoned the sergeant who
was waiting. The major nodded grimly and said, "He's
dead. Take a squad of men with you, in case Hansen tries
to resist. Bring him back to the punishment quarters."

Kuhn had reached the hotel lobby before he remembered
that his chauffeur would not arrive till nine o'clock. He decided to drive himself, and told the head porter to bring his
car round to the front entrance.

The cool air of early morning struck sharply at his breathing passages, and he could feel his heart protesting from the
exertion of hurrying downstairs. He felt in his pockets, to
make sure he had his heart tablets of nitroglycerin. Was it
wise to drive himself? He sat down and let himself go limp,
so that he would have to breathe as little as possible. He
closed his eyes, and the morning wetness brimmed out of
them. He was jolted into alertness by the clomp of boots,
and he looked up. A file of Security Brigade men was entering the lobby. One of them, who wore a sergeant's stripes,
marched up to the reception desk and demanded, "Which
room is the American's, Hansen?"

"Forty-one, but he's not here," said the clerk nervously.
"He hasn't been here for three days, not since the affair in
the Casbah."

"You're sure? We'd better search his room." The sergeant held out his hand for the key.

"What's the matter?" the clerk ventured.

"The Security Brigade man he shot has died."

Kuhn felt his heart miss one of its beats, and he remained absolutely still, to force calm. When the Brigade men had jammed into the elevator, the head porter appeared, bowing from the waist in expectation of a big tip. "Your car is ready, m'sieur."

Kuhn hoisted himself up and made his way slowly to the car, assisted by the head porter, who was staring at him with obsequious curiosity. "Damn them," he thought, "they all know Hansen is connected with me. I'll have to bluff it out, swear this was a terrible shock to me."

As soon as Kuhn started to drive, his fury was vented by the sense of action, and he was able to plan once more. He would have to go carefully, very carefully, in this business, but he'd manage it. He must wash his hands of Hansen, repudiate him entirely, help to put him behind bars, but at the same time he must not antagonize the rebel movement. He didn't want the Arabs to think that Hansen had been a decoy to trap them. If they thought that, all the Arabs would be against him, he would be farther back in his plans than ever before.

Kuhn swore to himself, grinding out his native German in the depths of his fury. "And on top of it all;" he thought, "here's Madame Lander taking care of Hansen, or maybe it's worse. After all I've done for him, if he and she are—"

Chapter Twenty-Three

MARI SCREWED UP HER EYES against the dawnlight and shivered with fear as she realized that the anxieties of her dream were with her in reality. Had Céleste come home? Was the Security Brigade man still alive? Did Yvette know she was here with Blair?

She turned her head on the pillow to look at him, and for one long moment the full tide of her tenderness for him coursed through her, free from the nagging obstruction of worry. Blair was lying flat on his back, with his knees slightly raised and his feet pressed against the bottom of the bed. The white of the bandaged shoulder made the tan of his lean face more pronounced, and the line of his jaw and wide mouth formed a rectangle of clean lines. Mari pulled up the sheet to cover him, and then she edged herself gently out of bed. She picked up her peignoir from the floor and thrust her arms into it.

Through the window she could see the sun, blood colored and ominous, rearing like an angry ball over the Casbah fortress. The curves of the city looked flaccid and colorless as a corpse.

Mari hurried out to the passage and along to Céleste's room. It was empty. The bed was untouched. Mari opened the mirror-fronted closets and riffled through her daughter's clothes, as she had done many times the previous day, trying to figure out what Céleste had taken to wear. The native *chadur* was the only garment missing. The slack wraiths of the dresses gave Mari a premonition of disaster. She stood still, with her heart racing, unable to summon her will to any action. But then a sound came to her, a sharp crunching of car tires on the graveled driveway.

Mari rushed out of the room to the stairway and went down three at a time, with her peignoir billowing out behind her. She reached the door just as a knock came on it. She fumbled wildly with the catch and opened to find, not Céleste as she had hoped, but Kuhn.

"The Security Brigade man is dead!" he said.

She did not grasp his words, for she was too surprised by his arrival.

"Eh?"

"The Brigade man who Hansen shot—he's dead."

Mari's mind leaped to meet the shock. Here was the terror out in the open at last, something with which to grapple.

"You're absolutely sure?" she demanded. "How do you know?"

"They're after him. I just saw a squad of Brigade men at the hotel. They said they were searching for him."

The sun's rays were so low that they shone under the brim of Kuhn's Panama hat and glistened on the rheum that filmed his lids. The old man's lips were stained with unhealthy mucus. Mari saw his stare run down her figure, and she pulled the peignoir tighter round her. Her mind was stamped with one urgency: *Blair must get away.*

"Hansen will go to prison for twenty years for this," said Kuhn. "Is he here?"

"No, he's not. Will you wait a moment? I must put some clothes on."

Mari went back blindly toward the stairs, and became vaguely aware of Yvette appearing from the back of the house, her face tight in a mask of disapproval.

"Show him in," said Mari 'mechanically, motioning toward the front door.

Mari groped at the banisters, unseeing. "Where can Blair hide?" she thought.

Mari went up the stairs slowly. She heard Yvette invite Kuhn into the drawing room, and then the old man's wheezing voice demanded, "Is Hansen here—the American?"

"Yes, m'sieur," came Yvette's voice.

"He is? You're sure?"

"Yvette!" screeched Mari. She ran back down the stairs and burst into the drawing room. "He's not here!" she managed to say. "He left here last night. You may go, Yvette!"

Kuhn glared at Mari. "Wherever Hansen is, they'll find him," he said. "Nobody can get away with killing a Security Brigade man."

Yvette made a sharp cry, as if she had been struck. "The Brigade man is dead?"

"Yes. Where is Hansen, do you know?"

Yvette pressed her hands together in anguish. "He's upstairs!"

"I tell you he left!" Mari burst out. "How dare you contradict me, Yvette. Get out of here!"

"I'm going to call the police," said Kuhn, and looked round for the phone. His breath began to come in sharp wheezes. Mari darted to the phone and stood in front of it. "Don't you believe me?" she cried.

Kuhn made a mumble and lumbered toward Mari, his brimming eyes fixed unblinking on her face.

"I want that phone," he said.

She felt behind her back for the instrument. She was trying to find the interroom switch so she could turn off the phone from the outside line. She managed it just as he reached her. Kuhn lunged toward her as if to push her away from the phone, and as he did so he made a sound that was half gasp, half gurgle. His face became distorted; the slack folds of flesh pulled up, displaying his dentures, then he fell back onto the ottoman and lay still.

Yvette shrieked, her scrawny neck cords standing out. Mari stood petrified for several seconds and then went cautiously toward Kuhn. Yvette kept screaming. The old man was alive, for his eyes were rolling and his mucus-stained lips were in a spasm.

Time seemed to poise itself, stationary, till Mari heard footfalls rushing down the stairs. Hansen burst into the room. Yvette cut short her scream and stared at Hansen, who was naked except for pajama shorts.

Mari pointed at Kuhn, trying to find words. "He's had a stroke," she said.

"Must be his heart," said Hansen. "He carries a phial of stuff for it."

He went over to the old man and searched his pockets. He found the heart tablets and wrenched off the screw top. He shook out a capsule and thrust it deep into Kuhn's mouth, far back on the tongue.

Yvette suddenly turned and hurried out of the room. Mari rushed after her, thinking the maid was going to call the police, but Yvette went into her own room, and Mari could hear a gabbled stream of prayers.

Mari ran back to Hansen. "You must get away!" she burst out. "They're after you! The Brigade man has died! That's what Kuhn came to tell me."

"Dead? Oh, God!"

"Hurry! We must get out of here! They're hunting for you. Kuhn said so."

Hansen looked down at the old man. Only Kuhn's mouth, which was twitching feebly, and his eyes, fixed on Hansen, now seemed to be alive.

"Lie still," Hansen told him. "You'll die if you try to move."

Mari pulled at Hansen's arm. "Hurry!" she begged.

He shrugged. "That settles it. I guess I'm for it now."

"No, no! We must get away!"

"Don't be crazy." The words were a mask for his instinct to escape. He could feel desperation coiling inside him. He made a conscious effort to fight it down, but he was already moving rapidly toward the stairs.

He bounded up the stairs, and she scrambled behind him. "I'm going with you!" she kept saying. She followed him, her voice turning into a wailing note of desperation. "You mustn't go without me! We can't be parted again!"

He turned and grasped her by the shoulders. "Listen. Suppose they catch me—do you want to go to prison, too?"

"I won't be left! There's nothing for me here without you!"

"Think of me then. How far could I get with you? We'd soon be spotted. No. I'll try to get over the border, I'll lie low somewhere, and when it's safe I'll get in touch with you."

Speechless with fear, she watched him fling on his clothes. An idea shot into her mind. "We'll go to my cottage!" she cried. "You can hide there for weeks. Even if they do search there, you can easily slip into the mountains—they're full of rebels the soldiers can't catch."

Without waiting for an answer she rushed into her room and pulled a dress over her head. In a frenzy of impatience she jammed her feet into shoes. She snatched up her handbag and ran back into his room. When she had nearly reached it she heard a noise that seemed to stop the blood in her heart—car tires on the driveway. She ran along the corridor to the bedroom overlooking the front door and saw a jeep pulling up. In it were men in the navy-blue uniform of the Security Brigade.

Mari rushed back to Hansen, crying out, "They're here, they're here!" He met her, his face gray.

"They're outside the front door," she gasped. "Oh, darling—"

He glanced at the window of the bedroom. "Can I get out there?"

"Yes, yes!" Her mind leaped to hope again, and they hurried together over to the window. "If you jump down, and then take that passage over there"—she pointed—"you can go through the back of the house. Turn to the right and you'll find the garage. Take the car and turn left and you can go out by the tradesmen's entrance and they won't see you—"

A loud knock came on the front door.

Mari explained rapidly how to get to the cottage. "Here, take this," she said, thrusting her handbag at him. "There's money in it, and the keys to the car."

Hansen took it and pushed out the window. He paused to look back at her, his bandaged head bright in the dawnlight.

"Don't follow me to the cottage," he said. "They'll be trailing you everywhere you go."

The knocking repeated downstairs, louder and more insistent.

There was a drop of about twice his height to the ground. Hansen let go and rolled with the fall. He landed lightly and ran toward the side passage.

Mari watched him till he was out of sight and then she walked slowly downstairs. By the time she reached the door the knocking was continuous. She opened up, and a Brigade man with sergeant's stripes said, "We've come for the American, Hansen."

"Hansen? Come inside." Mari pulled the door wide open and the four Brigade men filed in. Their dark uniforms and set faces made them seem like automata.

"You're just in time," she said. "Something terrible has happened. My guest has been taken seriously ill. He's in here. I think he's had a heart attack." She led the way in and the men stood looking down woodenly at Kuhn, who lay motionless on the ottoman.

"But this isn't Hansen," said the sergeant.

"He is the famous M'sieur Kuhn. Well, can't you do something?"

The black snouts of the Brigade men's carbines gleamed lethally. Mari glared at the guns as she strained her ears for a sound of the car leaving the garage, but she could hear nothing.

Kuhn seemed to be a little more eased. His breathing came evenly between his clenched dentures. "You'll be all right," she said, leaning over him. "I'm getting a doctor and ambulance immediately."

She went to the phone and called her doctor, asking him to come at once, then she called the hospital for an ambulance.

When she had finished the sergeant cleared his throat and said, "Where is Hansen?"

"Don't just stand there," she said sharply. "This man may be dying. Help me loosen his collar." The sergeant plodded forward and thrust his hairy hands inside the neckband of Kuhn's collar and burst it open.

The bloodshot eyes of the old man switched between Mari and the sergeant, and his lips began moving as if he were trying to frame words.

"Don't try to move, or say a word," Mari warned him, "or you'll have another attack." Fear filled Kuhn's eyes.

The sergeant straightened up. "I have my orders, madame," he said gruffly. "I am to bring Hansen back to the barracks. Is he here?"

Mari strained her ears before replying; *If only she could hear the car leaving.* "I think so," she said slowly, "would you like to come with me to find out?"

The sergeant motioned to two of the men to accompany him, and left the others beside the old man.

Mari led the way upstairs, calling out, "M'sieur Hansen!" She went into his room and made a great business of knocking on the bathroom door and listening, to satisfy herself that he was not in there.

"I must have missed him," she said. "He told me he was going out first thing."

"But it's only seven o'clock!" said the sergeant, his face clamped in suspicion.

"Perhaps you'd like to search the house?" asked Mari. "The word of Madame Lander is not good enough for you?"

"Where has he gone?"

"He said something about going down to the docks to see a ship's captain, a friend of his."

"The docks!" The sergeant wheeled around and barked at his men. "We must hurry!"

The men thudded down the stairs. Mari stood for several minutes, with her nails dug into her palms, praying that Hansen had gotten away safely, and then she heard the snarl of the jeep's exhaust falling in a rapid scale as the vehicle gathered speed down the driveway.

Mari went downstairs and ran round to the garage. The doors were open and the smaller sedan was gone. She came back to the house, full of the excitement of action. "I must get to him somehow," she kept saying to herself.

She went in to Kuhn and found him turning his head weakly from side to side. "Lie still!" she commanded. "Don't worry. You're going to live."

She thought: "You've got to. If you die they may blame Blair."

Mari remembered Yvette. She went toward the maid's room, trying to control her rage. "No use storming at her, the crazy old fool," she thought. "But I must shut her up. She mustn't tell the police what she knows about us."

Mari pushed open the door of the maid's room and saw
Yvette kneeling at the *prie-dieu*, her face set in stoniness except for her tight lips, which were moving rapidly in a mumble of prayers. The old woman took no notice of her.

Mari stood for a moment, torn with anxiety over how to
tackle her. "I must keep Yvette out of the way of the police,"
she thought, "they're bound to be here soon, nosing around.
It's my own stupid fault. I should have gotten rid of her
long ago. If she starts talking to the police that'll finish
everything."

The solution slipped into her mind, clear cut and final: "I
must take her with me. Yes, I'll take her along when I go to
Blair. The minute it's safe, I'll leave her behind somewhere."

Yvette left off her mumbling and rose to her feet, but kept
her face averted from her mistress.

"Don't worry, Yvette," said Mari soothingly. "Everything
is all right now. Your prayers have been answered. The
American is gone, and the police are after him."

"Gone, madame?" The old woman turned her head. "The
American has gone?"

"Yes. He won't be back. I promise you."

The rigidity of Yvette's face lessened slightly. "He has
brought mortal sin to you," she said.

Mari tried to look subdued, and said, "One who knows all
might forgive."

"Yes!" said Yvette, bobbing her head eagerly. "You must
ask forgiveness." She added, fearfully, "You're sure he won't
come back?"

Mari nodded.

"What is going to happen, madame?" asked Yvette, more
in her normal tone of voice.

"I don't know. I'm very frightened. You must help me,
Yvette. I am in great trouble." She watched the old woman's
face carefully, and was relieved to see it soften.

"What can I do to help?" asked Yvette. "Shall we go to
the priest?"

"Yes, we'll go to him," said Mari, fighting down the impatience that seemed to be trying to strangle her. "Listen,
Yvette," she said, "till we have been to the priest you won't
say a word to anybody, will you? We must be sure that what
we do is the right thing."

"We shall know when we go to the priest." The eyes of the
old woman, which had held that fixed look she wore when

she was praying, now seemed to have gained their normal focus.

"You are a good woman, Yvette. Now, go upstairs and pack a bag for me. Pack for yourself, also." She answered Yvette's look of inquiry with a persuasive smile. "We may have to go on a long journey," she said, and an inspiration came to her. "We may have to go search for Céleste," she explained. "She is still missing. I'm very worried about her, but I think I know where she may be."

Yvette went out, without any question, and Mari exulted to herself. "That's it," she decided. "I'm looking for Céleste. I'll tell the police I'm looking for her."

Chapter Twenty-Four

Hansen's right hand was sore from constant gear changing, but now that the belt of trees, which marked Mari's cottage, was growing clearer every minute he increased speed. His eyes were gritty from clouds of dust, whipped up by the car as it swayed in the ruts of the mountain track. Several times the wheels spun and the car threatened to plunge into the ravine, but each time he managed to swing it back.

Even now, he still snatched an occasional glance in the driving mirror, expecting to see that he was pursued. In every village he had raced through he feared a roadblock would trap him, or that a police car would appear in pursuit.

Why weren't they following him? The alarm must have gone out for him hours ago. Mari's car was so distinctive that it must have been spotted. Perhaps Mari had managed to put the police off the scent in some way.

Here was the last bend. He pressed on the accelerator, roared up through the wide belt of protecting thorns, and plunged into the shade of pines and terebinths.

He slammed on the brakes, in alarm. A truck was standing in his path.

His first impulse was to turn and go back, but then he realized that whoever was in the cottage would have heard him roaring up the steep ascent, and must be well aware of his presence. Probably he was being watched right now. Hansen turned off the engine, and instantly the quiet hit him. The cool shelf of the mountain seemed to be poised in an ominous vacuum, without sound or motion except for the soft whisper of a waterfall.

Hansen climbed out and walked toward the cottage, every nerve alert. The French windows of the living room were open, and he peered in, but could see nobody. On the table were the remains of a meal, only half eaten. A woman's robe was flung over a chair. Hansen walked along the front of the cottage, looking into the bedroom and the kitchen, then a flicker of a movement caught the corner of his eye. He turned and saw a figure emerging from the belt of pine trees, on the farther side of the cottage. It was a young man clad only in shorts.

"George!" called Hansen. "What the hell are you doing here?"

Behind George was another person, a girl in a sun suit. The pair had walked several paces toward Hansen before he realized that the girl was Céleste.

In the moments which it took for George and Céleste to reach him, Hansen's mind was feverishly revolving what this development meant to him. Were the police on Céleste's trail? Mari had said that she was going to call them in. If she had, this meant added danger.

"Why are you here?" asked George, as they drew together. "Are you chasing us?"

"No. I had no idea you were here. Have you two eloped?"

Céleste's look of suspicion eased, and she nodded eagerly, "Yes!" she said. "We're married now!"

Hansen whistled in surprise. "You realize that your mother is getting the police out after you?" he asked. "She's crazy with worry."

"I suppose so," said Céleste. "I was going to phone her from here, but I knew she would only send the police to get me. I'll write to her as soon as I can." Suspicion hardened her voice again: "What are *you* doing here, anyway?"

"That Security Brigade man died. They're after me. They want to pin a manslaughter charge on me, and they'll probably make it stick. I killed him by accident, but they're after my blood."

"Come with us!" suggested George quickly. "We're going into the *bled s'ida,* the rebel territory. You can hide there with us as long as you like, and while you're there you can help our movement."

"Mean to say you're going to take Céleste up there? Risk her life?"

"I asked him to take me," said Céleste.

Hansen turned to George impatiently. "Don't you realize that Céleste will be in double danger in rebel territory—from both French and Arabs? Your people will cut her throat the first time they suspect her of being a spy."

George's face fell swiftly into a pucker of worry. "I know it's dangerous," he said, "but that is the only way we could be together and—"

"You want Céleste to live in a cave, eating scraps, with the French Army chasing you both?"

"What else can we do? If we go back to Algiers they'll take Céleste away from me—they'll arrest me for abducting a minor, or something. In any case, the police are looking for me. The informer must have told them I was at the meeting in the Casbah."

"You can't hope to lick the French Army. Your real battle is in Paris. You must persuade the French people you're right, not that you can kill Frenchmen. Go bang the drum in Paris. You two can be happy there, and do a worth-while job."

"That's what I keep telling him," said Céleste eagerly, "but he's got this romantic idea that he must fire a rifle from behind a rock."

"All my friends and relatives are fighting," said George. His expression showed that he was being torn by cross-purposes.

"He's right, *sidi*," said Céleste, "we should go to Paris— that is where Arab freedom is going to be won."

"While you two are arguing," said Hansen, "is there anything for me to eat?"

They took him into the cottage, where Céleste prepared him a meal of canned soup and chicken. While she worked, Hansen observed the change that had come over her. Instead of the quiet, shy girl he had known, vitality now seemed to be alive in her. For the first time, he could detect in her something of the personality of Mari.

He ate ravenously and he had almost finished when the ringing of the phone cut into the quietness.

All three exchanged glances nervously. "Don't answer it,"

said Céleste, but Hansen shook his head. "We must," he said. "It may be the police checking up to see whether we've been seen here. If nobody answers they'll get suspicious. Have you sent the caretaker away?"

Céleste nodded.

"You answer it, George," said Hansen. "Try to sound like the caretaker. If it's the police, put them off."

George swallowed nervously and picked up the phone. He spoke in a slow cracked Arabic voice: "Who is it who calls?" Hansen and Céleste stood close beside him, straining their ears to get an idea of who was at the other end.

George's dark eyes widened, and he put his hand over the mouthpiece. "It's Michel," he said, "Madame Lander's chauffeur. He says he has a message for you from her."

Hansen suspected a police trap, and hesitated. "No, it can't be," he figured. "They'd never get Michel to rat on Mari."

He picked up the phone, just as Céleste cried, "Don't speak to him! I don't trust him!"

Hansen motioned her to be quiet and spoke into the instrument. "Yes?"

"M'sieur Hansen?" came Michel's voice. "Madame Lander wishes to know whether you arrived safely."

"Sure. But this is crazy, phoning me here. Do you want to advertise where we are?"

"Don't worry, m'sieur. I am calling from a phone booth. I have not been followed. Madame Lander says you are not to worry—everything is going well here. The police think you left Algiers by sea."

"Tell her not to be too sure. The police may want her to believe that."

"Is there anything you need, m'sieur? Madame says she will bring as much as she can, and there is a revolver in the bedside table at the cottage."

"Listen, Michel, get this. Tell madame that she must not come here. It is too dangerous. I don't want her to run the risk. Is that clear?"

"Well, I'll tell her, m'sieur, but madame seems very determined." The deferential voice seemed to alter its pitch slightly as the chauffeur asked, "Is Mam'selle Céleste there? I heard a young lady's voice just now. It sounded exactly like Mam'selle Céleste."

"Céleste? No, she's not here."

"Then there's some other young lady?" The servile voice

changed its tone and became inquisitory. "I'm certain I heard a girl's voice, m'sieur."

"Oh, I think that was the operator."

"But that was a man."

There came a pause, during which Hansen saw Céleste clutch George's arm, and her eyes were alive with fright.

Michel's voice came back. "Very well, m'sieur, I was mistaken. Er, may I speak to the caretaker again? I have several messages for him from madame."

Hansen sensed danger. He had an instinctive feeling that Michel did not believe him, and that he wanted to hear George's voice again.

"Too late, Michel," said Hansen. "The caretaker is on his way to town, to buy some things."

"Oh." Michel hesitated. "Well, thank you, m'sieur. I must go to madame." The chauffeur rang off.

Hansen put down the phone and snapped his fingers.

"Hurry!" he said. "We must get out of here, we're dead ducks if we stay."

Céleste and George started to speak at once. Hansen was already moving toward the door, and he spoke over his shoulder. "I've just realized," he said. "The police may be trailing Mari's servants. They're probably tracing that call Michel made here." Hansen gestured impatiently. "Let's get moving," he said. "We'd better take the truck."

"Truck?" said George. "The sedan is much faster."

"No, the police will be circulating the description of Mari's sedan. Any minute now, the nearest police post to this place will be alerted. They'll rush here to grab us."

He led them outside.

"I hope the truck will make it," said George. "It's ready to fall to bits."

"If it gets us out of the valley—that's the main thing. We'd be trapped here."

George started up the truck with an old-fashioned crank, and the engine spluttered into weary life. Céleste ran back into the cottage and came out carrying her *chadur* cloak, a pair of binoculars, and her mother's revolver.

Hansen felt savage fury at the thought of what Michel was probably telling Mari. He'd say Céleste was here. Mari would hit the roof, she'd think that proved he and Céleste were lovers. Oh, Christ, what a mess.

Céleste trained the glasses onto the village at the end of

the valley, where the track ran out into the highway. "All clear," she said, "there's nobody there yet."

"Soon will be," said Hansen. "Jump on!"

George took the wheel, and put the truck into low gear. Céleste sat beside him and Hansen climbed over the tailboard into the back. "I'd better stay here," he said. "If we see the police coming I'll slip off and hide in the thorns. You mustn't be seen with me—that would make it much worse for you."

The truck slid and shuddered down the steep incline, raising a ponderous surge of yellow dust that every now and then, as they zigzagged, came between the truck and the eye of the sun, so that they bounced down through a sulphurous murk. Hansen had to crouch on his haunches, hands gripping the back of the driver's seat, to lessen the shock of the violent bumping.

Every time they came in sight of the village at the end of the valley, Céleste tried to control the bouncing of her body sufficiently to look through the binoculars.

"Well?" bawled Hansen, over the clatter of the engine. "What are you two going to do? Are you going into rebel territory to be heroes, or are you going to Paris to do a real job?"

Céleste twisted round to face him, and shrugged, then pointed to George to indicate that it was up to him. She touched George's arm and he snatched a side glance at her. Céleste's face was calm and her lips were set in a quiet smile.

The gears of the truck began to take on an ominous rattle, but the vehicle still lunged over the ruts and holes as if it had some implacable will of its own. An acrid smell of burning rubber began to come from the tortured brakes. George had to wrestle with the wheel all the time to keep the vehicle on the track. Several times they lurched on the very edge of escarpments that would have hurled them down hundreds of feet. Gradually, the corkscrew slopes began to get less severe. They were all straining their eyes ahead to the village.

"How far away is the nearest police post?" asked Hansen.

"At El Ghazir, I think," said Céleste. "That's about twenty-five miles away."

Hansen looked at his watch. "We've taken fifteen minutes to get down. The police must be very close to us now."

He caught a glimpse of Céleste grasping the revolver. In her small-boned hands the black gun seemed to gain malevolence.

Hansen shouted at her, "Better let George have that!"
She smiled, but made no move.

"What about all the people in the village?" yelled Hansen.
"They'll tell the police we came through, give them our
descriptions, and tell which way we went."

George called over his shoulder, "The Arabs never tell
the police anything."

They all fell silent as they stared at the junction of the
track and the highway. The light in the valley was now in the
full intensity of high noon, making everything shadowless;
the neutral shades of the dun-colored village and the surrounding bluffs gave a hypnotic focus to the T formed by
the yellow of the track, where it ran into the black oily fatness
of the main highway. They trundled nearer till they could
pick out the long parallels of the tire streaks on the paved
road ahead.

Hansen broke the silence. "If you're going into rebel territory," he said, "you'll be turning right—you'd better drop
me off."

Céleste did not even look to George to try to persuade him
to turn left. She kept her gaze ahead, but Hansen could see
the white span of her knuckles round the black gun, gripping
the barrel.

The truck slowed down for the turn. George spun on the
wheel and pulled the vehicle round to the left, heading for
Algiers.

Chapter Twenty-Five

MICHEL EMERGED from the phone booth and collided
with a cadaverous man who hurriedly squeezed past to take
his place. Michel glared at him through the glass, but the
gaunt man did not notice—he was too busy getting his number. Michel noticed that he twirled the dial only once.

Michel remembered the need for haste, and left. He went
at a trot along the two blocks to the church. He snatched
off his peaked cap and went into the cool dimness, taking
soft-footed strides, and reached the line of penitents waiting
outside the confessional.

Madame Lander was still sitting on the bench. When she

saw Michel, she rose rapidly and came to meet him. Even in the shadows, he could see her eyes bright with eagerness.

"M'sieur Hansen arrived safely, madame," whispered Michel.

She let out a deep breath. "You told him that I'll follow him to the cottage very soon?" she asked.

"Yes, madame, but he said you mustn't go—it's too dangerous."

"You explained that the police are on the wrong trail—they think he has escaped by sea?"

"Yes, but he still said you shouldn't come." Michel cleared his throat nervously. "Something very strange occurred, madame."

"What?"

"There was somebody there with him. I distinctly heard a young lady call out something. It sounded exactly as if she were Mam'selle Céleste."

"That's impossible!"

"I'm almost sure, madame."

"You're crazy, Michel." But she was thrusting her face down toward his, peering at him in the shadows as if trying to divine the truth from his eyes.

"Michel!" She gripped his arm so hard that she could feel the bone of his forearm. "That's not true!" She had raised her voice, and several faces turned toward her in the gloom—pale ovals of disapproval.

"Well, perhaps I was mistaken," he said cautiously. "That's what m'sieur said when I told him I had heard a young lady's voice. I asked him if I might speak to the caretaker—I knew you were anxious about Mam'selle Céleste, and I thought perhaps the caretaker could reassure me she was not there—"

Michel avoided his mistress's eyes, fearing her rage at his implication that Hansen had lied.

"Well, and he said?"

"That the caretaker had gone. But I had been speaking to him only a minute previously!"

"Oh!" Mari made the word a shudder.

Michel peered at her intently in the gloom. Invisible hands seemed to be molding madame's face, thrusting fury into the lines of her mouth and eyes. She made an obvious effort to control herself and said in a small gasping voice, "That will be all, Michel."

Mari went back to her place on the bench and sat down blindly, letting the torture take hold of her. She remembered Boward's fuddled voice when she had awakened him with her phone call: ". . . yes, madame," he had mumbled. "I saw Céleste with him myself. She was in his arms. She slipped away from me on some pretext while we were having dinner, and after a long wait I went to search for her in the wood. This big man had his arms round her. No, I'm not sure who he was. I quarreled with her about it, and she begged me not to tell you. . . ."

A big man.

Mari tried to lessen her torment by taking some decision, but she was too stunned to think. Her mind was exploding with sharp memories—Blair denying he had been in the Casbah to meet Céleste, Blair persuading her not to call the police to look for Céleste, Blair's hostility to her at the dinner party in front of Céleste.

Here in the gloom, Mari's senses were acute to every impression, but her mind seemed to be anesthetized. She could detect the faint smell of decay and eternity; she could see the fierce sunlight transmuted by the stained glass into a soft rich glow, and she was aware of a mysterious new perspective made by the guttering banks of candles, leading up to the final focus of the High Altar; but her mind could not make anything of these stimuli; she was incapable of movement or thought.

How long she sat there she never knew, but she was aroused by a repeated tugging at her shoulder. She realized that Yvette was shaking her. "It's your turn now, madame. Father is waiting," the old woman was whispering.

Mari nodded her head and let herself be guided into the confessional.

The little space held a faint smell of melted tallow and carbolic. It was so quiet that she could her the priest breathing on the other side of the latticework.

She said, mechanically, "Forgive me, father, for I have sinned."

"How long since you made your last confession, my child?" The voice was so old that it seemed to be worn down to a smooth grain and to be part of the feel of sanctuary.

How long? Not since Blair had gone away during the war—those black months of waiting and slowly dying inside. She had sometimes come to pray here then, and she had kept a candle burning for Blair by the statue of Saint Anthony, the patron saint of missing travelers, till all hope had died. For it was hope, not forgiveness, which she had sought in the confessional during those months of torment.

"Not for eight years, father," she said.

The screen between them seemed to soak up her words, taking part of her, and she had a confused fantasy that the latticework could draw out her misery like a poultice. But as soon as she tried to form words, the torture began to jab at her; the renewal of her thoughts seemed to bring her stunned nerve centers to life.

"Well, my child?" came the patient old voice.

"I have sinned, father, and I am in great trouble."

She had to get rid of the pain. She stared at the latticework and began to pour out her distress, at first incoherently, but gradually, as pain narrowed the gap between her mind and her memories, she blurted it all out.

Slowly, as her pressing weight of torment projected itself to the latticework, Mari began to feel lightened, suspended in a vacuum. The pain slowly spent itself and she began to feel curiously detached, as though motivation no longer lay within her but in the wooden screen that had sucked up so much of her. She became aware that words were being intoned in the latticework, from the disembodied old voice of sanctuary: ". . . sint. tibe in remissionem peccatorum augmentum gratiae et praemium vitae aeternae . . ."

Her mind lost the thread of the priest's words, for now at last she was able to think. She was drained of the dead load of hopelessness.

She stepped out into the dimness. Yvette was waiting, and Mari caught her starched smell.

They went together toward the main door, through which the sun forced a thin rhomboid of yellow flame, so brilliant that wisps of smoke from the candles could be seen against it, like paintbrush doodles.

Mari felt a chord of sympathy with her maid, linking them in the mutual solace of sanctuary, but as they grew nearer to the door, Yvette's shiny face caught the light, which wrested out lines that the dimness had concealed. Mari's sympathy turned to pity.

When they emerged into the sun glare the heat struck sharply, unexpectedly, and Mari took in a sudden breath, as if she had been plunged into a new element. Once more she relived past torment. How often had she come out to these very steps during the war, drained of everything but despair. Oh, God, was it to start all over again? The fearful waiting, the not knowing, the great blank void inside her?

Yvette was grasping her elbow, trying to lead her forward. Mari realized that she had been standing still, as if trying unconsciously to let the sun soak out the numbness from her mind.

"Come, madame," said the maid firmly. Yvette's face looked masklike in the harsh glare; her skin was like dried wax that might peel off at any moment; only her eyes seemed to hold life.

In one stark flash the thought came to her: *"Am I going to be like Yvette—dead, wasted?"*

It mustn't happen all over again, that death of waiting. She couldn't go through that again. She must find out the truth immediately. Maybe it was all a mistake. She tried to fan a glimmer of hope, but her mind could not progress beyond a mental image of Céleste in Blair's arms.

Mari went to the limousine, where Michel was waiting with the door open. "Drive me out to the cottage," she ordered.

He gaped at her, in silent surprise.

"Yes, right now," she said impatiently.

Michel's narrow little face became lined with consternation. "But, madame," he said, "the police may follow you."

"No matter," she replied. "Perhaps it will be just as well." She had to face Blair and Céleste, she had to know.

Chapter Twenty-Six

THE LAST SHADOWS of the mountains fell behind, and the truck lost the impetus of descent. Now it faced a ruler-straight journey across the baking *gouban*, which stretched as far as the rim of vision, its endless wastes of sand hurting the eyes with a relentless glitter.

Heat began to weave round the truck, swaying and dipping like a wraith, and it gradually grew more dense till the view ahead was one mass of quivering air.

Now and then the haze would clear, giving a view far

ahead, and each time this happened Céleste held the binoculars to her eyes, to see if anything were approaching.

"You ought to have dropped me off!" shouted Hansen.
"If the police meet us here in the open, you'll be dragged
into my mess."

"No!" George yelled back at him. "The bloodhounds
could have picked you up anywhere in that valley!" George's
face was taut and dry from evaporated sweat. "We'll be
safe when we get to Djouma," he said. "I've got friends
there. They'll hide us till things blow over."

"We must split up when we get there," said Hansen.
"You two go to your friends. I'll make out somehow."

Céleste was touching George's arm, caressing it with her
fingertips. "If only we can get through," she said, "we may
be able to catch a plane to France from the Algiers airport."

George took a long time to make an affirmative grunt.
Hansen guessed that the young man was having second
thoughts about leaving Algeria.

Céleste seemed to sense this. "Just think, *sidi*," she said
coaxingly, "by tomorrow we may be in Paris, doing real
work for the movement."

"Don't count on that," said Hansen. "Your mother has
probably got the police looking for you."

"And for me, too," George chimed in. "I think that rebel
territory is the best place for us. I'm only going this way
because the police post was in the other direction."

The open back of the truck was grilled so fiercely by the
sun that though Hansen could feel his sweat ducts prickling,
his skin was completely dry; his tongue was swollen, and
every motion of his eyes made them hurt, for they held no
moisture. The bandage round his shoulder seemed to be
barbed wire.

"Mind if I get in front with you?" asked Hansen. "This
is cooking me alive."

They stopped while he climbed into the front seat, and
even in that brief moment the lack of movement in the air
made the heat close in stiflingly.

"All we need is to break down going across," said Hansen.

They listened anxiously to the note of the engine; it was
one continuous whimper. Far ahead, a mirage began to
dance. It was of a tremendous sheet of blue water, rippling in
feathery waves. They gazed at it in silent fascination, trying
to draw saliva into their mouths. When the mirage had

grown so close that they could pick out the individual pricks of sunlight on its crests, it vanished, and in its place were the hills, looking like the stumps of rotted teeth. There was a gap, straight ahead, where the dusty road vanished down into the gorge.

Hansen hunched himself forward slightly, mentally urging the truck to keep going till it reached the gorge; then there would be only the descent to the valley, and the safety of Djouma. He began to think of a drink, of letting liquid coolness run over his parched tongue and down into the dryness of his gullet.

They were only a few hundred yards from the gorge mouth when a bright stab of light hit their eyes. They all made a sharp intake of breath.

"A car!" cried Céleste, raising her glasses.

Yes, the light was the sun reflected off its windshield.

Swiftly it came into their vision, a closed jeep with a blue flag flying over the hood. "*Flics!*" said Céleste. "I can see the police sign."

Hansen swore, and wondered whether he had time to climb out onto the back of the truck, but he realized that he could find no cover there, nor anywhere around.

The distance between the two vehicles closed rapidly. Hansen could make out the pith helmets worn by the two flics. The jeep swung to its left, blocking the way and the driver held up an arm, gesturing the truck to stop. Hansen could see the sign on the windshield, POLICE, and the long squiggling Arabic word for it underneath.

"Tell them you've never seen me before," said Hansen swiftly, as George began to brake. "Swear that I bummed a ride from you. Céleste—put on your *chadur* and pull it round your face." She did so rapidly.

The truck lumbered to a halt, its brakes protesting, Hansen perceived, in the acute clarity of his strain, that the shadow of the vehicle was still tremulous from vibration.

After the roaring labor of the engine, a complete hush closed in from the desert, and seemed to slow down all movement and sound. When one of the policemen climbed out of the jeep and came toward them he appeared to be moving with exaggerated deliberation, and Hansen's mind raced between each footfall.

There are only two flics, he kept thinking, just two bastards who're going to send me to prison.

"Oh, God, we'll be parted," said Céleste frantically, clutching George's arm. "They'll take you away from me."

"No, they won't," said George. Hansen flashed a look at him and saw that his face had tautened.

The policeman walked round the truck toward its near-side, so as to stand in the shadow while he interrogated them. Under his pith helmet the man's face was brick red and dotted with the butter-colored freckles peculiar to fair people. He wore a revolver in a waist holster.

"Police pig," grated George under his breath as the man came round the front of the truck. "If only we could get as far as the gorge—"

"Oh, *sidi*," groaned Céleste. The face of the policeman ranged itself in the side window of the truck at elbow-level to Hansen, who steeled himself for the man's scrutiny.

"Show your papers," ordered the flic, in the tone reserved for Arabs.

The words galvanized George. He thrust in the gear and yelled, "Céleste! Get down on the floor!" The truck moved forward and the policeman jumped on the running board, pulling at his pistol.

"Stop!" he screeched, "or I'll fire!"

Hansen swung his fist with all his power in the face of the flic, who toppled off and sprawled in the sand. The truck lurched up onto the rough ground beside the road, so as to pass the jeep. The other flic scrambled out of the vehicle, shouting at them, and aimed his gun. A shot smashed against the metal frame of the cab, then another. Céleste, who had ducked low, writhed up with the revolver in her hand, but Hansen wrested it from her. He leaned out and took careful aim at the tires of the jeep and fired twice. The policemen ducked for cover.

"Lie on the floor, Céleste," shouted George again.

She crouched down between them, her face blazing with a savage exultance that reminded Hansen sharply of Mari. "Did you get them?" she was screeching. George forced her down lower with the flat of his hand.

Hansen peered back through the narrow window. One policeman was helping the other to his feet and hurrying him into the jeep.

There was still half a mile to the gorge. George had his foot hard down on the accelerator, and the note of the truck's engine was whining higher and higher up to its crescendo.

Hansen saw the jeep move off after them. The gap between the two vehicles began to narrow. He decided to wait till the police were closer before firing again. He broke open the gun and saw that he had four shots left.

Several loud whangs burst in their eardrums, in swift succession, as bullets hit the metalwork of the cab. Hansen realized that the police must have a rifle, to be able to hit at that range.

"You bloody fool!" Hansen yelled at George. "You've done it now. It's me they're after! Pull up, for Christ's sake!"

"It may be me they want!" George shouted back. "Anyway, we're all in this now."

Céleste was still crouching on the floor, her hand clutching George's thigh. She kept calling out to him to bend lower over the wheel. Her face was red with excited fear, and Hansen felt a sharp pang, for in this moment she seemed to be only a child. He raged at himself: "Oh, God, now I've dragged these kids into it."

The idea flashed into his mind of jumping out and surrendering, but the truck was going too fast.

He peeped back cautiously and saw that the jeep had turned off the road. "They're trying to head us off!" he exclaimed.

The jeep was rocking and tilting over the sand, beginning an arc that would bring it out ahead of the truck, but the police apparently decided that the going was too rough for them to make it in time. The jeep turned and bumped back onto the highway.

Hansen gauged the distances in an agony of suspense. The gorge seemed to be creeping toward them at a snail's pace, and the jeep was again overhauling them, but the delay had given George the edge he needed to get there first.

The somber shadow of the gorge lay across the highway, gathering the focus of their eyes. They plunged into the dimness and almost immediately the road began to tilt downward, and the truck gathered momentum. The cliffs reared up on each side of them.

George and Céleste made shouts of triumph, but a desperate feeling of being cornered was filling Hansen. "It's all of five miles to Djouma," he thought. "Even if we make it, our troubles will only be beginning there."

Several shots thudded into the tailboard of the truck and others hissed close by. Hansen kept snatching cautious looks out of the back window at the jeep, which was rapidly drawing near. He waited till a rifle bullet had cracked against the cab frame, then immediately showed himself and took careful aim at the offside tire of the police car. When he next looked the jeep had fallen back to a respectful distance, but seemed to be traveling all right.

Damn, only three shots left, better not waste any more.

Hansen stared ahead, trying to force his mind into a plan. The road ran gently downward for about a mile, then began a series of sharp zigzags down an escarpment, which fell away to the valley below. The truck reached the first bend without any more shots hitting it, and Hansen was surprised to notice that the jeep was a long time turning the bend after them. Good, perhaps he had disabled it after all.

The truck lurched crazily round the second hairpin bend, George spinning the wheel frantically. They skidded safely in the turn, and gathered speed on the next straight stretch.

Hansen peered up at the higher level they had just left, seeking out the jeep, and then yelled, "Weave! They're going to fire at us from the front!"

He could see the jeep standing still, and one of the policemen was aiming a rifle at the truck, which every second was rolling nearer into the line of fire. Hansen saw the cleverness of the idea: Now the police could aim straight at the fugitives when they were not shielded by the metal of the truck's cab.

George wrestled with the wheel, making the truck stagger from one side of the road to the other.

"Keep weaving!" shouted Hansen. A shot clattered on the hood, then another. A sharp pain hit Hansen's face. Céleste shrieked. The windshield was smashed. George threw up his arm to cover his face. Hansen leaned forward and seized the wheel, trying to keep the truck on the road. George recovered and grasped the wheel again. Céleste stopped her shrieking and squirmed up from the floor to wipe the blood from George's face with her hand.

Hansen realized that he was unhurt except for cuts from the flying glass.

The next rifleshot clanged on the metal roof of the cab. They were safe, for the moment anyway. The three of them were not exposed directly to the line of fire—till they came to the next bend.

"This is it," thought Hansen. The police could repeat this all the way down the long descent; they could stop on each level and fire at the truck when the passengers were exposed to view. There were at least twenty bends like this to come. "We'll never make it," he told himself.

Céleste was kneeling on the floor, her back to the engine, dabbing at George's face. Alarm for him filled her face. In that instant she seemed like a frightened little girl.

"Watch out," said George, "here's the next bend."

"We're finished if we just let them pick us off," thought Hansen. "There's only one way left. That jeep has got to be stopped."

As the truck swung out, preparing to get round the hairpin bend, Hansen yelled, "I'm going to stop them, I'm getting off. You go on!"

"No!" screeched George and tried to snatch at Hansen with one hand.

Hansen sprang out as the truck slithered round the bend. His whole body jarred as he landed on a debris of broken rocks. He threw himself forward, scrambling for the cover of boulders that were piled beside the road.

He watched the truck wobble up onto the banking, tilt at an alarming angle, then right itself and get back on the road. A noise like squealing pigs rent the air, and Hansen knew that George had slammed on the brakes. Céleste was leaning out, right in the line of fire.

"Get back!" yelled Hansen frantically.

No more shots came. He realized that the police had climbed back into the jeep and were speeding down the slope.

The truck was slowing up. In desperation, Hansen came out into the open and made violent gestures with his arms, indicating that George should halt on the next slope, and he would catch up with them there. George and Céleste appeared to understand, for the truck rolled forward again.

Hansen edged back into cover among the jagged slabs of rock. His mind was now poised and cold. All the rage and fear had been drained out of him.

"I'm for it," he thought, "I hope the kids get away."

The jeep came into view, hurtling down toward him, at the front of a great plume of dust. As it neared the bend its engine spat with a reduced throttle. Hansen waited till it was broadside onto him and the two policemen were exposed, then he aimed carefully at the driver. The man's lips pulled back from his teeth in an expression of almost comical surprise, and he lost control of the wheel. The jeep slewed round, making little sideway hops, and smashed to a stop against a shoulder-high rock.

There was a long moment of suspended motion, and then the flic on the offside wriggled out of the vehicle and squeezed himself flat on the ground. He stayed close by the chassis for protection. He was holding the rifle, and Hansen saw the long nose of the gun point toward him. It was not more than twenty feet away.

Hansen ducked into cover, and looked round rapidly. He figured he might be able to edge his way higher among the great mass of rocks and still keep out of sight of the police. He moved cautiously, but the police spotted him at intervals, for bullets spattered on the rocks only a few inches from him. He had a confused idea that if he could get a view of the jeep and confirm that it was disabled, then there was just a chance he might be able to slip away.

The blood from his cuts was trickling down into his eyes, and the face wounds were prickling with sweat. He had to keep blinking his eyes to clear them.

"You go round that way," he heard one flic call. "I'll cover here."

He had to act swiftly, or he'd be picked off. Damn, only two bullets left. He saw a tall slab of granite, the size of a car, which reared up almost perpendicularly out of the mass of dynamited rock. Hansen wriggled toward it, using his hands and knees to claw himself along. He was dizzy with fatigue, and he had difficulty in focusing his eyes. The edges of the rocks were razorlike and blistering to the touch. By the time he reached the upthrust block of granite he was in the last reserves of his strength.

He rose in the lee of the tall rock and snatched a look round it. The jeep was below him, less than his own height away. He saw the flic with the rifle, huddled up against the rocks, pointing the gun straight at him. He ducked back at the instant the bullet whined past. Hansen showed himself immediately and fired at the policeman, then crouched back as the rifle went off again. At the end of a second he heard a clatter, as if the rifle had fallen to the ground. Hansen stood upright and stuck his head out at a different place, in case this were a ruse to trap him. He saw the policeman clasping his shoulder, with one arm hanging limp, and simultaneously Hansen became aware that the other man was still in the driving seat, and was aiming his revolver at him. Hansen fired again, and saw the driver slump forward over the wheel. Hansen watched both men warily, and leaned out to get a good look at the jeep. Its nearside front wheel was buckled up at a fantastic angle.

The policeman in the open was bending to pick up the rifle, his arm still hanging slack. "He's got guts," thought Hansen.

He turned and looked down at the valley to see how far the truck had gone. He knew even before he looked,—it was waiting for him on the next level down, stationary on the blazing yellow of the road. He could see George and Céleste peering up cautiously. He waved to them and started to climb down.

The descent to the truck was not more than a hundred feet, but his muscles were jumping with exhaustion, and a sudden searing pain in his right foot told him he had strained a tendon. He dropped clumsily from one rock to another, several times misjudging and falling awkwardly. Thorns and scrubs tore at him. He had almost reached the truck when there came the sustained whing of a bullet that ricocheted somewhere near. He was too far gone to care. His lungs were a bellows of pain and his breath came in retches. He gathered every part of his energy for the last few yards, and then his friends were waiting to haul him up onto the truck.

He felt the breeze begin to press against him as the vehicle moved forward. His ears were pounding so much that he could not hear what Céleste was saying. He could see her lips working.

The truck had roared down several slopes before Hansen could master a twitching of his exhausted muscles, and his lungs resumed their normal rhythm.

"Did you stop them?" Céleste was asking eagerly.

"Their jeep's smashed up," he said. "They can't follow us. I may have killed one of them."

"We'll get to Djouma all right!" cried George. "Once we make it we'll be safe. I've got plenty of friends there."

"Your friend we had breakfast with—are we going to him?" asked Céleste.

"No, we must go into the medina, the slum quarter. We can lie low there."

"Don't fool yourself," thought Hansen, "we'll never get out of there alive. Half the French Army will be on our tail in a couple of hours."

A few more turns, and then they got their first view of Djouma, with its new concrete minaret, gleaming purely in the sun. The white town looked strangely calm and peaceful.

Chapter Twenty-Seven

MARI LEANED FORWARD impatiently on the car seat and tried to peer ahead through the jam of mule carts and pannier-laden Arabs. "Keep sounding the horn, Michel," she ordered irritably. "What's holding us up?"

"Looks like a roadblock, madame."

Heat was collecting rapidly inside the halted limousine. The sultry air seemed to be bleached by the sun, so that it lay listless between the blind walls that bordered the street. The heat was shuddering in eddies over the hood of the car. Mari fanned herself impatiently, but Yvette, with her usual reaction to anything disturbing, wore a look of self-sacrifice.

Behind the car was a farm truck loaded with squawking fowls, and the raucous noise of the birds frayed Mari's nerves.

"Stop hooting," she ordered Michel. "We've been here at least five minutes. You'd better go and find out what has happened."

"Very good, madame." Michel climbed out and edged his way through the crowd of Arabs, whose white robes caught the light so violently that they hurt the eyes. Sloping sunrays split the street into two triangles—one muted in shadow, the other a solid blaze. The dense throng was shuffling in between the blocked traffic, and Mari could tell, from the excited noise and gestures of the people, that something big was happening.

The first stirrings of fear began in her.

An urge for action made her decide to find out for herself what was happening. She opened the door, against the press of the crowd, and stepped out into the noise and heat. Immediately, she could sense the hostility of the Arabs. An invisible current of herd tension among them communicated itself to Mari, by the crowd's refusal to make way for her. Usually the Arabs concealed their dislike of the French behind a blank façade, with only their liquid black eyes revealing their thoughts, but now she heard the word of contempt—roumi—mumbled all around her, and much of the jostling seemed to be deliberate. She found a vent for her anxiety by pushing impatiently through the crowd, thrusting her handbag ahead to clear a way.

Most of the Arabs had the lean faces of country peasants, their skin rucked up round the eyes in myriad wrinkles. Several of them were bent beneath panniers containing gourds, locust beans, or seed. Mari realized that this was market day, and the town was crowded with Arabs from far around.

A barefooted old man ahead of her was leading a scrawny cow by the halter. The animal pricked up its tail and defecated, so that Mari had to pick her way awkwardly to avoid the mess. The Arabs round her made high-pitched titters of malice and their teeth caught the sunlight in unfriendly grins. Anger began to overcome her anxiety.

At that moment she caught sight of Michel, who was shoving his way back toward her. His sharp little face was tight with eagerness. "Yes, it's a police roadblock!" he cried. "They're searching for M'sieur Hansen!"

The shock wave in her mind stopped her ears against what Michel was saying. She managed to catch one phrase. "The whole town is sealed off."

Mari forced herself to concentrate.

"And, madame," Michel was saying, his wet black eyes on hers, avid to see the effect of his words, "the police say there are two Arabs with him—a man and a woman!"

"Then it can't be Blair!" cried Mari, but Michel's busy eyes seemed to bore recollection into her. "Unless he and Céleste—"

Her words trailed off as she realized what was in Michel's mind. One Arab might be Mari's caretaker, and the woman could be Céleste dressed in Arab's clothes—she remembered that Céleste was wearing the *chadur*.

Mari was jostled by the swaying crowd, and several of the Arabs clustered close around, brazenly listening.

"They've wounded two policemen seriously, madame," said Michel. "The police are certain the fugitives are hiding somewhere in town. The roadblock is to prevent them slipping out—other police are posted all round the place. Troops are on their way here to search the whole town." .

Mari was surprised to realize that she could still think calmly. "Doesn't the caretaker of my cottage live here in Djouma?" she asked.

"Yes, he does, madame. I have his address in my notebook."

"Go to his place. Find out all you can. See if he has come back to town today. I'm going to phone the cottage. Where can I make a call?"

"The only place is probably in the hotel in the main square. It's only a *fonduq*, a native inn. You'll have to pass through the roadblock."

"Leave the car in a side street, and after you've been to the caretaker's house I'll meet you at the hotel."

Mari shouldered her way toward the police block, which was under the arched gateway of the town.

The pulse of excitement in the crowd seemed to be growing stronger. Many of the Arabs went out of their way to elbow her, not attempting to conceal their dislike of the unveiled woman. Several of them, in the safety of the crush, ran their fingers against her exploringly. .

This insolence in the usually docile Arabs was part of the growing sense of trouble.

They stick together, thought Mari; they probably all know where the hunted Arabs are; there may be a riot when the roundup starts.

Mari became suspended in a horrible emptiness of indecision; the cells of her body were alive to every stimulus except that of motivation. She tried to mouth expletives, to force herself into a rage, but her mind kept returning to one syllogistic line of thought: "If Blair lied to me, and he's running off with Céleste, then he's here in Djouma, he'll be caught and they'll guillotine him. If he wasn't lying, he's not here, and we'll be together again very soon.

"I'll soon know," she told herself. "I'll phone the cottage, and if there's no answer I'll know he has been lying to me all the time."

Her thoughts broke up into a kaleidoscope of fragments. She thought of the dinner party, with Blair hostile to her in front of Céleste; then of the words he had whispered to her in the darkness only a few hours ago; the way he had tried to persuade her not to call in the police to find Céleste.

"If there's no answer from the cottage," she said to herself, "I'll stay here till he's caught. I want to see him handcuffed. I want to see him taken away. I want him to know that I'm watching."

She had to form the words with her lips several times to give them weight, for her brain was still fighting her instinct.

"They'll guillotine him," she said out loud, heedless of the jostling crowd. Some dark sense of horror forced her to imagine the diagonal blade falling on Blair's neck, his head falling into the basket, and the executioner picking it up by the ears and calling out, "In the name of the people of France, justice is done."

At that moment she passed by the stall of a Mozambite butcher and there, on the wooden block, was a sheep's head, with the wool singed off and the scorched skull grinning, the eyes staring blindly.

An awful tremor ran through her. "It can't be true," she whispered.

Her need to get to the phone became overpowering. She pushed forward fiercely, only vaguely aware of growls of anger from the peasants she shouldered.

Somewhere among all these people, or inside one of these white buildings, Blair might be in hiding. He and Céleste.

Mari looked around, taking in her surroundings for the first time. A group of half-naked little urchins were squealing excitedly, trying to raise laughs from the older Arabs by insulting Mari in their slurred dialect. Nearly all their heads were scored with ringworm. She scattered the children by dropping coins on the ground, and they dived for them like animals.

As she came nearer to the roadblock, she began to notice the open hands, painted in red and blue, which marked many of the house doors as a talisman against the evil eye. Several times the throng jammed her momentarily against the bulging cakelike windows. She tried to peer into the interiors, in a wild fancy that she might see Blair.

Strung across some of the side streets were fluttering lines of grubby pennants, a sign of market day, and she became aware that most of them were of green or white, placed

alternately—the nearest the Arabs could achieve to the forbidden flag of the independence movement.

Abruptly, Mari found herself free of the crowd. She was
in the shadow of the arched gateway, beneath which the
police had erected a trestle. There were only three flics—all
rookies by the look of them—and they were keeping back
the surging mob by swinging their long bayonet-tipped
rifles at anybody who came too close. They were stopping
all traffic, not allowing anyone to leave, and only letting in
a trickle of Arabs, examining each one carefully.

"Officer," said Mari, to one of them, "I must get to a
phone."

She saw the young man's eyes examining her and his tone
was respectful: "I am sorry you are delayed but bandits are
trapped inside the town. We await the arrival of the troops
to catch them."

"Bandits?"

"Yes, one of them is the American, Hansen, who killed a
Security Brigade man." She sensed his relief at talking to a
friendly compatriot, amid the hostile murmur of the alien
mob.

"But you'll never catch them! There must be thousands
of people in town today."

The young policeman waved his bayonet warningly at the
swaying crowd and said, "It is not always necessary to
search."

"You mean?"

"We have our informers," he said, and tried to look knowing.

Chapter Twenty-Eight

A BRAYING NOISE filtered down into the rancid basement. George sprang up onto the sacks of dried beans that
lay below one of the window slits, and cocked his head,
listening intently. His eager face was made golden by a thin
pencil of light, which pointed sharply down through the
glass.

Hansen and Céleste froze into immobility, so as not to
make a sound.

"It's a police loud-speaker," George announced. "It's saying something about a reward."

"Probably for us," said Hansen.

"*Sidi*, let's leave here," Céleste burst out. "I feel trapped. Your friend must have been gone at least an hour."

"No, he'll save us, if anybody can. He's been a leader of our movement in this city for years. We can trust him. It'll take him some time to arrange a place for each of us to hide."

"I won't do it!" cried Céleste. "I refuse to be parted from you!" She said this so often that neither of the men made any comment.

The air was so close that both the men had thrown off the Arab clothes that the *moutcha*, the store owner, had given them for disguise, but they had laid them out carefully, on sacks of powdered chilies and crushed dates, ready to fling on at a moment's notice. Neither of the men had shaved, and their faces were half mooned with stubble, and laced by dark scabs from cuts caused by the broken windshield of the truck.

From the ceiling hung sugar loaves in blue paper, and strings of onions, and on the floor were great jars of muddy fluid in which chick-peas were soaking. Among the smells, Hansen could pick out the rancidity of stale olive oil, the creeping odor of mice, and, impregnating the whole space, the black stench of rotting meat. A few bluebottle flies buzzed torpidly, and beetles scuttered with a high squeaking noise.

The braying of the police loud-speaker could be heard again. This time it was more clear; it was coming nearer. Hansen could not make out the French-accented Arabic, which was distorted by the amplifier, but George caught the sense of the words. "Yes, they're offering a reward for us," he said, "and there's something about anybody sheltering us being arrested."

The noise came once more, still more clearly. The loud-speaker had a mechanical ferocity about it. They all tensed, listening.

"They have our names!" George exclaimed. "I distinctly heard that time. They're giving our descriptions."

Céleste scrambled up onto the sacks, beside George. She put her hand on his arm, nervously, as he listened.

A key grated in the lock and the door swung open. They all tautened. The storekeeper appeared and came down the steps toward them, at a maddeningly sedate pace.

"Keteer felous," he grinned. His black-stumped teeth made his mouth look cavernous in the gloom. "You are worth much money. The police pigs are offering half a million francs for you, dead or alive."

Hansen swore. "That's fifteen hundred bucks!"

"And they offer it merely for information leading to your capture." The Arab reached the first of the lances of light, and his face was suddenly given a velvety patina like polished mahogany. "Not only that, anybody found sheltering you will be arrested."

Hansen felt a stab of fear that the *moutcha* might betray them. The Arab seemed to sense this, for he smiled, his teeth catching the amber glare like rows of wet cigar stubs. "You think too much of your money, you Americans," he said. "You are safe with me."

"*'Anam, Allah 'alaik,*" said Hansen, "Allah reward you. I don't want you to risk your neck for me. If I'm caught here you'll be sent to prison."

"*Inch'Allah,* if God wills it. Our greatest danger is from the renegade Arabs. Yes, we have them even in Djouma. They are sure to learn something soon, and then it will reach the ears of their French masters."

"We must get out of here," said Hansen.

"It is all arranged," said the Arab. "Each of you will be sheltered by a member of our movement. You," he said, looking at Céleste, "will hide in the women's quarters—"

"Oh, no, please not," said Céleste, her face screwed up in alarm. "We don't want to be parted."

She looked frantically at George for support, but he said quietly, "You must, *sidi,* that will be safest for you."

"Safe? Without you? No, I won't."

The *moutcha* cut in sharply: "If you stay together the chances of being caught are far greater."

"We'll risk that," said Céleste. She was smiling as she gazed at George, trying to fill him with her own resolve.

"No—" he began.

"*Sidi,*" she said. "There is going to be fighting—anything may happen. Whatever happens, let it be to both of us."

George swallowed nervously. "Yes," he said after a pause. "We'll stay together."

"You don't seem very sure," said Céleste sharply.

The thought flashed in her mind, "Can it be that he's scared?" She tried to face up to this thought. "After all," she told herself, "he's no soldier, no hero, he's always told me that himself. But surely he'd want to be with me, see this through together?"

She spoke up firmly, to steel George's resolution. "We'll take our chance together outside," she announced. "We'll try to slip out of town together while there's still a chance."

The storekeeper shook his head. "The whole town is tightly cordoned by troops."

"He's right," said George, his eyes still on Céleste. "We must stay in town."

"Together," she added.

The *moutcha* shrugged impatiently. "So be it," he said. "The only place you can go together is to the Reguibat."

"The thieves' quarter!" exclaimed George, looking alarmed. "We'll get our throats cut!" He tried to make a joke of it. "Even worse, we'll smell so bad we won't be able to go near each other for weeks."

"And I?" asked Hansen. "Where shall I go?"

The *moutcha* looked at him steadily. "I shall be honored to have you beneath my roof."

"You mean—nobody else will take me? It's too dangerous for them?"

"Come to the Reguibat with us," cut in George eagerly. Too eagerly, thought Céleste. Did he feel safer with Hansen around? Again the thought crossed her mind that George was afraid.

"No," said the *moutcha*. "Three of you would be too many. I have a better idea." He made a motion with his hand from a position George and Céleste could not see, indicating he wanted to talk to Hansen alone. "First of all," the *moutcha* went on, "I will show you two to the Reguibat. There's no time to lose."

He went up the steps and opened the door, nodding his head for George and Céleste to follow him. Céleste clutched George's arm, in a moment of fright, and the contact seemed to strengthen her. They shook hands with Hansen, and not a word needed to be spoken.

When they had gone, Hansen slumped down onto the sacks and waited. Hunger pains began to rumble round inside him, and he felt around among the sacks till he found one filled with dates. He took a handful. The close heat made the cuts in his face prickle with sweat, and his fingers became clammy from the sticky fruit and the moisture of his hands.

He was still chewing when the door opened again and the *moutcha* appeared.

"I owe you for these dates," said Hansen. "Add it to the half-million francs I owe you for not grabbing that reward they're offering. I shan't forget this. If I ever get out alive—"

The Arab made a deprecating gesture. "I am proud to shelter a man who has killed a dog of the Security Brigade," he said. "My only son was bastinadoed by the Brigade." His tone grew brisk. "There is much for us to do—the other two are best out of the way. They'd be dangerous. They have too much to live for. Love mixes badly with war. You know how to use dynamite?"

Hansen nodded. "You have some?"

"Plenty." The cigar-stub teeth showed in a brief smile. "This is good dynamite—stolen from your American Army dumps."

"What's your plan?"

"We wait until sunset, when the French will sound curfew for the Arabs to stay indoors. Then when most of the troops are in the streets and our people have the shelter of the houses, we trap the French inside the town by blowing up the main gates. We dynamite those tanks at the gateway. We blow up their other tanks and trucks. We shoot down the French. They'll have no place to hide."

"Sounds possible. Where is the dynamite now?"

"Most of the sticks are already in place to blow up the tank roadblock at the main gate. We have put dynamite in the sentry's staircase in the main gate. We need more dynamite there—and we need somebody reliable to do the dynamiting." He looked at Hansen expectantly. "Everything depends on us being able to blow up those tanks at the roadblock. We'll have picked men waiting to cover that gateway so that none of the French can get out alive. And it's through that gateway that you can escape with your friends."

"I'll help you," said Hansen. "What do you want me to do?"

The *moutcha* began pulling the sacks to one side. "Here's the rest of the dynamite," he said. "We'd better take this to our men at the main gate now. They're waiting. We must make sure to blow up those tanks, or they'll mow us down with their machine guns."

The booming note of the police loud-speaker outside was

now so loud that Hansen could feel its vibrations in the soles of his feet. It sent a current of resolve into him, and he went forward to help lift the dynamite.

Mari managed to drag her eyes away from the old-fashioned stand phone, but it remained in her retina—the circular instruction disc greasy from many fingers that had laboriously traced out its Arabic words. She could still hear it giving out that terrible ringing sound in the earpieces. "No answer," the operator had cut in to say, but still Mari held on, gripping the instrument so hard that when at length she did flop the receiver back on the hook her fingers were cramped tight.

The air seemed to be growing more fetid. Mari feared that she was about to faint, so she sank down into a wicker chair. Her whole being was concentrated on trying to cope with the shock. *Blair had been cheating her all the time— cheating her with her own daughter.*

Her faculties seemed to have been made raw and sensitive; she could detect an odor of urine and bedding from the crowded sleeping quarters of the *fonduq,* and she was acutely aware of flies that buzzed; a mangy mongrel dog rubbing itself against her chair.

The barefooted proprietor came and bent over her. "Is there anything else madame wishes?" he asked. She realized that he wanted his *baksheesh,* and she fumbled irritably for a coin. Then she saw Michel. The glazed peak of his cap caught a blur or radiance in the light of the lobby as he shouldered his way to her. His small wedge of a face was eager with sensation.

A withered old Arab was following Michel. He was toothless, with a skin like long-stored apples, and his filmy eyes were staring around in bewilderment. Mari recognized him as the caretaker of her cottage.

"Madame!" said Michel. "The caretaker saw Mam'selle Céleste arrive at the cottage on Wednesday morning. She was with an Arab, a young man of not more than twenty!"

"An Arab? He's sure?" Suspense suffocated Mari. "You're sure?" she repeated in Arabic to the old man, but he spread out his hands to indicate that he could not understand her.

"He speaks the mountain dialect," said Michel. "I've got the story out of him. Mam'selle Céleste and the youth kept calling each other '*sidi*' and they were very affectionate to each other. He said they made shameless, public caresses, like the roumi. They gave him money to go home for the night, while they stayed at the cottage."

"How does he know the young man was an Arab?"

"He says the youth spoke the pure tongue of the Mahrgreb."

"How tall was the young man?" In her impatience, Mari raised her hand high in the air, to Blair's height, to mime her question, and looked interrogatively at the caretaker.

The old man shook his head and held up his own gnarled, black-nailed hand till it was only a little higher than Mari's head.

That's much shorter than Blair. The relief that burst in Mari was so overwhelming that it swept everything else from her mind and senses. She stood there for a long moment, letting it wash through her. *Blair wasn't at the cottage with Céleste, it was somebody else.*

Her tumult of relief was dashed by remembrance that Blair was in danger. She turned to Michel and ordered, "Ask him if he knows where Blair Hansen is."

Michel put his lips to the old man's ear and whispered, but the Arab only shook his head.

"He wouldn't tell, even if he knew, madame," said Michel. "These Arabs all stick together."

While Michel was translating for her, Mari had an idea. She opened her handbag with trembling fingers and pulled out a roll of bills. "Tell him I'll double the police reward," she said. "Say I'll give him a million francs if he'll tell me how I can find Blair Hansen."

Michel whispered again, and the eyes of the caretaker rested on Mari dubiously. His slack old lips mumbled a reply.

"He says he doesn't know," Michel translated, "but the hunted men will not be taken alive. All the Arabs will fight to shield them, for one of the fugitives is a leader in the independence movement."

"A rebel!" Mari burst out. "He must be the Arab Céleste was with at the cottage." Her mind jolted away from this onto the main terror. "Blair Hansen—why is he with an Arab rebel? What has happened?"

Michel spoke to the old man, who mumbled a reply. "He says he only knows there is going to be fighting," Michel reported. "The Arabs are getting out their hidden arms. There will be rioting and killing. Many of the older people, and the women and children, are being sent out of town to safety."

Fear spurred the impatience that was mounting in Mari. She had a wild impulse to rush into the streets and call out for Blair.

A swathe of noise cut into the lobby; the police loud-speaker was moving into the main square outside. The words were beating out remorselessly: "Wanted for manslaughter —Blair Hansen, aged thirty-five, American, two meters tall, dark hair *en brosse*, narrow face, shoulder bandaged and wound on back of head. Also wanted, charged with conspiracy against the Republic, Djoj Warouk, an Arab aged twenty-one, slender build—"

The words whipped her mind into a crescendo of fear, in which the old man's words were the peak: *They'll never be taken alive—there's going to be fighting.*

"I must stop them!" she burst out.

Michel's small face puckered in surprise. "But how, madame?"

"I'll find some way. I must. Let's go outside." She edged her way out into the heavy weight of sunlight that lay on the main square. The crowd was thicker than ever, surging to and fro, a great white ferment coming to the boil. There was a continuous bubble of mob cries, passed from mouth to mouth, angry sounds that gave the menace form and substance. Mari sensed that the Arabs were working themselves up into one of their blind explosions of fury. If they flared up nothing would stop them, not even machine guns or tanks; they would use their knives and rifles fanatically till they were all wiped out. It would be another massacre like Sétif.

Most of the dark faces, set in the white burnooses, were turned toward the center of the square, where the latest troops to arrive were climbing down from their trucks.

Mari shouldered her way toward the soldiers, with some half-formed idea of speaking to the officer in charge. As she passed through the crowd, its hostility found a target in her. Many of the Arabs mouthed the involved Arab obscenities, and several spat at her. She was too absorbed to be aware of anything but her urgency.

She came close enough to the troops to see their red faces

and smell their sharp odor of sweat. Some of them wore handkerchiefs stuck in the back of their kepis, in Foreign Legion style, to shield their necks from the sun. The young men wore tight expressions, to conceal their awareness of the crowd's hate. They were holding their guns with both hands, their fingers ready to touch the triggers. The long bayonets struck exclamation marks of fire in the sunlight.

Several whippet tanks lumbered into the square, caked with dust. The heat rose from the metal of the tanks in thick shudders of air. The drivers, naked to the waist, wore sweat cloths round their necks. The long guns reared out of the tanks in a silent threat.

Mari fought down an hysterical desire to scream. She had to do something quickly. If the shooting started the Arabs would be wiped out—and Blair with them, too. He mustn't try to fight, he mustn't resist. He must let himself be captured. How could she find him?

She stood on tiptoe, looking round frantically for an officer. She had no idea what she would say to him. All she knew was there must be no fighting.

The ugly mood of the Arabs became more pronounced when the loud-speaker truck moved toward the medina, for as its booming died away, the pattern of hostile crowd-noise became more sharp, in contrast, on the motionless air.

"Oh, God in Heaven," she thought, "this is all my fault. I should never have persuaded Blair to escape. I might have got him off. I'd have spent every franc I have, getting the best lawyers from Paris. Blair killed the Security man accidentally. Perhaps they'd have sent him to prison only for a little while. Prison, that's better than dying. They'll kill him if he resists. Oh, if only I could get to him."

The noise of the loud-speaker started again, booming and reverberating. The sound was trapped soggily by the baked walls.

Chapter Twenty-Nine

THE ARABS TRAPPED inside the town were packed against the main gateway so tightly that their hoods made one continuous flow of white. A brimming quiet slowly began to lap outward from the French roadblock under the archway, till a menacing stillness filled the mob.

Hansen could hear only a few muttered words—whispered rumors that one of Messali's chieftains had arrived in town, that the fugitives had already escaped, that the French were bringing more troops.

Here and there, Hansen would catch glimpses of Arabs pulling out the forbidden guns from under their robes, and making gestures of bravado. The man next to Hansen was fingering an old-fashioned Springfield rifle, which still carried the red-painted mark to show it was obsolete U.S. equipment. Another Arab was flicking his thumbnail on the blade of a *khusa*, a double-edged knife.

Hansen sensed that only the smallest spark was needed to make the Arab fury blaze up out of control. One frenzied shout of "*Y' Allah!*", one rifleshot at a French soldier, and the riot would be touched off.

Hansen whispered to the *moutcha*, who stood close beside him: "Think the crowd can wait? They seem itchy on the trigger."

"They have my orders. They all know that sunset is the time."

Hansen glanced up at the sun. It was almost directly overhead. At least seven hours to go. He felt a longing for it to be over.

Two rows of soldiers were keeping open a narrow lane through the crowd for those Arabs trying to get through the roadblock. A file of elderly people, and women and children, were shuffling in two lines between the soldiers, waiting to be screened by the Security Brigade men. Each Arab's appearance was being checked against a number of printed photographs, which the Security Brigade men had posted on little hand boards. Behind the group were three heavy tanks, their black oily snouts glistening in the sun. The Brigade men were using the tracks of one tank as a desk, spreading out documents and photographs on it.

Hansen's back was aching from the strain of stooping to conceal his height. He was so hot, in the stifling robes, that every few seconds a metronome of dizziness flicked across his consciousness. Sweat was prickling into his shoulder wound.

He realized he would have to sit down somewhere in shade, or else he'd pass out. He made a tentative effort to edge out

of the packed mass, but the press of the crowd was so
heavy that he gave up.

The metallic bray of the loud-speaker crackled over the
heads of the crowd: "All persons not resident in Djouma are
advised to leave." The voice kept repeating it.

Hansen realized that the French were trying to empty the
town as much as possible before nightfall; then the troops
would impose a curfew, make everybody go indoors and stay
there while a house-to-house search was made. This was a
well-rehearsed exercise; those heavy machine guns and the
tanks would open fire at the first sign of trouble from the
Arabs.

If only the Arabs would wait till sundown, before they
blew their top, then there'd be a better chance for him to
escape under cover of the fighting. And leave the kids here?
The French would turn the town inside out and George and
Céleste would be arrested for the killing of the policeman.

The mob had grown so silent, in its pent-up exasperation,
that the voices of the troops and the Brigade men could be
heard clearly.

Hansen felt the desire for action coiling inside him. Seven
whole hours of this still to go. He looked at the three heavy
tanks that formed the roadblock under the great archway.
He imagined those tons of steel lifted up in a great white explosion. These Fascist bastards had stuck their noses in too
far this time. The Arabs would have the last laugh—something to balance against the thousands of Arabs massacred
by the French at Kabylie.

When that dynamite went off it would trap the French
inside the town and destroy their main weapons—the tanks.
A few more hours, and he would be climbing to freedom
over the rubble of this gateway.

Dizziness struck at him again. "I'd better get back," he
whispered to the storekeeper. "My wound is troubling me."

"Yes, let us return to the store."

The two men turned and leaned their weight against the
Arabs behind, to edge their way out. The crowd slowly
made way as they recognized their leader, the *moutcha*.

The hazy heat seemed to have entered into Hansen's head.
His thoughts were as tremulous and unsubstantial as the
wavering eddies of air. He thought of water running over
his dry tongue; he imagined lying down somewhere cool, and
straightening out his cramped frame; he heard Mari say

to him pleadingly once more, "We mustn't be parted again!"

Her voice seemed to be echoing round inside his skull, each reverberation breaking off into smaller diminuendos.

"You'll be killed!" she was saying. "Please don't risk your life."

He shook his head, to clear the fog of fatigue and strain, but the voice of Mari kept on, as if from far away.

Hansen took a grip on himself. He mustn't pass out, or he'd be finished. He looked round for the nearest shade and then he heard Mari's voice again: "The only thing that matters is for us to be together—somewhere, somehow. We can do it, if you'll only listen to me."

Incredulity rose up in him, and then he realized the truth.

Mari was speaking over the police loud-speaker.

He stood still for several moments, trying to focus his mind on the great fact.

She was here, she was right here in this town.

He found himself forming the words with his lips. "She's here."

When her voice sounded again he turned automatically in the direction from which it came. He went blindly toward her, thrusting through the crowd, trying to figure out where the loud-speaker was situated. The voice was hollow and muzzy from the amplifier, but it was Mari, he was sure of that. Her words were tumbling into each other in her urgency: "If you give yourself up," she was saying, "and avoid bloodshed, then we can be together after a little while. We've waited so long, we can wait a little longer."

"Oh, Christ, she's crazy," he thought. "She wants me to go to jail for five years, maybe more. An Algerian jail. If ever I got out of there alive, I'd be lucky."

But she was here, maybe he could get to her. She might be able to hide him someplace, perhaps in her car.

He turned to the *moutcha*. "I'll meet you back in the store," he said. "I know that woman who's speaking."

"Be careful," said the Arab. "It may be a trap. Are you sure she's a friend?"

"I'm sure. She may have a plan. I'll be at the store soon."

Hansen broke clear of the crowd and stumbled up the street toward Mari's voice, which slowly was growing clearer.

"It was all my fault," she was saying. "I should never have let you go. We should have stayed and fought the case in the courts."

Hansen saw the long shadow of the minaret across the road, and when he came to it he saw a police truck, stationary in the broad square in front of the mosque.

A crowd of Arabs was standing sullenly round the vehicle, staring up at a woman who stood at the microphone. Hansen knew immediately she was Mari.

He moved toward the truck, screwing up his eyes against the glare, to get her into focus. Her voice was uneven in pitch, as if she were on the brink of breaking down.

Hansen edged closer to the squad of troops that kept a space cleared round the truck. He saw that Mari's dress was sticking to her with the heat, her shining black hair was wisping over her cheeks, and her lips were dry and strained.

Hansen heard Mari's voice echoing back at him from the sun-baked walls: "If you're smart we can still have wonderful years together. Think of that."

Was she crazy? Did she really think he would meekly give himself up? Spend years in a stinking Algerian jail?

Even the tones of Mari's voice seemed peculiar; they were vitiated, bloodless. Hansen tried to focus his gaze on her more distinctly, but the light seemed to be a shimmering curtain between them.

She didn't really want him to give himself up. This must be her way of letting him know she was there.

That was it, she had a plan. Maybe she had worked out a means to get him away.

"Watch out," she was saying. "Watch out for me as well as yourself."

He kept listening to her, and after a while she repeated, "Watch out for me, as well as yourself."

That was odd. Why did she say that? Why watch out for *her?*

When Mari had finished an Army officer helped her down from the truck, holding onto her for a bit longer than was necessary. Hansen moved closer, but the press of the crowd was too much for him to see her clearly.

He heard her voice, but he could not make out the words. Then he saw the officer escorting her toward the *fonduq,* the Arab inn. Mari was walking slump shouldered, as if weary.

A few curious Arabs were trailing behind her. Hansen joined them.

Why did she want him to watch out for her? Was she going to make a sign, or leave a message?

Abruptly, the realization slid into his mind, as he stared over the shoulders of the Arabs in front of him. Anybody who followed her was being watched. She wanted to warn him of that. The French guessed that he would try to make contact with her. They had men watching. They hoped to catch him by using her as their bait.

Chapter Thirty

HANSEN MOVED AWAY diagonally from Mari, but kept her in view all the time. His trained eye soon picked out the men who were shadowing her. There were two of them, both dressed as Arabs. When Mari entered the inn they ranged themselves casually in the doorway, in such a position that one of them could watch everybody who was approaching from outside, while the other kept the interior under observation.

How could he get in to her? Hansen became aware that most of his weariness had gone. Once more he was keyed by tension. He looked carefully for several minutes to see whether there were any other watchers, and decided that the two in the doorway were the only ones. He should be able to handle them.

He crossed the square, keeping his face well hidden, and his frame stooped. He shuffled past the two men in the doorway. Hansen went across the crowded foyer, forcing himself not to look back to see whether the two men were following him. He saw no sign of the officer or Mari and guessed that the Frenchman had insisted on escorting her to her room.

Hansen mounted the greasy-railed stairway to the landing, which was filthy and ill lit. There was no other floor; she must be somewhere along here. Hansen strode along the corridor and realized that it extended round the central courtyard. As he came to the first corner he heard the officer's voice from somewhere round the bend. "Very well, madame, but that is the latest permissible time. You must leave the town by then."

There was the faint sound of her voice, as if it were on the other side of a door, and then the officer's voice came again. "You will be here if we require you again, madame?"

Hansen took a swift glance round the corner and saw the officer touching his cap to a door that was closing. The Frenchman's steps sounded along the landing, and Hansen turned back. The officer overtook him and hurried toward the stairs. Hansen waited till he had gone and then went to Mari's door and knocked.

"Who's there?" came her voice.

"Me. Open up. Hurry," he said softly.

As he spoke he caught a motion out of the corner of his eye. Somebody was peering round the bend in the corridor. Two white-robed figures came into view. They looked like the couple who had been shadowing Mari. They must have decided to investigate him.

The knob twitched feverishly and the door was flung open. Hansen had a split-second impression of Mari standing in the entrance and then the two men were running toward him.

The peril poised Hansen's nerves. His thoughts raced fast and clear. Probably these were Brigade men, so they wouldn't have reported their suspicions to the Army officer; the Brigade and the Army hated each others' guts.

Hansen slipped into the room a few inches ahead of his pursuers. One of them had a revolver but before he could level it Hansen hit it away, then lunged up with both hands at the men's heads and crashed them together. Both men sagged down. Hansen caught hold of one and smashed his fist into his face, then grasped the other by the hair and slammed his head with all his might on the floor. The two men collapsed into stillness. Hansen dragged the bodies clear of the door and Mari slammed it shut.

Hansen pulled open the men's robes and verified from the uniforms beneath that they were Brigade men. He took their revolvers, and Mari helped him gag the Frenchmen with their hoods and strap their hands behind them.

"Must hide them," Hansen gasped. "If that officer comes back—"

He looked around. There was a battered old wardrobe over by the narrow-slitted window. He dragged each of the Brigade men over to it in turn, and thrust their unconscious bodies into it. Not till then did the trembling exhaustion hit Hansen again. Waves of dizziness sucked at his brain. He held onto the door of the wardrobe. He felt Mari against him, holding him to her naked breast. An odd disconnected thought shot into the fog of his mind. "She must have pulled her dress off as soon as the officer left her."

The heat of her skin came through to him. She made a small moaning sound and tightened her grasp of him and her nails dug deep into his flesh.

Her black mass of hair was loose over her face. She threw back her head to look up at him and her lips were moving tremulously, trying to find words. He lifted up her chin, and their mouths met, and her tongue was searching against his. He could feel the sweat on her bare back and the thrust of her breasts.

A knock came at the door.

Hansen looked round wildly. For one moment he thought of hiding in the wardrobe where the two Brigade men were tied, but he realized that this was the first place any searcher would look. Hansen picked up the revolver, and motioned Mari to ask who was there. Her voice contorted with fear as she called out, "Who is it?"

"Michel, madame. You told me to report."

"Oh, I don't need you, Michel. Come back at five. Wait a second." She broke off as Hansen gesticulated and she leaned nearer to hear his whisper.

"Tell him to have the car ready, about fifty yards outside the main gate," said Hansen, close against her ear. "Tell him to wait there without fail. If they try to move him away, he's to pretend there's something wrong with the car. Say that you'll pick him up there about sunset."

Mari repeated this to Michel, screwing up her face in curiosity as she did so.

"Very good, madame." The chauffeur's steps moved away along the landing.

Mari and Hansen went into each other's arms. She writhed herself against him and her lips plucked at his skin, but when she looked up at him and noticed his cut and scabbed face she pulled him over to the bed and made him lie down.

Hansen let himself go limp. The pillows smelled of decay, and the air was stale and hot. He lay still, making a luxury of feeling his breathing resume its normal rhythm. He half-closed his eyes as Mari fussed over him. She fetched eau de Cologne from her handbag and bathed his forehead, then loosened his clothing.

"We must get out of here," he breathed, "before those two Brigade guys are missed."

"There's no place we can go. Anyway, you must rest first."
She bent down and brushed her lips against his cheek.
"What's happened? Where were you? What are you going
to do?"

She held her ear close to his lips while she questioned him.
Instinctively, they spoke in whispers, in case anyone were
listening outside.

When he had finished explaining what had happened he
said, "Now let's go. We must hurry."

"I don't have to leave till five. They say I must be out of
town by then."

"Yes. There's going to be fighting. You must clear
out."

"Five o'clock. That's four whole hours. Darling, I want
you for those four hours."

"God, you must be crazy." What was the matter with her?
She could never get enough of it. This was no time for hitting the sack. Still, he'd better play along with her, or she'd
create a scene.

"This may be all we have left," she whispered. "Suppose
we don't get through?"

"We will. Better go to the car. I'll meet you there at
sunset."

"But how? You'll never manage to get through."

"Yes, I will. Trust me. You'd better go now, in case they
come for you again. Be ready in the car, have the engine
running—"

"Oh *chéri*, I can't leave yet."

Her hair was against his face, her lips moving warm and
restless over his skin, and he felt her fingers impatient with
the robes that encumbered him. Hansen opened his eyes and
saw her crouched above him. In this strange striped light,
with her great eyes catching one of the yellow bars from the
sun, she looked like a caged animal, a beautiful feline,
adapting her caressing body to his, rhythmic with a need
that met his, and melting the danger and the tension with
the power of her urgency. Hansen felt himself shuddering
with the tumult of climax, and then he had to fight against
letting himself sink into spent nothingness. But the release
was too complete.

His next awareness was that he had come out of oblivion.
Then came a sound that cut into the stupor of his mind. He
raised himself on one elbow, and Mari tried to push him

back. "It's only the crowd shouting outside," she said. But his instincts were alert to threatened danger.

Hansen sprang up and went over to the window. As soon as he looked through the slats of the blind he knew, by the lengthened shadows outside, that noon was now well past. The sun was a molten ball edging down toward the tip of the mosque's minaret. Down in the square was a churning tide of white and brown—the close-pressed bodies of the crowd. A low growling noise of menace rose from the people, and while he stared he saw the reason. Over by the mosque the pattern of the crowd ended in a crude semicircle, formed by soldiers, and in the cleared space were the khaki shapes of troops gathered round the doorway.

"They're going in!" said Hansen. "The troops are going in the mosque. This will start the riot!" He wheeled round to Mari. "I've got to go," he said. "This will bust up our plan."

"No, don't go!"

He picked up the two revolvers of the Brigade men, and gave her one. "You may need this," he said. He thrust the other in his pocket, and pulled his robes about him.

"You mustn't go!" she cried, holding the gun gingerly.

"Do as I say," he said curtly. "It's the only way we'll get out alive. They may come here any moment. Be waiting in the car at sunset, as I said. I hope to have Céleste with me—"

"Don't risk your life for her! She got herself into this. Let her damned Arabs get her out!"

Hansen looked at her silently. The orange slits of light through the blinds struck lateral gleams in her eyes, and along the barrel of the revolver, and he could see the rapid breathing that moved her naked torso.

They both started as a peremptory knocking came at the door. "Open! At once!" came a strident order. The murmurs of other voices could be heard outside the door, and there were several clunks like rifle butts coming to rest.

Mari made a croaking noise of terror. "The window!" she gasped. "Get out of the window!"

Hansen gestured frantically for her to be quiet.

"Yes, he's in there!" came the voice behind the door, then a shout, "Open up!"

Hansen dashed to the window and ripped down the blind with a savage pull. The window was narrow and glassless, covered only by some cracked screening. He jabbed at it with his elbow and scrambled up onto the sill, and as he did so he heard the men outside smashing at the door. Hansen squeezed himself sideways in the narrow space, which was scarcely eighteen inches across. He got his head through and looked down. The ground was about fifteen feet below. The jagged edges of the screening were tearing at him. He tried to jerk himself free, and looked back frantically into the room.

The door began to give. One panel broke and a rifle butt slithered through. Mari was standing as if petrified. The light poured through the blindless window, bathing her starkly in brightness. She raised the revolver and pointed it at the door.

"Stand out of the way!" yelled Hansen. "You'll get hurt!"

He heaved himself against the pull of the torn wires and felt them give. He got through just as the door opened.

Uniforms of Brigade men darkened the other side of the room. Hansen twisted himself round to prepare for the fall, and as he did so he saw the bright stab of Mari's gun. It roared again. He tried to claw himself back, but he was already slithering out. Just as he began to fall, he saw the flashes of the Brigade men's guns. Mari's white body suddenly flowered into red—bright wide petals of horrible red —and then a pain slammed agony into his shoulder.

Hansen felt himself falling, and he had a vague impression of white-robed bodies rushing up to meet him, and then there was darkness.

Hansen awoke with the feeling that he was caught in some machine that was ruthlessly hitting him with pistons. Between each thump of agony he saw the *moutcha's* face bending close to him.

"You are safe, my son," he said.

The Arab's face came more clearly into focus, and looking beyond him Hansen was able to see that he was back once more in the basement of the store.

The pain was shut off by a memory that hit him harder; he relived the sight of Mari's body splattered into redness. He knew he should be full of rage, but his mind seemed to be numb. He found himself struggling up, but the gentle hands of the Arab restrained him. "You must rest," said the *moutcha*. "You are badly wounded."

Hansen tried to find words, but they would not come. His mind was ripped by the memory of Mari's body being burst by the bullets.

The Arab explained what had happened. "They fired at you when you fell. Our men began firing back. There was much shooting, but we got you into an alley and along to here. Then the French loud-speaker told the troops to fall back into riot positions. We managed to get our men off the streets before the French could mow down many of them. Both your young friends are safe. They are waiting near the gateway ready for the explosions. Then you can escape also. We start at sunset."

Hansen looked up at the window light, which now was nearly horizontal, and pinkish in color. Must be almost sunset now.

"I must leave you," said the *moutcha*. "I am going to the main gate to take charge."

"You? No, that's my job," said Hansen. He tried to move but the pain in his right arm slammed at him again. He managed to say, between his teeth, "I'm going with you."

"Impossible. Your arm is shattered. You must stay here."

Hansen forced himself up onto his elbow and looked at his right arm. Somebody had ripped off the sleeve and tried to set the broken bone with a rough splint, but the dressings and the splint were matted with dried blood, through which fresh blood was welling. The pain slammed again, then again. There was room, in his frenzy of pain, for only one thought: Mari's dead. I must get the bastards who did it.

"I'm going with you," he said again. "I'm going to blow up those tanks."

Chapter Thirty-One

THE TIP OF THE MINARET still held a glowing driblet from the sunken sun, but the rest of the town was softened by the haze of evening. The serrated outline of the buildings was merging into the backdrop of the mountains, and the first stars were winking in the east.

Michel closed the hood of the limousine. Whenever troops had passed by on their way into town, he had pretended to be doing repairs. Now he was alone. A stifling quiet seemed to have been dropped over the earth.

He strained his ears. After several moments he heard some orders barked near the gateway, and in the stillness the sound was a comfort, holding back the menace of silence. A bugle blast sounded abruptly, and Michel jumped. The loud-speaker began to blare inside the town. A searchlight was turned on, and the blue-white glare accented the keyhole shape of the main gateway.

"The curfew!" he thought. "The French are going to start the roundup now. God, the Father, where is madame? Why doesn't she come?"

She will get herself killed. Me too. She doesn't care. This *grande passion* of hers will get us all killed. This Hansen has brought nothing but trouble from the start. Madame takes it for granted that I'll risk my neck for him.

The quiet grew more intense, as if the night itself were holding its breath.

"Why have the soldiers left me alone?" thought Michel. "They know this is Madame Lander's limousine. They know that she and the American are lovers. They know she's come here to find him. This is the most likely place to find him. *They know that, too.*"

Panic hit Michel. A wild urge to get away filled him. He started the engine of the car. Immediately, out of the corner of his eye, he saw the kepi of a French soldier appear over the balustrade of a nearby house, then another kepi to the left. Something caught a glint of light—a bayonet.

So this was a trap! He was caught! Michel sobbed in terror. The soldiers were waiting in ambush to catch madame and Hansen when they came here. They would all be killed.

His thoughts poised between escape and duty. If he drove off now, he told himself, he would be safe—unless they fired at him, thinking he was going off to a rendezvous with madame.

Fright closed his mind to everything but one obvious fact—he must get away from the limousine. That was the center of the trap. Michel cut the engine and climbed out. He had no idea of where to go, except to get as far away from the car as possible. His teeth clamped together in terror. He stumbled along the darkening road, not daring to look back, expecting every second to hear a command to halt.

Some rationalization of his cowardice made him walk

toward the main portal of the town, in a hazy notion that
he might meet madame, that he would not be deserting her
if he went in the direction from which she would probably
come.

The Brigade lieutenant made a gesture ordering silence
and motioned his men to follow Michel. The squad slipped
quietly in pursuit from shadow to shadow on rubber-heeled
boots. Their dark-blue uniforms merged into the gathering
darkness.

As the soldiers moved in pursuit of the chauffeur, other
shapes, lighter figures, emerged from concealment and glided
after the soldiers. They were in white, the white robes of
Arabs. Every now and then, as they darted across a place
where the shadows did not reach, there came a glint from
daggers, or from the gleaming long barrels of old-fashioned
rifles.

The Arabs increased their pace to keep in sight of the
soldiers, for the squad was closing in on Michel. The lieutenant, who was in the lead, broke into a trot as Michel
came to the great arched gateway of the town. The lieutenant
cocked his revolver suspiciously. In that instant a great in-
verted cone of light clawed up into the sky. The flaming
blast hurled back the lieutenant and most of his men. The
rest were flung flat by the shock wave.

Behind them, the Arabs were deafened and blinded by the
explosion. They shielded their heads with their arms. When
their faculties returned they stared in awe. The gate was
gone.

The searchlight was muffled by an ugly cloud of gray and
black which billowed upwards from what had been the great
gateway.

There came a rattle of machine guns and rifle shots and a
wild chorus of shouts.

Then, thinly at first, then rising in pitch, came a noise
that chilled the spine, a wild unearthly wail, the ancient battle cry of the Arabs: "Y'Allah!"

Primitive urges let loose in the Arabs. They howled the
cry of wound-maddened animals. They leaped on the fallen
Brigade men. Their daggers flashed; they were still rising
and falling when their leader roared, "Look! There is
Warouk!"

Through the menacing cloud of dust over the shattered

gateway staggered the figure of George. He was covered with
dust and looked like a wraith. He slipped and slithered down
the rubble, into the shelter of its mass.

"*Y'Allah!*" The Arabs howled their glee and surged forward to help him. By the time they reached him the noise of
firing had increased from the other side. A dull red glare
became visible. Machine guns began to rat-tat their tattoo
of death.

George was grasped by the eager hands of his friends.
They lifted him and began to retreat to the greater safety
of the buildings.

"Wait!" shouted George. "Céleste is back there!" He
twisted to look back in terror at the swirling dust cloud and
the ominous glare.

From it slowly emerged a figure of red and gray, a great
frame that slipped and swayed. Its right arm hung helpless,
but the left supported a shapeless burden which clung tightly
to the tall form, impeding its progress.

"Hansen's got her!" shrieked George. "He's got Céleste!"
He struggled to get free and ran back. He scrambled up the
rubble.

George and the other Arabs grasped Céleste, who still
clung to Hansen.

Céleste seemed dazed, and held on frantically to Hansen.
It took a score of eager hands to pull her loose. She was
smothered in dust from head to feet, except where a red
scalp wound pulsed angrily.

Céleste looked back and shrieked. She was the first to
realize that Hansen was steadily climbing back where death
waited.

He stood silhouetted against the growing glare—gaunt
and elemental. He leaned against the up-pointing snout of a
wrecked tank, then reached into his pouch and took out a
grenade. He extracted the pin with his teeth, waited calmly,
then threw it. One of the machine guns stopped its tattoo. He
took out another grenade and lobbed it deliberately; then
several others.

Céleste struggled like a wild thing, scratching and swearing, trying to get back to Hansen.

By the time he had thrown his last grenade and backed
away down the slope, Céleste had fainted clean away.

The Arabs picked up Hansen and the girl and bore them
off, yelling their cry of victory. . . .

The huts on the town's outskirts rushed past the probing headlights of the limousine. Violent flashes from back in the town lit up the faces of the riders.

George, who was driving, twisted his head away from the road and looked back anxiously at Céleste, who was in the rear seat with Hansen, tending his wounds. "Sure you're all right?" George repeated, more loudly this time.

"I'm fine," she said curtly, taking her eyes from Hansen only to lift her clothes and wipe the blood from her forehead.

George slackened the speed of the car. "This is far enough," he said. "You're safe enough now, Céleste. I'm going back. You go on with Hansen. We'll all meet later up in the hills. I told you where."

"Good for you, George," thought Hansen. "That's a power play. You sure need one after being in such a hurry to get away. But no go, George. When you left Céleste behind, you left her for good. A dame can go for a coward, but never for a coward where she's at stake."

The stupid mockery of it all filled his mind: Mari dead because of her lust for him, smashed to a bloody pulp because she wanted a few more hours of his loving. Even if she'd lived they couldn't have stayed together much longer. They had used up what they had in common. And beside him was this legacy of Mari, Céleste, who once had been such a bleeding heart, such a pure little virgin. Now she was touching him with hands that were tender but knowing, with no eyes for the boy who had failed her.

Hansen remembered Céleste's arms and legs clamped tight around him as he carried her to safety. She might have been her mother, an excited, warm animal. And the things she had panted in his ear—wet from her own wound—things which she'd panted swiftly as if afraid a bullet might stop her before she got them out. She'd sure grown up fast in the last few days.

What a stupid bitched-up mess life was.

"Very well, George," Céleste said calmly. "We'll meet you in the hills."

So it's okay by Céleste for George to go back to fight, if he would, thought Hansen. She wants to take up with me where her mother left off. Bitterness of futility engulfed him.

As the car halted Hansen said, "Okay, George, we'll both go back."

"No!" cried Céleste. "You mustn't go!"

"Don't worry." Hansen smiled grimly. "We'll be back. One of us is bound to be back."

His parting grin was in mockery of the whole human circus.

THE END